TOTALLY LOSING FACE

AND OTHER STORIES

I0666988

HILLEL
GROOVATTI

SELF PUBLISHED

Edition

First Edition, January 2016. Fourth Edition, September 2020.

Work of Fiction

This book is a work of fiction. The characters, incidents, and dialogue are drawn from the author's imagination and are not to be construed as real. Any resemblance to actual events or persons, living or dead, is entirely coincidental.

Copyright

Credits

- Author Picture: Deborah Hayner
- Book Illustrations: Cyrus Hunter
- Cover Design: AVDesign
- Cover Picture: Daryl "Matz" Manialak
- Editors: Emma Kaufmann and S. Carmody

Printed by CreateSpace, an Amazon.com Company

First CreateSpace printing May 2016
Printed in the U.S.A.

ISBN: 978-0-692-61965-0

Amphibian Ark

A portion of the proceeds from the sale of each book will be donated to Amphibian Ark who hope to ensure the global survival of amphibians: www.amphibianark.org.

Quotes

"Sex is interesting, but it's not totally important. I mean it's not even as important (physically) as excretion. A man can go seventy years without a piece of ass, but he can die in a week without a bowel movement."

—Charles Bukowski

"Twenty years from now you will be more disappointed by the things that you didn't do than by the ones you did do. So throw off the bowlines. Sail away from the safe harbor. Catch the trade winds in your sails. Explore. Dream. Discover."

—Mark Twain

"I tell you, we are here on Earth to fart around, and don't let anybody tell you different."

—Kurt Vonnegut

Acknowledgements

I'd like to acknowledge a number of people for contributing to the creation of this book and for supporting and helping me along the way. First, I'd like to thank Cyrus Hunter for finding enough inspiration to artfully create exceptional illustrations for the book. A big thanks to Emma, Ani, Carmody, and Deborah for contributing their creative juices. Also, one day on vacation I popped into a tattoo parlor in Boracay, the Philippines, and convinced one of the artists, Daryl "Matz" Manialak, to help me create the cover picture. Many thanks to him and if you're ever in Boracay needing some ink, drop on by and tell him I sent you. And finally I'd like to thank the following people for supporting me throughout the creative process: M&P, Yo, Grig, MikeCZ, Haz, Carmody, and Chigger.

Dedication

To LPF, with love.

CONTENTS

Hsiao-mei's New Lover

I needed some, just enough to get me by. I sifted through my numbers and nobody was available. Finally, I decided to call my old standby, Hsiao-mei. She was like a soldier, always ready to follow orders. All I had to do was call and arrange a place to meet. She was very good looking, but a head case. I couldn't stand being with her for very long, but she's always been there for me in times of need.

We arranged to meet at a fast-food restaurant near the main train station in downtown Taipei. I parked my motorcycle downstairs as a light cleansing rain began to fall. The locals call it *mao-mao yu*. I creatively translate that to mean "peach fuzz rain:" there's just enough to notice, but not enough to cause alarm.

I spotted her upstairs sitting alone by a big glass window overlooking downtown. I was hoping she'd be there for me and was very glad she was. I sat down and said the usual chitchat, but she wasn't on tonight. Something was eating at her. She sipped her tea and looked out the big glass window onto the street below watching the hordes of people walk by. She sat motionless; didn't say a word. I sat across from her and turned away from the window. I glanced around the restaurant and watched all the customers suck down their greasy food and cackle like a gaggle of geese.

The silence between us was becoming annoying. She eventually loosened up and began to speak while writing invisible Chinese characters on the table with her finger.

"I have a new lover," she calmly explained. For some unknown reason, she refused to state his nationality other than proudly mentioning that he was a foreigner, as am I.

"He's not my boyfriend because he knows my past," she clarified. She always claimed to be a bad girl, but never elaborated. I just thought she wanted to be spanked!

"He knows what love is," she continued. "You may think you know what love is, but you don't. Having sex is easy. Animals have sex, but he makes love. He's willing to do anything I want to please me. Wherever I want it, he gives it to me. We once did it on a bus full of people heading to the airport."

She took a long, slow, satisfying sip of her tea and shared a laugh with herself as she gazed intently out the window. "I think he is God," she matter-of-factly revealed. "I do not know you well enough to feel comfortable, but he makes me very comfortable. I wear special clothes when I know I'll be with him. I want to surprise him and make him feel as good as he makes me feel. Sometimes I'll ride with him to work, and I'll pleasure him right there in his car."

She gently placed her fist on the table and gritted her teeth. "I cannot see him every day," she pouted. "He has a girlfriend who is very beautiful. She is much more beautiful than me. He must see her, so I can only see him sometimes," she sighed deeply. "He is going to Thailand for New Years with her. I can only see him nine more times before he leaves, and then I cannot see him for two whole weeks," she said as if they would be apart for years.

She turned and looked at me like I was a cancerous tumor. "He is my master. I will marry another man, but I will always have sex with my lover, always! I will have his children, but lie to my husband and say that the children are my husband's. I will always love him. I will never find anyone better than him!"

Realizing that my chances of getting into her pants were somewhere short of impossible, I told her that I was going to go home. She said nothing in response. She simply put both hands lightly around her paper cup and blew slowly. She seemed to be praying. That is how I last left her.

An Open Window

There's an open window on my right
And a closed door on my left
The sun is dipping
The sky's an angry wild beast
My bird has taken flight
Chaos is in control
There's an open window
Yes, an open window
Closing quickly
'Bout to shut
I should've seen it coming
But was always too busy running
From here to there, going no where
But busy just the same
Busy just the same
Looking back, I see what I lacked
But now, do I have the knack
Or should I just accept my plight
Might have missed the flight
Because, there's an open window
Letting the air out
And there goes your clout
A window screaming
Your mind is teeming
And you wonder why
And you want to fly
But does your pane
Contain a stain
Does your frame
Withstand the rain
There's an open window
Shouting your name
There's an open window

Screaming in vain
And the wind is loudly gusting
As the light
quickly
begins
to
flicker
and

wane.

Will the Thrill

His name was Will, but I called him "Will the Thrill" because he always had something exciting to say or do. He was a big, loud, brash American. The way Americans are supposed to be. He had two solid tree trunks for legs, above them was a huge barrel chest, and screwed onto a thick neck was a square chiseled face.

When Will said something you believed it without question. When he spoke people listened and then commented. He knew where he came from, where he was going, and what he stood for.

He grew up in Iowa and then moved to North Carolina where he studied briefly at Chapel Hill. He wanted to be an international businessman, but quit school after a few years, got bored of it.

He had to be a first-born child. You can't help but imagine him giving orders all his life. And teaching? He said he taught English to kids for a year in Japan. I tried and tried to imagine him teaching children: "A is for apple! Get it. A. Apple. SAY IT! Drop and give me twenty you whimpering snot-nosed twerps!"

Before Japan, he was in the army. Says he saw a lot of bad things during his stint. He's been all over the planet, except Antarctica, but that's on the list. He's done it all and seen it all.

He said resolutely that he only dates Asian women. Period. His last Asian girlfriend in the States was rude to his parents one night because she didn't show up for dinner. Made excuses. "That's bullshit," said Will. He dumped her on principle, but his face would soften a little when he spoke of her.

Got his head straight after Japan and went back to school. Likes it. Was just traveling this time for the summer.

Although he's only twenty-five years old, he seems twice as old as that. He's lived life. And when asked about life he said, "The war didn't get me, but I know I'm gonna die, early. Hell, I was just over in Thailand. I was fucking this whore and right in the middle, the rubber broke. I went, 'Oh FUCK!' I'm terrified to take an AIDS test. I probably got it right now."

A Little Yes

An eager yes would have been nice.

That's what I wanted.

An iffy maybe was her reply.

Long pause.

Maybe was all that she could muster.

It took the air right outta me.

Maybe it is.

And a maybe look was written on her face.

A definite no poured out of her body.

Her legs were screaming hell no.

Her back was saying no way and her arms were a definite fuck off.

But I was all over yes.

Look at me.

See what yes looks like.

I know you can read me like a book now.

Look at yes.

No, no, no.

I was there for yes and only yes, and I was not going to be denied a yes, oh no.

Her voice was calm and quiet showing no signs of yes, so I pushed it and jumped at her words.

I wanted to get closer.

Forget the signs.

So many games.

So tiring.

I ultimately made that abysmal plunge to make her say yes.

She cocked her head in an instant and her eyes grew huge.

With laser heat beaming from the back of her skull and through her dark squinched eyes, she etched NO! right through my screaming heart.

I jumped back and yes disappeared into a cloud of confusion.

She didn't just say no, she said NOOOOOOO! Without even saying no, oh yes.

And yes wiped off my face and disappeared from my mind, while retreat and collect your wounded was left in its place.

I just wanted a little yes and this is how she treated it.

I can have a little yes with others who know how to say no when they mean yes!

There are many other yeses in this town, baby!

And I'll be good goddamned if I'm ever, ever going to yes with her again.

So I said goodbye to no, and she said yes to goodbye.

Taichung Kung Fu

I **was in** Taichung, Taiwan on a busy Friday night eating and drinking with a few locals. I suddenly felt the urge to take a piss as you normally do after a few beers weigh heavily on your bladder.

Having recently arrived for the weekend in Taichung and visiting this local establishment for the first time, I was unfamiliar with the location of the restroom. I enjoyed trying new local restaurants and usually stayed clear of the foreign hangouts. Taichung has its fair share of foreigners, but they tend to stick to their bars and the majority doesn't stay around long enough to learn the language. I firmly believe that if you're here in Taiwan, you might as well learn the language and practice as much as possible. And mingling with the locals in their hangouts was the best way for me to improve my language skills.

I had been living in Taiwan for six years and got by decently on the strength of my Mandarin skills. So I confidently approached a red-faced old man who was wandering around the restaurant and asked in Mandarin, "Excuse me, where's the 'wash hands' room?"

He looked drunkenly at me, then down at his watch and casually replied that it was 8 o'clock.

I was slightly perturbed that my Mandarin was misunderstood. Was it too noisy in the restaurant? Was I drunk? No way! So I asked the question again very slowly making sure my tones and my pronunciation were correct, "Where is the 'wash hands' room?"

He squinted at me as he swayed back and forth and barked out, "8:00pm!"

I probably should have asked someone else at this point, but I was NOT going to be misunderstood. I had put too much time and energy into learning Mandarin. He probably just wasn't used to listening to foreigners speak Mandarin Chinese. Or maybe he was an aboriginal who didn't speak Mandarin well. In any event, I asked him again very slowly, "Where is the 'wash hands' room?"

He practically screamed, "8:00pm!!!"

Seeing this was getting me nowhere and my bladder was about to burst, I decided to attempt something my kung-fu teacher had been preaching to his students: Use your opponent's strength to your own advantage.

I suddenly pictured the two of us sparing, me and the old man. We were using different fighting styles, so different that we were back-to-back swinging wildly at each other. I had to somehow enter his drunken zone in order to engage with him. But how?

I thought about asking him the same question for a fourth time then stopped myself. "Use his power," I heard my *shifu* say.

I looked down at my watch and said, "Oh, 8:00pm!"

"Yes, yes, yes," the old man said with a broad smile, thankful that this stupid foreigner understood his Mandarin. Now we were engaging.

"Wow! 8:00pm," I repeated with a smile.

"Yes, yes."

"Do you know what I really have to do right now?"

"No?"

"I have to find the toilet, so I can release this uncomfortably large 'little inconvenience'?" In Mandarin, a 'little inconvenience' is a piss and a 'big inconvenience' is a shit. "Do you know where the toilet is," I asked feigning abdominal pain.

"Oh sure, right over there," he replied pointing down a dark hallway.

"Thank you very much, you saved my life," I said jokingly.

I walked down the hallway and found the toilet or WC (Water Closet) as they refer to it. Success! Sometimes you have to go with the flow to get the flow going.

Lessons from the Big Leagues

Used to play ball in the streets
With my friends in our bare feet
Dreaming the summer away
Waiting for a better day
High School seems like yesterday
Stayed on the lofty path I laid
Had passion, had desire
And a right arm full of fire
College days were a maze

Of babes and booze and full-on rage
Had a knack for the game
Quickly made myself a name
I hit the real world running
Played the field with pistols gunning
Slugged it out in my minor's hat
Biding my time, whittling my bat
One glorious day, the phone she rang
My manager, big bucks he sang
Then came the big leagues
New balls and leaches
Big money and beaches
Catching grounders, snagging flies
Signing cards, telling lies
Meeting babes, eating pies
Rain delays and superdomes
Cold beer in Styrofoam
Playing ball far from home

Look Ma, I'm on TV!
Sometimes I felt it was all a dream
The money, the fame, the scene
Old timers used to say
Soak it up now, before it goes away
One thing's for sure, I paid my dues
Gonna get what's coming before I'm through
I wanna be a better man
I wanna be a better man
One season I found myself in a strange funk
Couldn't hit my mark, couldn't hit bunk
Then the devil took me by the hand
Guided me towards the Promised Land
In a mental lapse
Started injecting
Synthetic rainbows
Right into my ass
I wanna be a better man
I wanna be a better man
Suddenly found my mark
Started hitting balls outta the park

Then I was everybody's darling
Talk shows and Rodeos
State parades and cameos
Kissing babies, selling fries
Home runs and RBIs
Grand standing in Cleveland
Highballing in Oakland
Pounding beers and snorting mills
Smoking grass, popping pills
Living it up, burning bills

Look Dad, I'm MVP!
One day on a wicked mean streak
Hitting my stride, way past my peak
Locked on third, waving at the fans
Wild pitch, go for it man!
Split for home in a fury
Catcher got back in a hurry
Approaching home I dug in deep
I launched my body in a heap
Collided with the catcher in a BOOM!
They swept me up with a broom
My doc, he said with a moan
I think it's time you called it quits, headed for home
My dreams they were shattered
My world it was scattered!
My mind raced, my heart sank
My body, my temple had just been tanked!
What price fame?
What price fame?
So now I'm living in a crack house
Living in a crack house
Got a big gut, can't bust a nut
Feeling like a punk, can't make a buck
Flying like a puck, stuck in a rut
Face full of cuts, smoking old butts
I wanna fade away
I wanna fade away
I'm living in a crack house
Living in a crack house

Got bitch tits and nasty gits
Gummy mitts and smelly pits
Runny shits and funky dits
Full of hits and dirty bits
I'm living in a crack house
Living in a crack house
Feeling like a white mouse
Feeling like a white mouse
Living in a crack house
Living in a crack house.

Mastering the Squat Shitter

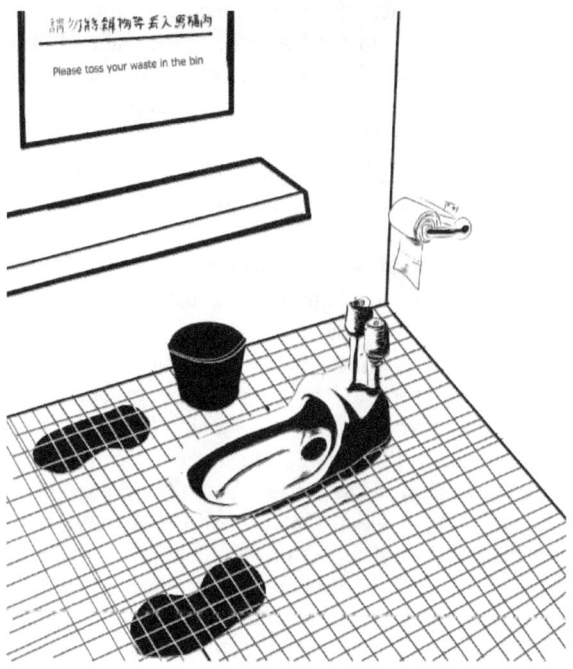

Upon arriving in Singapore, the Lion City, I was overcome by an incredible urge to deposit some waste. I pushed my luggage cart aimlessly around the airport until I noticed a bright blue and white sign with an arrow that said, "Toilets." Bingo. I followed the arrow and sure enough I ended up in a toilet. And luckily it seemed to be of the modern, clean looking variety.

An attendant smiled brightly as I entered. I returned the smile, then felt horrible for leading him on. I didn't want to give him the wrong idea, so I said in a gruff voice, "Shit a brick, where?" just in case his English was bad. Much to my surprise he responded in damn good English, "Fair sir, the stalls on your left will definitely meet your needs," then he smiled brightly again.

"They're extremely nice at this airport," I thought. I left my cart with the attendant after trying unsuccessfully to park it in a location so as to not block the entrance. I ventured to the stall area and only one of the six stalls was available. The other five were occupied by the smelliest shits in the world. Their gaseous expulsions bounced off the acoustic walls of the toilet like a bomb blast. "Good gravy!" I gagged after inhaling far too much of their offensive odor. "How about a courtesy flush! You're killing me and all the inhabitants in here! As well as the plants! I mean you're pealing the paint on the walls!" I barked out hoping they would get the hint and flush! The attendant came over and sprayed some deodorizer trying in vain to freshen up the putrid air.

If I didn't have the urge to take a massive dump, I would have waited outside until the air cleared, but I had to go. I felt a ten-pound baby wiggling inside of me.

I held my breath and walked towards the available stall. I could see it was available because it had a blue sign near the handle indicating that it was not occupied. A red sign denotes that the stall is inhabited. That's a nice feature. In some countries, they don't have this simple courtesy. Instead people are forced to try every stall door and knock wildly sometimes breaking down the door and barging in on you when you're right in the middle of your business. And when someone knocks, what's the proper protocol? Do you knock back? Yell? Grunt? Fart? Who knows?

But I digress. Where was I? Oh yeah, so I approached the available stall holding my breath whilst five stinkers chimed away at their porcelain instruments. As I neared my stall, I noticed a sign above it that read, "Mind Your Head When Squatting?" Strange, what did that sign mean? The ceiling was fifteen feet high and the stall door was about ten feet high. Surely management did not want me to worry about hitting my head on the ceiling or the doorframe. Maybe they received a lot of basketball players in this airport. But even then, they'd have to be like giants in order to hit their heads. Odd.

I kicked the door open (I don't like to touch too many things in these public stalls) and voilà, there in front of me was the dreaded squat shitter: a little pear-shaped porcelain boat set right into the ground. It looked like a large banana split cup.

I was about to turn around and conduct my business elsewhere, but by this time the head of my turd was sticking right out, and I really needed to eject it. So I quickly decided to give the old squat shitter a go. Why not? When in Rome. I was told later that squat shitters are healthier to use than regular shitters. I'd like to see the results from that report!

This squat shitter was not your standard disgusting rural Mainland Chinese train station squat shitter, no, this was Singapore so the shitter was nice and clean, and it sported some helpful bells and whistles. One of the hardest things about using a squatter is trying to figure out where to put your feet. If you're too far back, you'll miss the porcelain boat and lay cable on the ground behind the shitter. If you're too far up you may miss the front lip of the porcelain boat and piss all over the ground in front of the device, and urine could get all over your shoes or worse, you could slip when you stand up and fall into the shitter!

No need to worry, this squat shitter was designed with embedded footpads so you could be assured of lining up properly. It also came fashioned with an automatic flusher and a stainless-steel table secured into the wall, which actually came in handy later on.

Now, one end of the porcelain boat had a round hole filled with water and the other end was dry porcelain. It was difficult at first to determine which way to face, but I correctly decided to use the footpads as guides. I dropped my drawers and naturally aligned my feet facing towards the door and anus over the drain hole. Note: due to plumbing constraints, some squat shitters are bass-ackwards; in other words, the drain is closer to the door. In any event, always position your ass over the drain hole, not over the dry porcelain, because turds laid on the dry tarmac do NOT flush well. Water flows towards the drain hole and the water pressure usually happens to be very low. If it's high, then water will splash off the turd and hit you in the face, and nobody wants that!

As an extra bonus, by placing your buttocks over the drain hole, you may even receive a refreshing splash of water up your bum—if you drop a big enough piece of shit and you're hovering close enough to the drain— which definitely wouldn't happen if you dropped a steaming beauty onto the dry tarmac.

I was all set to free the dirigible clogging my anal orifice when the change in my pocket began to eject at a rapid rate. Then I felt my cell phone begin to drop. I quickly learned that you must lean a bit forward when you squat and grab your pants with one hand and pull them towards your knees to avoid this problem. Luckily, I caught the change and my phone before they fell into the shitter and quickly placed them onto the convenient stainless-steel table beside the commode.

The final thing to note when squat shitting is to make sure your penile member (if you have one) is pointed downward towards the porcelain. When I shit, I also like to expel my urinary juices. I don't know if everyone is the same. Some may prefer to do one or the other, not both. If you're like me, make sure your penis points downward at a 90-degree angle when squatting. If it doesn't, you're bound to piss all over your pants or shoes (Hence the sign on the door: Mind Your Head When Squatting). I sussed out this potentially humiliating problem before any damage could occur by grabbing my lizard with my free hand before urinating and directed it towards the porcelain.

So there I was holding my pants and underwear in one hand, my cock in the other, leaning forward at a nice angle, making sure to hover over the drain, feet aligned properly, facing the door, and then I opened my cheeks and freed the baby.

I let out a massive fart afterwards, but unfortunately, the squat shitter does not allow for your typical low basal fart sound to reverberate around the porcelain bowl like you naturally get from a standard crapper. Had I been using a standard shitter and expelled my long brown piece of art followed by a long lustrous fart, the sound alone would have resonated in the basin for a good ten seconds. I was a bit miffed at being denied this little joy. But one nice benefit to the squat shitter, your cheeks never touch the porcelain, so it's more hygienic. And since your cheeks are spread out further while squatting, there is less fecal matter attached to the sidewalls of your ass, yet another bonus and good for the environment—less toilet paper.

My knees were a bit uncomfortable during the whole ordeal, but I think I got a good thigh workout. A serious downside to the squat shitter is the squat position is not very conducive to reading, unless you're really good at squatting. And if you're not used to using a squat shitter, during a long session your knees could give way, you'll start wobbling uncontrollably, and you could fall back into the porcelain and right onto your own excrement. But by following the guidelines previously mentioned and with enough practice, anybody can master the squat shitter.

One final safety tip: make sure there's enough toilet paper in the stall before you enter. Some places in Asia sell it in tissue packets in a coin-operated machine hanging on the wall outside the john. You may have to go through a few pairs of perfectly good socks before you get used to this. Luckily for me, this particular stall had toilet paper.

After I completed this particular mission, I unfortunately happened to use up the meager amount of toilet paper provided; and at dinner the night before I overdid it (The restaurant's *chou tofu* was to-die-for) to such an extent that I had quite a large parcel to deliver to the government, or wherever these things go, and, of course, it wouldn't flush down the drain. I accidentally undershot the hole and it landed smack-dab on the dry porcelain, a major no-no. The automatic flusher sent water gushing over and around my goods and my pants got a nice brown-water spritz. But my turd wasn't budging. It just sat there. I flushed again, but no movement occurred. It seemed permanently adhered to the tarmac.

I looked around the small stall for something to push it with, but there wasn't anything and I didn't want to use my socks! There was a trashcan in the stall; however, but I wasn't about to pick up a disgustingly stained trashcan. Thus, I had a dilemma on my hands. I thought it was bad form to just leave a steaming duce in the bowl for the next guy. So I improvised, as you often do in Asia, and flushed it again, then gently nudged my brown torpedo towards the drain using my shoe (Luckily, I didn't have to kick it!). Instead my nudge freed it enough for the water to send my poo swiftly on its way.

The Fart Lover

The joy of farting never seems to lose its luster
While people age and pictures fade, a good fart still goes a long way
My best friend can muster one up at will
He stops and poses, squinting his face tightly
As he sticks his ass up high in the air
He clenches his right fist and raises it
Then all at once, he squeaks out a polysyllabic tone
That almost sings as it rumbles out full-blown
He simultaneously pumps his fist up and down to his self-made beat
As the long-winded wonder slowly ends, he marvels at his feat
Thrusting his hands out and up, as if signing his creation
Then he chuckles with glee and inhales cautiously
If it smells, he makes a face and quickly waves his musky abortion away
And if it doesn't, he giggles softly and lets out a crazed cry of satisfaction
He farts early in the morning and late at night
And anywhere in between with much delight
He gasses planes, trains and automobiles
Planting his smelly seed wherever he roams
Never with the slightest care to atone
I don't know if it's possible
But if I could bronze a fart
I'd bronze one of his for all to enjoy
As much as he does.

Gareth's Dilemma

It was late September as Gareth strutted into the break room where myself and all the secretaries were eating dinner. I was managing an English language school in Taipei, Taiwan and Gareth was one of my new recruits. He smiled and said "hi" to all the ladies in his slow Canadian drawl. The secretaries all smiled back and tried to attract his glance. He had recently arrived in Taipei, just finished teacher training and was scheduled to teach an adult night class in about an hour.

He paced the front of the room with his head hanging down. He played with the knobs on a broken radio, erased the whiteboard, and occasionally looked up when he thought of something to say. He was like a shy puppy. The secretaries thought he was extremely handsome. I thought his eyes were too small and close together and his jaw was too big. But he seemed like a cool guy. He was about twenty-five, very reserved and not too animated, but he had a dry, humorous side.

He started making me laugh talking about "douches" and "enemas" knowing the secretaries, with their limited English abilities, wouldn't understand.

Once the secretaries left the room, I decided to ask what was troubling him. I really wanted to just sit back and enjoy my English newspaper during the break, but he looked so pathetic I thought I'd try to help him out.

He leaned on the big glass window looking out over Taipei onto a busy intersection below. The cars and the scooters whizzed on by. "There're just too many women and not enough time," he muttered as if this was an agonizing statement. "I mean, what if you get a girlfriend, how can you be faithful with so many beautiful women running around here? Okay, what if you do find a great one, and she's the hottest chick ever? How do you know it's the right time? What if you don't want to settle down, yeah? What do you do?"

He looked all bothered and sexually repressed so I said, "Maybe you just need to get laid."

"Oh no, I don't need that! I got laid twice yesterday by two different women! I didn't even want to! One is a friend you know. She calls me up and has me come over, and then she cries and I didn't want to, but I had to, you know."

"Yeah, I hate when that happens," I said, almost feeling sorry for the guy as he looked out the window, touching it gently and drawing circles with his index finger while making sad faces to no one down below.

⊙⊙⊙

As the cold rains of winter arrived in late December, Gareth came into the break room again and didn't even look at the secretaries; just sat down quietly in a chair in the back of the room and looked out the window as the raindrops slowly slid down the long windows.

The secretaries quietly filed out of the room after they finished eating. I was almost done with the daily crossword and had forgotten that he was even in the room.

"Man, you ever been in love?" Gareth blurted out.

"No, can't say that I have," I said, looking up from my newspaper.

"It sucks, let me tell you."

"Why's that?"

"I met this woman, this beautiful, enchanting, engaging, wondrous, incredible woman! And she is unbelievably gorgeous!"

"Sounds great so far."

"She's married."

"Uh-oh."

"Yeah, she won't let me call her. I have to wait until she's ready to see me. I literally have been waiting by the phone for days, and every time it rings, I pray it's her, but she hasn't called for over a week. I can't wait. I can't think straight. I have to see her! I'm dying to see her, to hear from her, but she's treating me like a toy that she can just throw around whenever she wants to. I can't live like this! I love her and want to spend the rest of my life with her if she'd only get divorced and fucking call me!!! I'd marry her tomorrow, I really would!"

⊙⊙⊙

Winter left quickly and the unpredictable "plum rains" abruptly arrived in April. Summer was right around the corner, and we were gearing up to open a slew of new children's classes. The secretaries were in a heated argument in the break room over how many classes to open and who would teach them. I let the ladies figure it out while I ate my chicken leg and rice dinner.

Gareth entered the room as I finished off the last of my meal. He practiced his limited Mandarin skills on the secretaries and then approached me once the ladies left. "Hey," he said, "you ever want to do something else here? Like 'real' business? Like importing or exporting or something?"

I tossed my Styrofoam dinner container in the trash and said, "Importing or exporting what?"

"I don't know, anything. There just seems to be so much opportunity here and people are making money hand over fist, and they just don't even seem to know what they're doing."

"You can make good money teaching English," I added.

"Naw, I'm thinking much bigger. Look ahead, try to predict the future. What's going to be an important product in five or ten years? Let's figure that out and get into it. Let's make some real money man!"

◇◇◇

Summer was finally coming to a close. The monsoons left and the typhoons were gathering steam. A lot of the summertime English teachers were leaving back home, and I was planning a little vacation to clear my head.

I went in to observe one of Gareth's adult classes and a few days later called him into my office to discuss his review. He wasn't using the book very much, wasn't giving his students enough opportunity to speak and worse yet, he wasn't correcting them: Typical new teacher mistakes. But his students really seemed to like him.

"So Gareth, how do you like teaching here?" I asked.

"It's not what I want to do for the rest of my life," he said. "In fact, this is probably a good time to tell you that I'm leaving after this class is over."

Not what I wanted to hear. The hardest part of my job was finding good teachers. I spent most of my time hiring and training teachers, and just as they were getting good, they would invariably want to leave. I closed the folder containing his review and leaned back in my chair and said, "Now why would you want to leave Taiwan so soon?"

"It's complicated. It's nothing to do with you or the school. I've had a great time teaching here, just something came up."

"Like?"

"Like, I got a girl pregnant."

"The married one?"

"No, that was ages ago. She doesn't want to have anything to do with me. I met another one, she's rich, comes from a good family and her father does something in the government."

"Sounds great, are you getting married and moving back to Canada?"

"Hell no! Well, I'm moving back to Canada, but not getting married. I'm too young for that."

"So what did you tell the girl?"

"I told her I'd pay for an abortion, but she doesn't want one, she wants to marry me. What would you do?"

"Wear a rubber!"

"Well, it's too late for that."

I tried to talk him out of it and tried to get him to stay, but his mind was set. He finished his last class a few weeks later and left Taiwan, for good.

He left me an old box of rubbers on his last night; they were the "ribbed" kind for extra stimulation.

Anticipation Builds

Anticipation builds.
His eyes close and his heart immediately begins to beat faster.
A vision etched in the deepest sections of his conscious mind erupts.
So real.
So mesmerizing!
Can he bring it to life?
Can he bridge the dimensions?
The images are so crystal clear.
It has to be done.
It has to be exorcised.
It has to be brought to life.
It cannot stay locked in his sunken head, forever.
It has to meet reality, become one with reality.
It festers in his head and longs for freedom.
BIRTH!
It's pounding in his head and he feels it every night, begging for a chance to come out and play.
It used to be a gentle knock, and now it's an obnoxious pounding.
Boom!
Boom!!
BOOM!!!
It's coming out!!!
Walk through the red door and into the white room.
She's eating.
She's enjoying the fruits of her work.
She stands erect with mustard smeared on her face and ketchup dripping from her naked breasts.
Come.
He follows.
He sits down to eat.
He asks for a special meal and eyes her face for a response.
Within a wink, she brings out his special meal and carefully places it on the table.

She lowers a piece of French bread closely next to his salad and encourages him to eat. He eyes the salad as she picks up a long sharp knife.

She grabs the French bread and butters it till it's dripping wet and then lunges it into his fresh green salad.

He watches her emotions as she slams the bread into the salad, thrusting it repeatedly into the thick white dressing.

Harder and harder she slams the bread into the salad, the table is vibrating so rapidly it's about to shatter.

He can't stand it anymore; he rips the heated bread away from her throbbing hand and throws it on the floor.

He suddenly grabs the juicy green salad and slams the bowl on top of his head.

Leaves and dressing slowly slide down his face.

Abruptly, he stands and spits directly on her mustardy face.

Afterwards, they both sit down quietly.

She licks her lips as he stares out the window at a dog pissing on a tire.

Preschooler Hitting the Gutter

The ambient industrial noise of Friday night rang out like a gong in the huge Asian metropolis. The ever-present humidity injected the city with fever-like symptoms. The heat made every moment exceed its normal time frame. Darkness loomed high above gritty yellow streetlights while a massively thick layer of soot encased everything. The masses wearily traversed the uneven streets on their way home as the scent of garbage and dust clung to the smoggy air.

An exhausted young mother walked home with her young son and daughter in tow. The youngest, a daughter of about three or four, had to urinate. As the family came out of a dingy alley, the mother wiped the soot from her brow and spotted a metal grate over an open gutter on the side of a busy street. The mother picked up her preschooler, crouched down above the gutter, pulled up her young daughter's torn dress and pulled down her daughter's underwear to the little girl's dirty flip flops. The young mother clutched the preschooler close to her chest with one hand while she stretched her daughter's little legs over her own bent kneecaps with the other hand.

The young son watched on in devilish curiosity as his mother gave the word for the girl to go. The little girl struggled with the unfamiliar position, nestled tightly against her mother's abdomen, legs outstretched over her mother's knees. Finally, the girl let a thick stream of urine fly right towards the grated gutter without a drop missing its mark. The little girl's older brother laughed and pointed and jumped up and down as the cars barreled by.

Old Port Mac

Cheers to old Port Mac
Forests of Eucalyptus green
Ports of blue seem so serene
Light chocolate beaches
Unmolested by tourist leaches
Oh look, there's a koala with a soggy bottom
And there's a nice quiet pond that's all turned rotten
Hey now, watch the gray-haired bowlers in white
Take in a drink and sit down for a bite
Watch the old mingle with the young
Hear the tight-lipped twang of the local's tongue
Hell, the living's easy, mate, when you don't have a care
Say that you're from the States and you might get a stare
When the evening comes
You better watch your bum
You might get a smack, or a pinch or a poke from someone's thumb
The local dance club springs to life
As throbbing music penetrates the crowd like a knife
Young girls dance in groups, legs wide open
The wankers stand with fists clenched just a-hopin'
For a little root or a little blue
And the boys bump and pinch and say, "Oh girly, you'll do"
As the liquor takes its toll, blokes pass out in stalls
And half naked birds teeter in the halls
A yellow river flows through the centre of town
Tan mounds of vomit can be seen all around
And you duck and bob and weave as you make your way
G'day, Mate, the locals sneer and say
Hope you enjoyed your stay in Mac
Right! You know I'm never coming back.

The English Virgin

I was supposed to go to Thailand to hook up with a friend who I had met while traveling in Japan. Unfortunately, there was some confusion, and I ended up in Taiwan instead. I figure things happen for a reason, so since I was in Taiwan, I decided to make the best of it and travel around for a bit.

After about three weeks of traveling around the island, I wound up in a small town about four hours by train southeast of Taipei called Hualien. I don't like big crowded cities so that's why I headed towards Hualien, which is a much smaller city than Taipei and Kaohsiung and near the ocean.

Hualien is famous for *Taroko Gorge,* which is just a nice gorge, nothing much more to say about it. However, you would have thought the second coming had just arrived, judging by all the tourist buses that showed up to see the old gorge. Granted, it's in a beautiful green canyon with a very nice view, but that's about it.

After visiting the "gouge" of Hualien, as a referred to it, I checked into a run-down hotel right in the middle of a night market. A Taiwan night market, as its name suggests, is an outdoor market that's open only at night. Every city in Taiwan seems to have its fair share of these markets. Thousands of people flock to the night markets to take advantage of cheap prices, crowded conditions and plenty of noise. This Hualien night market was nestled in a long, narrow, densely-packed street, where customers purchase everything from stylishly cheap fake-brand-named goods to stinky tofu, which, incidentally is the worst smelling substance known to man. It's some sort of thick fried tofu that vendors sell in large chunks on the side of the road and the locals eat it up like candy. Every time I walk by a vendor selling stinky or *chou tofu*, I literally want to vomit because it smells like raw sewage.

Needless to say, I wasn't sleeping that well, since my room was above the incessant reverberations from the night market below my hotel window, so I would often purchase a few large cans of Taiwan's famous beer—aptly called *Taiwan Beer*—to help me sleep. The beer tasted okay, except it gave me the worst hangovers I've ever had. Rumor has it, they use formaldehyde as a preservative in the beer, hence the guaranteed headache the morning after.

There isn't really much to do in Hualien. Besides the night market, there's a movie theatre, a number of karaoke parlors, a few *Pachinko* gambling joints which house loud slot machines that run off of small steel balls, and that's about it for fun in Hualien. I did discover one really nice restaurant though, which specialized in lamb and offered a really nice view of the ocean.

The restaurant served lamb, lamb's milk cheesecake and lamb's milk for your coffee. It reeked of lamb when you walked in. I got used to the smell and really enjoyed sitting down at the restaurant, looking out at the beach, reading, writing and pondering life. And the staff really seemed to like me and often tried to speak English with me. Hualien really kind of grows on you after a bit of lamb's milk. But it suddenly dawned on me that my funds were rapidly depleting, and I needed to do something fast to increase my cash flow in order to continue my travels.

It's really amazing how things just happen to work out while you're traveling. I was looking for a job; low-and-behold I walked by an English school one day and a woman rushed out and accosted me. "Hi, you

Englishy teacher?" she asked.

"Strangely enough, I am," I lied.

"What you name?" she asked.

"Burby Tetherbaugh," I said. She tried to pronounce my name, but couldn't. I had to chuckle at the way her tongue got completely twisted in her mouth as she spat out my name, "Booby Teetertow."

She informed me that her name was Ms. Liu, before inviting me in to take a look at her school. I walked through the front door and two young secretaries sitting behind a reception desk greeted me with giggling smiles. The school consisted of three very small classrooms, a small reception area, a small teacher's lounge area, and a small library composed of English teaching books and supplies. After looking around, Ms. Liu encouraged me to observe a class already in session. I had nothing better to do, so I quickly agreed.

"Right now?" I asked.

"Yeah, yeah," she said, pushing me in the direction of the classroom. I guess she really needed a teacher fast.

She guided me to a classroom, knocked on the door and immediately entered. The class of fifteen eight-to-twelve-year-olds crammed into the tiny room erupted with giddy excitement as I entered. They were so cute! A few parents sat around the back of the room, smiling from ear to ear. Ms. Liu said something in Chinese to the teacher, Ms. Yen, then to the class in Chinese and finally pointed towards me.

I waved to the class and then sat down at the back and smiled to the friendly parents sitting next to me. The young local female teacher stood up in the front of class and spoke at length in Chinese. Then she wrote on the whiteboard:

This is a _____. These are _____s.

She held up flashcards and had the students insert the words from the flashcards into correct English sentences using the grammar points written on the board: This is a ball. These are balls. After the students were comfortable with those grammar points, she held up flashcards and called on individual students to formulate correct sentences. She rounded off the class with a quick spelling test. Ms. Yen was extremely patient and very encouraging to the students. Consequently, the kids and parents loved her. All in all, teaching English seemed very easy, and I was one hundred percent certain that I could do it after seeing how easy it was.

After the class was over, Ms. Liu asked me if I'd be willing to teach at the school. I said, "Of course!"

"Great, can you work this weekend?"

"You bet, but I don't have a work permit," I said, wanting to make things as legal as possible.

Ms. Liu said she was willing to sponsor me to obtain a teaching visa so I could legally stay and work in Taiwan. However, I'd have to work a minimum of twenty hours a week at her school. That sounded good to me. How difficult could this English teaching gig really be? After all, I spoke the language fluently. And once I grew tired of teaching, I would eventually have enough cash saved to leave and continue on my travels. I could avoid all of this of course by making one phone call to my folks and ask them for money, but that would be too much like giving in.

Ms. Liu gave me some paperwork to take home and fill out. It was all in Chinese, which incidentally I cannot speak, read or write. She also gave me an address in Chinese of a government office that I needed to visit to sort out my paperwork so that I could legally teach English in Hualien.

The next day, at the urging of Ms. Liu, I hailed a cab and went to the aforementioned government office to start the process of getting a work permit. I gave the cabbie the Chinese address, and before long he dropped me off in front of an old green building that looked like it had been constructed in the 1930s. Inside, there were several officers lounging around behind long wooden desks.

I noticed one of those mechanical number machines, which spewed out numbers printed on slips of paper. I picked a number, 49, and patiently waited for my number to be called. I was the only customer there, but I politely waited anyway, not wanting to cause a disturbance. Meanwhile, the officers stared and smiled. Finally, a woman came up and said, "You wanna me helpa you?"

"Work permit," I said, slowly and succinctly, and then showed her my number. She smiled and said something to everybody in Chinese and they all laughed and laughed. Then she told me that the number machine was broken. Ha, ha! "Why was that funny," I thought. She led me to one of the uniformed officers sitting behind an orderly desk, and he smiled enthusiastically like he was so happy to be helping me.

"Work permit," I said.

"Sorry, Engrishy berry bad," he replied.

"I can tell."

"Pardon, what?"

"Nothing, nothing," I said, knowing that this was going to be a long day. I somehow managed to explain to him what I needed, and he gave me some additional forms to fill out. After carefully filling in the requested information, I gave them back to him, along with a letter of intent from Ms. Liu's English school and a copy of my University diploma translated by Ms. Liu into Chinese because I was told by her that my diploma had to be translated. The officer shuffled through my paperwork and spotted something that wasn't right so he had one of his bored coworkers come over and take a look. The two officers had a long discussion in Mandarin, which I completely could not understand and then the first officer looked up and smiled.

"Engrishy virgin," he said, still smiling brightly as ever with some nasty-looking teeth.

"What?" I replied, somewhat confused.

"Engrishy virgin," he replied.

I was hung over, but I wasn't that hung over. "What? English virgin?"

"Right, right," he nodded, giving me a cheesy smile.

"Why?" I asked.

That question seemed to throw them for a loop. They went off speaking Chinese amongst themselves, and then he fired back, "You speaka Chinese?"

"No," I replied.

Undaunted, he said, "How you say *'gui ding'* in Engrishy?"

"Dude, I don't know. I told you I don't speaka Chinese."

"Oh, right, right. Uh, *gui ding*?" he said, and then had a pow-wow with his coworkers. "Ruluh," he said happily, after conferring with his coworkers.

I picked up a ruler on his desk and said, "This?"

"No, no, RU-LUH," he said loudly. I scratched my head and looked around for help. It would have been nice if I'd known a group of foreigners in town who I could have asked for help, but I didn't know anyone in town. I could have called Ms. Liu at the English school, but her English wasn't much better than that of the officers. Luckily, the officers were now consulting a Chinese-to-English dictionary, which one of them conveniently had on their desk. It took them a very long time just to find the Chinese word, for some reason. They were flipping pages back and forth, scribbling imaginary Chinese characters on their palms with their fingers, and finally they found the word and showed me the translation: RULE.

"Oh, oh. This is your rule. You need an English virgin because this is your rule. I get it," I said, still very confused.

"Yeah, yeah, yeah," he said happily and then pushed the paperwork back at me and smiled.

I flashed him a bright smile, while I said under my breath, "Why does he need an English virgin, the sick bastard?"

I've heard of under-the-table stuff, but what kind of weirdo wants an English virgin in exchange for a work permit? Well, if that's what it took, I would scour the countryside. Maybe he just wanted a sexually inexperienced teacher or a nanny for his kids? Anyway, and more importantly, how the hell was I going to find an English virgin in Hualien?

Wait a second! How in the hell would this guy know if she was a virgin or not? How would I know? And did he want a male or a female "Engrishy" virgin? Probably female, but maybe not. I could only imagine what he wanted to do with her. My mind was racing at this time. What to do? What to do?

When you travel, there are things you just have to accept, like culture shock, getting ripped off and diarrhea. This was one of those things that I just had to accept. If I wanted to get a work permit, I needed to submit an English virgin along with my paperwork. This was evidently the way business was conducted here. I don't condone it, but I was going to have to work with it in order to process my paperwork, it was that simple. At least they weren't asking me to eat tiger penis or renounce my religion. All they wanted was an English virgin, and by gawd, I was going to find one and give it to them.

I walked out of the office and onto the busy street. Scooters and taxis bustled by as a few vendors hocked their goods displayed in little metal carts covered by big, bright umbrellas. "There's got to be at least one English virgin in this town," I thought.

First, I decided to check the phone directory for foreign names. I figured I'd call and say, "Hey are you an English virgin?" Yeah right! Anyway, the phone directory idea didn't work. None of the public phones had phone directories. After pondering the matter further, I decided to hit the bars and try to find the foreign crowd.

While I was in a taxi on my way to some random bar located on the outskirts of town that the hotel receptionist had told me about, I started trying to profile a virgin. What exactly would a virgin look like and how could I spot one right away? Was there a special look? Did a virgin exude virginity in some way? I figured a younger person was more likely to be a virgin, but I didn't want one that was too young, who knew what they were going to do with her! The more I thought about it, the more I felt there was really no way to tell if someone was a virgin just by looking at them fully clothed. I pictured bringing her into the work permit office and saying, "Uh, excuse me, here's an English virgin" and then some gloved nurse would slap her on a gurney and perform an inspection. That wasn't going to happen. I mean, I'm sure the foreign affairs' guy wasn't going to spread the virgin's legs and do a search right there and then in the office. This was Taiwan and all, but I just didn't think that was going to happen. I wouldn't let it happen!

As luck would have it, I ran into a few foreign guys from Canada at a small run-down bar that the English-speaking taxi driver suggested. After chatting with them, I decided that being real upfront and asking them if they could introduce me to some English virgins would be out of the question. Instead, I made up an excuse that I had a thing for English girls. They told me that I was in luck. They knew a girl named Suzie, who lived in town and worked with one of them at the English school across from a McDonald's restaurant in the center of town.

The very next day I went to the English school where Suzie apparently worked and pretended that I was looking for a job. They gave me a tour of the office, made me sit through another class and handed me some paperwork. Suzie was nowhere to be found so I went to the McDonalds across the street and camped out. As I walked in, I noticed a blonde foreign woman complaining at the front counter about a large black hair in her hamburger. She was obviously very British on account of her British accent. I ordered and then sat down close to her and sparked up a conversation. As luck would have it, she was the woman I had been looking for. Her name was Suzie and she hailed from Essex, England. She was about 5'7" with long legs, blonde hair, not too thin, but not too thick.

When she was about to leave, I popped the question. "Say, I need some help. Would you be willing to go with me to the foreign affairs' office and assist me in getting a work permit tomorrow," I said brimming from ear to ear. Then I added, "For some reason, I need to be accompanied by another foreign person."

She was as nice as could be. This whole thing seemed ridiculous, but I just wanted to follow the "ru-luhs" so I could get a work permit, make some money and continue my travels. If luck was on my side, I would be successful in my quest and not end up in jail. Suzie amazingly agreed to accompany me. Of course I didn't tell her about the English virgin bit, I figured easing her into it at the foreign affairs' office was the best route to take.

I met Suzie the following day at a movie theatre near the hotel where I was staying and she was looking pretty good but dressed a bit ragged. She was wearing torn blue jeans and a baggy old tie-dyed blouse. I kind of gave her a strange look as I was checking out her attire. She looked at me and said, "What?"

"Oh never mind. I was just hoping you would have dressed up a bit. I don't want them to object to my work permit thing based on your appearance. But never mind, you look fine."

"Thanks Burby," she said rather pissed off. "What is it again I'm supposed to be doing there?"

"I don't know. I think it will speed up the process if you're with me, for some reason."

"Why?"

"I don't know."

"Well, I've only been here a few months myself, and I don't speak a word of Chinese other than '*xie xie*' and '*gan ni*'," she said.

"What's that mean?"

"Thank you and fuck you."

"Oh, those two are important," I said, trying to commit them to memory. Then I continued, "Look I don't really know why they need you, but you don't mind going do you?"

"No, I've got nothing better to do today. I don't have to teach till 6:00pm."

"Oh, do you have a work permit, by the way?"

"No, most places just do things under the table here. Your school is obviously trying to do things the legal way."

We talked about teaching and she said some things that were a bit disturbing like it wasn't easy to teach and the kids could be brats. I thought she was just a complainer. How difficult could it really be? You just go in there and talk, and they listen, then have them repeat a few sentences and that's it. But she said you have to lesson plan, spend time controlling the class, correct pronunciation mistakes in class, assign and grade homework, interact with parents and show progress. I told her I'd been a camp counselor once, so I didn't think I'd have any trouble with the kids. She just laughed.

We continued chitchatting along the way. "Have you been to *Taroko Gouge* yet?" I asked.

"Gorge. *Taroko Gorge*," she corrected.

"Oh yeah, Gorge. Have you been?"

"Yes, it's very beautiful and very peaceful," she said, and I had to agree that it was. "Taiwan really is a very green and beautiful island once you get out of the cities."

We showed up at the foreign affairs' office with paperwork in one hand and a possible English virgin in the other. I failed to actually confirm her virginity with her beforehand, but figured she'd pass. The same smiling-faced officer was there. I saluted him and then said, "I've got what you wanted." Then I got a bit concerned, what were they really going to do with Suzie? So I added, "Just look, no touch, right?"

He looked Suzie up and down and obviously seemed satisfied with her looks. He couldn't keep his eyes off of her. Then he sifted through my paperwork and said in broken English, "Engrishy virgin?"

I smiled and said, "Yes, Essex." Then I winked at Suzie.

The officer seemed confused.

"Oh come on now. Don't act like you don't know what's going on," I said.

"Wait. What? Did I just hear him correctly?" Suzie said. In hindsight, I guess I should have told Suzie about the whole English virgin thing beforehand so she wouldn't freak out. Actually, she probably wouldn't have come had she known beforehand, so the best way, I felt, was just to let it happen and deal with it at the point of conflict.

"Yeah, yeah, it's some sort of Chinese thing," I said, trying to placate Suzie. I looked back at the officer, and he had a blank expression on his face like he didn't understand. I was thinking, "Oh, no, I went through all this trouble to get her and bring her here and now he's playing dumb. Maybe he doesn't like her. What are the odds that there's another English woman in town? I may have to scour Taipei."

"Excuse me, Burby, what did I just hear?" said Suzie, grabbing my arm.

"I'll tell you later," I said, sensing the hostility in her voice.

"No, I think you should tell me now, right NOW!"

"Okay, okay, look, they told me in order to finish my paperwork; I needed to bring in an English virgin." After I told her that, I quickly turned to the officer and smiled. He smiled back.

"A what? Is that what this is all about? Are you planning on selling me into some sort of pornography ring or something? You're a right bastard!"

"Shhh! No, no, no. Look I just need a frickin' work permit; in order to do that they said I needed to bring in an English virgin. I have no idea why and no idea what they need you for, but they need you. I need you." Then as an incentive, I threw in, "Just play along, I won't let anything bad happen to you."

"What! Well, I am English so at least you got that right. I came here to help you, but nobody ever said anything about bondage and slavery."

"Bondage and slavery? Whoa! Nobody's selling you into slavery," I said confidently.

"Oh yeah, well that's what it sounds like to me. Look, my father's in the government and he'll have all of you in jail in a flat second! I'm having no part of your sick, twisted, disgusting plan. You're an asshole," she said to me. Then she turned to the officer and said, "And you're a pig! I'm reporting you all right now! *Gan ni!*"

The officer clearly understood her Chinese insult and stood up quickly in extreme anger.

"Whoa! Uh, please realize that these people are all government officials, so if you want to report something, then report it to them," I said. "But please wait just a second until I at least have the work permit in hand. Come on!"

"What's your plan? Are you going to inspect me or something and then sell me to the highest bidder? Take pictures? Group sex? S&M? You're all sick. All of you!" she yelled. Then she directed her attention to the erect officer. "I want to see your superior now! NOW! Don't act like you don't understand the word 'Superior.' Hello, boss, leader! Go, now. *Xie xie!*"

I'm surprised the newspaper reporters hadn't arrived, what with all the ruckus Suzie was making. I could see the headlines now: English Virgin Ring Busted.

A portly looking uniformed gent eventually came out with a tiny little uniformed woman clinging to his official looking side. The portly gent spoke to the officer dealing with our case for about ten minutes, all in Chinese. Then the portly gent barked something to the little woman at his side in Chinese and she promptly turned to us and said, "Accuse me sir, miss, what probwem?"

"No problem," I said.

"Yes, there is a problem, a very big problem," Suzie exclaimed. "These people are trying to sell me into prostitution!"

"Shhh! Let me handle this," I said.

"I'll do nothing of the sort," she responded. "These two men are sick bastards, and they want to sell me into prostitution," she exclaimed to everyone within a mile radius.

The little officer nodded her head rapidly, smiled and then said very politely, "Accuse me? Swowy pwease."

I decided to just come out with it and put a tent over the whole circus. The gig was up. "Look, this gentleman told me to bring in an English virgin. So I brought her in, and now he doesn't want her and I don't know why. I just want a friggin' work permit, okay?"

"Accuse me? Engrish virgin?"

"Yes," I responded.

The officers spoke amongst themselves for another ten minutes, and it seemed to be getting heated. Finally, the translator turned to us again and said, "Accuse me?"

"Goddamnit! These people are completely incompetent," Suzie screamed. "Look, these two people are bad people! Bad! Very bad! They want an English virgin for some sick, psychotic reason. This twit drags me down here to help this officer in his diabolical scheme and doesn't even have the common decency to tell me about his plan beforehand. Now I want these two arrested! *Comprende?*"

"Accuse me? Pwease swowy, speaka swowy."

"Arrrgh! Honest to God, I'm going to kill somebody," yelled Suzie. "Did you get that?" They apparently did, because they all put their hands on the guns hanging from the holsters around their waists and the little interpreter grabbed a big stapler. "Can't anybody freaking speaka Englishy in this godforsaken, backward country!"

Frustrated, Suzie demanded a piece of paper and a pen and told me to write everything down for the translator. So I wrote: *The kind officer told me I needed an English virgin to complete my work permit paperwork, so I brought in an English virgin (the loud girl standing next to me) but the officer doesn't seem to like her.* I handed the paper to the translator. She showed it to everybody behind the desk and then they all began speaking Chinese amongst themselves again while the smiling officer handling my case flipped through his Chinese-to-English dictionary.

I tried to calm Suzy down, but nothing seemed to work. Then I attempted to make small talk with the officers as they discussed the issue at hand and frequently consulted the dictionary. "So have you ever been to *Taroko Gouge?*" I asked.

"GORGE, you fucking imbecile!" Suzie screamed.

I wanted to gouge her gorge right about then, but I just kept quiet after Suzie's latest outburst and let the officers suss it out.

"I know, I know," yelled my officer. They spoke amongst themselves again and then promptly all started to laugh like something was the funniest thing they'd ever heard. They were crying from laughing so hard.

"Honestly, these people! I hope you all have heart attacks while eating fried chicken feet," Suzie screeched.

The little translator tried hard to contain her laughter as she turned to us. "Accuse me, accuse me, we know, we know," she said, steadying herself on the desk with one hand and wiping her eyes with the other.

"Yes, we know you know, now tell us," said Suzie, trying to stay calm.

"He no say 'Engrish virgin,' he say 'ENGRISH VIRGIN'," said the translator giggling and nodding her head.

"Oh, well that clears it up!" said Suzie in disgust.

"We don't understand," I said.

The translator took out a piece of paper and scribbled one word on the paper; the one word that would make it all okay and get me the hell out of this terrible mess. She wrote: VERSION.

It took a few second for it to register, then I laughed, what else could I do?

"What is all this about?" Suzie demanded.

"Well, you're not going to believe this," I started.

"Try me," she said, still frustrated and about to unleash her fury on everyone again.

"The officer told me he wanted an English virgin to complete my paperwork, right? However, what he meant to say was 'English Version.' He needed an English version of my paperwork and not an English virgin. I misunderstood him. Isn't that funny?" I said as my face turned ten shades of red.

She threw up her arms and then a dead calm appeared on her face. "Fucking hysterical," she said, and stormed out of the building.

Afterwards I learned how to say the word "sorry" in Chinese: *dui bu qi*. I said that phrase about a hundred times to the officers and then clarified with everyone exactly what piece of paperwork I needed to give them in order to process my work permit. As it turned out, they only wanted an English version of my diploma, which I had on me. I quickly handed them a copy along with the other requested forms.

They smiled and said I could come back in a couple of weeks to obtain my processed paperwork, but I'd still have to fly to Hong Kong to get everything finalized for some strange reason. Since I had never been to Hong Kong, I was looking forward to checking it out. Ms. Liu kindly offered to forward me the money to purchase a plane ticket.

I met Suzie that night outside of her school.

"Look," I said, as she rolled her eyes and quickly walked past me. "I'm sorry, I'm really sorry, *dui bu qi*!"

"I am not talking to you!" she said. "Just, go away. Goodbye."

"One minute of your time, that's all I ask. Please!"

She abruptly halted, crossed her arms and said, "What?" She looked at her watch and added, "One minute."

"I'm so sorry. You must think I'm a bad person."

"No, daft, dense, and dumb come to mind."

"Yes, I'm all of those, and you forgot stupid, idiotic and retarded."

"Yes, I did."

"Look, I really didn't mean any harm. I just thought it was their custom: You needed to bring in an English virgin to get a work permit. I really didn't know. I've only been here a few weeks okay? And I really, truly, honestly appreciate your help. So let me make it up to you and buy you a beer." She didn't look to be in a forgiving mood.

"I'm a really nice guy once you get to know me," I added. "I'm here in Taiwan all by myself, and I don't know anyone. It would be nice to just sit down with someone, have a few beers and talk, in English. That's all I'm asking. Really." She wasn't buying any of it.

"I'm sure," I continued, "that after teaching those little monsters all night long your throat is probably pretty raw and thirsty. One little cold brew sure would taste good and do you right. And it's Friday!" She started to look a bit forgiving.

"Come on," I said, "I've never felt so bad in all my life. You really are a super person to offer to help me out and all, and now I just want to say 'thank you' and make it up to you." I flashed her my wounded puppy dog look. She seemed about ready to give in.

She exhaled heavily, smiled angrily and practically shoved her middle finger up my nose! "Fuck right off!!!" she yelled and walked away.

What a shame! I really wanted to find out if she was a virgin or not. Oh well. I had my evil way with her over and over again in my mind. Right there in the safety of my imagination, she definitely wasn't a virgin!

A few weeks later I flew to Hong Kong, completed my paperwork, flew back to Taiwan and completed my paperwork at the foreign affairs' office in Hualien. The officers all laughed when I came in and the guys shook my hand. They were so nice.

So now I'm a legal foreign worker in Taiwan. I've moved out of the hotel and found a very nice apartment near the beach that I'm sharing with a few locals who are slowly helping me learn Chinese. I've already taught a number of English classes at Ms. Liu's and should begin teaching more classes soon. I've also signed up a few private students who I've met around town. Suzie still won't talk to me, but all in all, life is good and stinky tofu isn't really that bad once you get past the smell. It incidentally goes really good with *kung-pao* chicken and a tall, ice-cold bottle of *Taiwan Beer*.

Flying Rebar

Two gray-haired, retired couples from New York waited outside in a long line at the Vincent Willem van Gogh Museum in Amsterdam. Friends for many years, the two couples were vacationing together this summer.

"Har, this line is just not moving, and it's almost 3:00p.m.," said Harold's wife, Bestelle, impatiently. "The museum closes at five."

"Well, gang, what do you want to do?" asked Harold, confirming the time on his watch and then looking curiously at the other three adults.

"We could try that other museum over there," said Walter, pointing to an avant-garde museum nearby. "There's no line and we can come back bright and early tomorrow morn to give our respects to old Vincent van."

"That one," said Harold, pointing at the avant-garde museum across the street. "Looks pretty artsy-fartsy, maybe that's why there's no line. What do you think Stell, Edie?"

The two ladies looked at each other and agreed, "Fine with us."

The four tourists nonchalantly walked over to the avant-garde museum, strolled in without a wait, paid the entrance fee and proceeded upstairs to the first exhibit.

"Now that's more like it," said Walter. "No waiting, no lines. Just in and out. They run a smooth operation here."

"Speaking of operations, did I ever tell you about my hernia operation?" asked Harold.

"Oh, Har! Please," begged his wife, Bestelle.

"Yes, you have Harold, numerous times, in all its glorious detail," said Walter's wife, Edie.

"Well, a good story is always worth repeating," said Harold.

"Honey, spare us," said Bestelle.

"All right," said Harold, frowning at his wife.

The foursome entered the first display room of metallic objects: Thrashed wrought iron gates, swinging I-beams, twirling stainless steel spheres. One display consisted of a welded metal box with a hulking amount of steel placed on top of it to make the entire work of art look like a gigantic metal tree.

"Hey, I could do that," said Walter, referring to the display.

"I think any farm-hand could do that," said Harold, equally unimpressed.

"Honey, have an open mind, this is art," said Bestelle.

"My mind is open, but you'd have to pay more to have that piece of junk removed than you would to purchase the metal to build it," groaned Harold.

As they meandered past the numerous metallic objects, they walked by a display with an artist verbally directing a metal lifting device. **Work in progress: Flying Rebar**, a sign read. The artist stepped around an array of creatively arranged piles of rebar and yelled at a confused worker commandeering the metal lifting device. A large welded mass of metal was swinging from the lifting machine, as the artist helped push the swinging mass of rebar and simultaneously pondered the best position for his work of art.

"Move it over here, no there," the artist ordered.

The worker moved the lifting device back and forth as he grunted and dripped sweat all over the ground. The artist held a chain with a hook in one hand and tried to visualize where the work of art should hang from the ceiling to give it the most desired effect.

"It must assume a flying motion, hence the name—Flying Rebar," he confidently told the worker.

"It won't hold from the ceiling," said the worker.

"We'll make it hold!" yelled the artist.

"Hey, that display kind of reminds me of the time I was working construction on the Lower East Side," said Walter as the foursome continued walking.

"Was that the time your thermos fell from the fiftieth floor?" asked Edie.

"Yeah, it was. Damn near hit a taxicab," said Walter.

"You're lucky it didn't kill someone," said Harold.

"I'm lucky the coffee Stell put inside the thermos didn't kill me," he said with a chuckle.

"I heard that," said Bestelle.

They walked into the next room which had various forms of modern products artistically arranged: Soap bars swimming, milk cartons exploding, tea pots percolating above cups and saucers designed to look like baby birds in a nest begging for food. Blenders a-blending. Toasters a-toasting. Toilets a-flushing.

They walked past another display entitled **Trash IT**. The work of art consisted of numerous mangled computer products mashed together.

"This looks like someone put their trash into a trash compactor and is now trying to pass it off as art," said Harold, pointing to the display.

"Shhh, Honey, the artist may be around here," said Bestelle.

"Don't shush me," said Harold. "If the so-called artist were here right now, I'd tell it to his face what I think of his art. Nothing wrong with that is there Walt?"

"No, if you're an artist your art should stand up to criticism. But I think the guy who designed that trash display probably got run out of town a long time ago," joked Walter.

"Well, his art is giving me the runs, I'll tell you that," joked Harold.

The two wives just shook their heads.

They walked into the next room, which had various erotic pictures on display: Nudes, dildos, dicks oozing life, dripping wet pussies. Cock sucking. Muff diving. Ball licking. Titty tonguing. Spent men. Satisfied women.

"Oh my!" said Edie.

"Well, they can do what they want behind closed doors, but do they have to sell it to everyone?" said Bestelle.

"Sell it? They're trying to cram it down our throats! And would you look at them, not a one is wearing a prophylactic. Shocking, simply shocking," said Walter with a grin.

"I'd say, and how about a little romance first?" added Harold, snickering for effect while the two wives waved the men off.

The group quickly exited the porn area, then slowly wandered through a few more display rooms, soaking up the art. Between two of the sections, they noticed a small dark theatre with rows of seats and two projector screens hanging above a stage nestled in front of the seats.

"Hey gang, let's go in this mini theater and rest our weary bones. All this porn, oops, I mean art is getting me all hot and bothered," said Harold.

"Good idea, I need to adjust my pacemaker," joked Walter.

They entered the theatre, eased into the comfortable seats and began watching the presentation projected on the two screens. On one screen was a movie about an avant-garde artist and on the other was a continuous display of the artist's works. "Life is art, you just have to find your way to express it," said the artist on the left screen.

The two couples sank into the soft seats and intently watched the program, along with a few other attendees.

About five minutes passed, then a man carrying a dirty green backpack and dressed in a worn-out World War II army trench coat loudly descended into the theatre. He was thin, with long, graying brown hair tied into a ponytail. He jumped onto the stage with authority, while the projectors continued to display images above him. The grungy-looking man, who did not resemble the avant-garde artist on screen in the slightest, put his crusty old backpack in a free corner below one of the hanging screens and removed his filthy trench coat. He took out an old checkered tablecloth from his backpack and shook it; dust flew everywhere. The tablecloth sailed in the air several times in slow motion as the dust seemed to collect on the projector beams and float in suspended animation. He gently laid the red and white cloth on the dark stage.

He leisurely removed his grimy old boots, shook the dirt out of them and placed one at one corner of the tablecloth and the other on the diagonal corner. Abruptly, he jumped up in the air several times and began loosening up and stretching.

"This oughta be good," whispered Harold loudly.

"Shhh," said Bestelle, elbowing him. "He's performing!"

"Don't shush me! I hope he takes a bath on stage. He smells like one of Walter's movements," joked Harold.

"He smells like yesterday's lasagna-induced one," replied Walter.

"Honestly, you two. He's performing! Shhh," said Edie.

After the man loosened his neck, cracked his fingers, jogged in place and windmilled his arms, he finally looked like he was ready to perform. He took an old fedora hat out of his backpack and placed it in the corner at the right of the stage. He carefully knelt down and placed a large white piece of paper on the brim of the hat. Immediately afterwards, he jumped on top of the tablecloth at the center of the stage and quickly raised his hands in the air, hoping for thunderous applause. None was forthcoming.

Undeterred, the performer pulled out a paper bag from his backpack, walked to the front of the stage and shook the item open. He walked backwards to the black wall behind him as if balancing on a tightrope; bent down as easy as you please, and then stood the paper bag up against the wall as he excitedly eyed the audience. Abruptly, he jumped to the center of the stage and raised his arms in the air and smiled, again looking for applause. Again, none was given.

Still undeterred, he stood on the tablecloth and began to make big kung-fu-ish movements while he whistled. He appeared to be limbering up.

He struck an awkward pose and suddenly dropped his trousers to his ankles and quickly raised his arms proudly in the air. Perplexed, he studied the audience, as if anticipating oodles of appreciation. Again, none was given.

Feigning sorrow, he proceeded to remove his shirt and kick off his trousers. He reached down and dropped his holey, filthy underwear to his ankles. They floated down and rested atop his dingy yellow socks. Standing naked on stage, he confidently raised his arms in the air, self-assured that this grand display would obtain some sort of reaction from the audience. One person slowly clapped while a woman giggled.

"Oh dear," said Edie, as she put her hands over her mouth.

"I guess they don't believe in circumcision here," Walter whispered to Harold.

"Or clean underwear," Harold fired back.

The performer spit onto his hands and rubbed them together. Once his hands were sufficiently lubricated, he began to masturbate. His dick grew and stiffened in no time at all. The performer made long stroking movements on his elongated schlong and thrust his upper body back and forth as he slowly turned in circles. After a few rotations, he stopped turning and pointed his cocked member towards the audience. Following a momentary pause, he kicked his grubby underwear into the air, then carefully turned to align himself with the paper-covered hat resting quietly in one corner and made a few Sumo-esque feet stomps on the floor for added effect.

Stroking his stiff unit rapidly, he properly aligned his feet with the hat in the corner of the stage and grunted loudly. The audience watched in amazement as a stream of semen spurted out of his dick, flew across the stage, and made a crinkling sound as most of his essence hit the paper target lying on top of the hat. The performer turned to the audience in all his glory and raised his arms in the air and smiled profusely. A few people in the audience responded with applause.

The performer, whose penile shaft was still throbbing, grubby socks still hanging at his ankles, stretched out his arms and proceeded to dance what looked like an Irish jig all over the stage. Afterwards, he joyfully pranced backwards towards the wall behind him and painstakingly crouched down, until his ass was directly over the small paper bag standing conveniently open against the back wall.

"Oh no," whispered Edie.

The performer placed his hands together in a praying fashion, grunted again and then launched a loud juicy fart followed by a long stringy piece of shit. It landed in the bag with a thud. He swiped his greasy asshole with a single stroke from one hand and capped it off by wiping the excess caking his mitt in a long artistically flowing pattern on the back wall behind the two hanging projector screens.

"Without art, we are doomed to die a meager existence," proclaimed the artist featured on one of the screens above.

The performer returned to the tablecloth, put his arms down by his sides and bowed graciously and deeply to the audience.

A few people heavy-handedly clapped while looking around perplexed at the other members of the audience. One excessively pierced college student stood up and cheered with gusto. "Encore, encore," he yelled. The performer placed his hands over his heart and politely declined the offer.

As the sparse applause died down, the performer quickly ventured to the back wall and reached for his hat. He crumpled up the soiled paper resting on its brim and wiped off his fedora on the back wall. He leapt to the front of the stage and held his hat upside down, hoping for tips from the audience.

The two New York couples stood up and quickly filed out without tipping the performer.

"The least they could have done was warn us beforehand," shrieked Edie.

"My word!" complained Bestelle. "I don't have to leave New York to see that!"

"I think I need a cigarette," said Walter.

"Well. I thought there was something more he could have done with it, like maybe add some strobe lights and music," added Harold.

"I agree, it seemed a bit raw," said Walter. "Maybe he could have used glittering toilet paper and a real crapper, instead of that old bag."

"And how about some lubricant?" said Harold. "My God, you're going to rub yourself raw using saliva!"

"Oh, you two are incorrigible," said Edie.

"Well, I've seen enough!" said Bestelle. "Let's call it a day for the art scene and see what else there is to Amsterdam."

"I don't think you can top that," said Edie.

As they walked to the entrance, Walter sarcastically thanked a guard who was standing stiffly at the exit. "Hell of a show, gent," said Harold.

"Glad you enjoyed it," he said, smiling.

"Say, how many performances does that shitter and masturbator do a day?" asked Harold.

"Come again?" asked the guard in good English.

"There's a guy shitting and masturbating in your little theatre. Isn't he with the museum?" asked Walter.

"Shitting and masturbating?" repeated the guard. "I don't quite understand."

"We just saw some guy jack-off into a hat and excrete into a bag onstage in your theatre," exclaimed Walter. "Don't tell me he's not part of the exhibition."

Edie and Bestelle held their purses in one arm and put their hands on their chests in shock. "Don't tell me he's not part of the show," Edie said sternly. The guard looked perplexed.

The foursome guided the guard to the mini theatre where the performance had just taken place. They glanced around the empty room, but could not find any traces of the performer. All his props had completely vanished as well. "He was just here," they all agreed.

"If you go to that back wall you'll definitely see and smell his signature," said Harold.

The guard turned on the lights and walked down to the back wall to investigate. He could smell something rotten, but the wall was black, so he couldn't clearly make out the performer's signature. The guard turned around and shrugged his shoulders.

"Can't see it?" asked Walter. "Well, I'd wash that wall if I were you."

"And be on the lookout for a renegade jack-off, shit-in performer," said Harold.

The stunned group walked out of the museum. They took a deep breath outside, looked at each other and began to chuckle.

"Don't blame me," said Walter. "I only suggested going to the museum. We all entered at our own risk."

"Well it's good to know that performers like that have a stage to perform on, and we were privileged enough to see possibly his one and only performance," said Harold.

"Oh honey," said Bestelle.

"Let's eat, I'm starved," said Walter.

"How can you eat after watching something like that?" said Edie. "I'm sickened, simply sickened!"

"How can you not think about eating after a thing like that?" said Walter.

"Walt, what do you make of that whole performance? What was he trying to say?" asked Harold.

"Maybe that life should be enjoyed, before everything turns to crap," said Walter.

"Yes, I think you're right!" said Harold. "Masturbating represented the beginning of life, while shitting represented the end of life. So once you're born you need to make the most of life and enjoy it, hence the dancing in between the self-gratification and the defecation. And the more gratifying your life is, the bigger the signature you will leave when you die."

"Yes, yes!" said Walter. "It truly was a marvelous performance! I wonder if he'll be preforming again or maybe he's just a one-shit wonder!"

"You two! You really should be committed," said Edie.

"Men! You just can't take them anywhere," said Bestelle.

Just then, a massive mound of rebar came flying out of the second story window of the avant-garde museum and landed directly on the foursome, crushing them instantly beneath a huge pile of welded metal.

The artist, the same one who had been manning the metal moving machine at the museum's work-in-progress display, stuck his head out of the second story window to view the results below. "Oh my God," he screamed. "Oh my God! Don't touch it! Don't move a thing! It's a masterpiece! I'll be right down. Don't touch it!"

Across the street, in full view of the entire event stood the shitting-and-masturbating performance artist, smoking a cigarette. "Ha! Well, that pretty much settles it, rebar really can't fly," he said to himself and then turned and walked away.

The Celebrated Chef of Guangdong Province

When I first moved to Guangzhou, China, in 1999 to work for a U.S. computer accessory company, I remember hearing a story about a foreign couple that ventured into a local pet store. The husband intended to purchase a puppy for his loving wife. They spent an hour in the store looking over the puppies, playing with them, and cuddling them. The puppies were all so cute; it was very difficult to decide. In the end, they chose a small black and white half-breed with a lot of pep.

The owner of the store sat the happy couple down in an adjoining restaurant and offered to feed them while he readied the puppy. They ate a very satisfying meal, and then waited anxiously for their puppy. Finally, they asked the owner if he was done "preparing" their new pet.

Surprised, the owner told the man and woman that he had already given it to them. Horrified, the couple abruptly realized that the pet store was not a pet store after all, but a restaurant specializing in dog meat. To make matters worse, they had just been served and eaten the puppy that they had lovingly selected to be their pet!

To westerners living in China, it seems that there is little the Chinese will not eat. A good example occurred when I was once on a business trip in a city in the northwest of China called Urumqi and was politely asked by a factory owner to attend his daughter's wedding. It was an honor I could not refuse.

At the wedding, I found myself seated at a small, cramped table along with nine other people in a huge ballroom filled with guests. Along with eleven other courses, we were served a strange sausage-shaped meat with a hole in the middle. The meat was extremely tender and tasty, so much so that I had three huge helpings of the satisfying dish.

Curious, I asked one of the waiters what type of meat I had eaten.

"Coin meat," he calmly replied in Mandarin Chinese.

When this particular meat was sliced it looked a bit like an ancient Chinese coin which also had a hole in the middle of it: hence the name "coin meat."

"Yes, but what type of meat is it?" I asked in Mandarin.

"Donkey dick," he joyfully replied.

My eyes almost popped out of my head when I realized that I had just eaten three heaping helpings of donkey dick!

"Very tasty?" he asked.

Trying to contain my shock, I swallowed deeply and replied with a somber, "*Hen hao*," which means "very good" in Mandarin.

My stomach actually churned a bit. I couldn't believe that I had just been served and eaten donkey dick! At a wedding! But the meat was actually very edible, and the Chinese believe that ingesting the penis of any animal is supposed to make men more potent. I can't say that the donkey dick made me any more powerful in the sack than usual, but it sure was scrumptious.

While living in China, I always tried to eat most of the food served to me, but there were some things I just wouldn't knowingly eat: like insects, tiger penis, bear claw, and chicken butt. Street vendors in some parts of China actually serve chicken butt on a stick with a telltale hole in the center of the meat: It's considered a delicacy.

One night back in Guangzhou, my Taiwanese coworker, Lizard Ma (He chose his English name because he liked lizards, go figure), decided to take me to an old restaurant to try a new dish that was sweeping the city. Lizard wouldn't tell me what the dish was beforehand because he wanted to surprise me. He always got excited when treating me to something new and famous and I could tell by his giddiness that this dish was very special. However, I was skeptical because he had ordered some pretty gross dishes for me in the past.

Since the restaurant was nearby, we walk from our downtown office. Along the way, the traffic was gruesome and the air was so thick with pollution that I felt like I needed a respirator just to inhale. The smog trapped in the offensive stench and oppressive heat of the booming metropolis like a blanket. Accentuating the smog, the bright city lights glowed high in the sky and reflected off the pollution displaying a crimson sooty haze for all to see.

In addition to the massive amount of vehicles on the roads, there were also huge throngs of people scampering around. So much so that the sheer volume of humanity scuttling about on that busy autumn Friday night made me queasy. I just tried to put it out of my mind as I had grown accustomed to doing.

We walked down a long, narrow lane, past a deformed beggar bowing repeatedly for small change, past a young girl singing for tips and playing an out-of-tune guitar horrifically, past a "barbershop" specializing in blow jobs, and past two street urchins relentlessly trying to get us to enter a massage parlor and a karaoke bar respectively.

After making our way through the riff-raff, we eventually entered an old, brightly lit traditional restaurant that was jam-packed with people. Chinese landscape pictures loosely hung from grease-stained walls and a massive framed menu displayed food options in Chinese characters above a large serving hatch which exposed an active kitchen practically glowing from the numerous flaming woks in action.

All the tables were taken, so we stood over a young family that seemed to be finished with their meal and were just jibber-jabbering. As is the local custom, Lizard and I spoke loudly to each other, trying to make it uncomfortable for the family to just sit and chat at their table while hungry customers were waiting. The family got the hint and quickly left.

As soon as we sat down, a busboy instantly appeared and cleaned the table. As he was wiping, I looked up at the menu hanging on the wall and tried to decipher it based on the limited amount of Chinese characters that I knew.

"What are we going to have?" I asked Lizard.

"You will see," he said, smiling cleverly.

A waiter rapidly appeared with a pot of hot tea and asked us impatiently for our order. Lizard motioned to the waiter to come closer to him so that he could whisper our order without me listening in. But the restaurant was very noisy and the waiter could not hear clearly, so Lizard had to speak louder than he wanted to. Consequently, I overheard a bit of what Lizard was trying to conceal. It sounded like he was ordering "girl soup." I could only imagine what that was.

"What?" I asked, quickly grabbing Lizard's shoulder and turning him towards me.

"Don't worry, it's the house specialty and is very famous," he said.

"What is it?"

"You will see," he replied, excited that I was concerned.

The waiter chimed in and said that the restaurant had stopped serving that special dish.

Lizard let out a heavy sigh and was very disappointed, but ordered a black dog dish instead.

The Chinese believe that black dogs are the tastiest of all dogs, followed by yellow dogs, and then by multicolored dogs. The worst tasting dogs of all, according to the Chinese, are white dogs, go figure.

I was curious, having never tried dog before, so I decided to give it a shot: when in Rome or "*ru xiang sui su*" as the Chinese say.

After the waiter left, Lizard and I chatted in Mandarin. He had been living in Guangzhou for two years now. His wife and two kids were living with him as well. He had moved them over from Tainan, Taiwan, and was thoroughly enjoying the excitement of being in Guangzhou.

Interestingly, there were so many Taiwanese residing in the area that they actually had their own Taiwan-style school strictly for the children of Taiwan workers. Lizard said that the school's enrollment was well over two thousand students!

While Lizard and I were chatting, four local men were sitting at a table practically inches away. They were drinking *Tsingtao* beer and were red faced, rowdy, and feeling good. The guy nearest to our table turned towards me and smiled, his face was so bright red from drinking alcohol that it looked sunburnt.

He said to me in Mandarin, "You speak good Chinese."

"Not as good as you," I replied in Mandarin and smiled, knowing that you can never accept a compliment in China.

"No, no, no," he said quickly. "Your Chinese is very good. Where're you from?"

"My mother," I said, giving him the old joke.

"Ha, ha, me too! Do you speak Cantonese?" he asked (In Guangdong and Hong Kong the local dialect is Cantonese).

"No, not yet," I replied.

"Me neither, I'm from Beijing."

"No wonder your Mandarin is so good," I said, knowing the Chinese think that people from Beijing speak Mandarin the best.

"No, no, no," he said rapidly, smiling from ear-to-ear.

He drunkenly grabbed a big bottle of beer, two glasses, and then handed them to Lizard and me.

"I toast you two," he said, pouring us a small glass of *pijiu* or beer.

Lizard and I said, "*Hao, hao,*" meaning "good, good."

I ended up slamming numerous shots of *pijiu* down my throat as Lizard and I traded toasts with the gentlemen from the other table. We all chatted for a while and toasted each other over and over again saying the traditional toast: *ganbei* (which literally means "dry cup").

After Lizard and I were feeling no pain, the Beijing man seated at the adjacent table came over and sat down with us. He introduced himself as Lao Liu and then told us the story about why Mr. Sheng, the owner of the dining establishment, did not serve his specialty at the restaurant anymore.

The gist of the story I have translated below.

◊◊◊

The childless couple, Mr. and Mrs. Sheng, had been trying to have a male child for years, to no avail.

One day Mrs. Sheng came home and told her husband that she had some very important news.

"Old Love, please tell me that you are pregnant!" Mr. Sheng said anxiously. "And please, please tell me that it's a boy," he said, as he hovered over the dinner table, bracing himself for some good news.

In a country where every couple was granted only one child (thankfully this policy ended in 2016), the male child was more highly valued because only the male child could carry on the family name and take care of the parents when they get older.

That never really made any sense to me for two reasons. Firstly, given that there are really only a handful of last names in all of China, who cares if you're a Wang, Li, Ma, or Chen? They're all related, one way or another. Secondly, since most Chinese couples only wanted a male child, you'd think that somewhere down the line daughters would become very prized possessions that would warrant a fairly large dowry from the hordes of unmarried males.

Unfortunately, the male child, through centuries of tradition, is a big face gainer. As a result, according to some sources, underground abortions of female fetuses were off the charts.

Nevertheless, Mrs. Sheng was not pregnant. Instead, she revealed quite gravely to her husband that she had lost all the couple's savings by making a bad investment.

When Mr. Sheng heard the news that his wife had lost all their money, he exploded! Mr. Sheng pounded all the walls in their small apartment, slammed the doors shut, and blamed Mrs. Sheng for everything he could think of.

"We were saving that money for our child and to open up a new restaurant. Now what will we do?" he cried. "Stupid woman! If you could only get pregnant with a male child, maybe our luck would change; but now, there's no use getting pregnant because we can't afford a child and probably never will be able to! I knew I never should have married you!"

"It was your cousin's investment idea," she retorted in tears. She'd only invested because she thought she could trust her husband's cousin.

"*Tamade*," he screamed, which is a colloquialism that means, "fuck his mother."

"Had you stolen some money from a bank or cheated my cousin out of his money," he continued, "then I might have had a little respect for you, but now, I, I can't even look at you!"

After the heated argument, Mrs. Sheng felt so angry and depressed that she didn't speak to her husband for a week, and he gladly followed suit. Finally, her parents came over and tried to smooth things out.

Mr. Sheng was reluctant to talk to his wife, but had no qualms about yelling at his in-laws and telling them what a stupid daughter they had raised.

After Mr. Sheng ran his mouth, his father-in-law became very incensed over the disrespectful way Mr. Sheng was speaking to all of them. The argument almost came to blows. Just before it did, the in-laws left and Mrs. Sheng retreated to her bedroom, completely distraught.

As the weeks past, Mr. and Mrs. Sheng slowly began speaking to one another again, but only in a perfunctory manner.

To escape the situation, Mr. Sheng started staying out later and later at night and coming home drunk. He tried to restrain himself from having sex with his wife, but some nights when he couldn't resist the urge, he would mount her from behind and use his forearm to bury her head into the pillow so that he wouldn't have to see her disagreeable face and be reminded of the money that she had squandered away.

Mr. Sheng needed to recoup his losses fast, so he pondered numerous ways of earning money quickly. One inebriated night, he chatted with his crazy cousin, Bowen, who worked as a janitor at a big hospital and frequently thought up wild moneymaking schemes. After many bottles of beer, Bowen came up with an ingenious new idea "guaranteed" to make them both rich.

"With so many couples in China wanting boys," said Bowen, "the abortion rate is over the top and all of those abortions are female fetuses. Needless to say, the hospital that I work at is overflowing with these fetuses." Bowen leaned in, "And who do you think has to dispose of them? Me! That's right! Me! So get this, I have a fantastic idea! Why don't you try to prepare a female fetus dish? It would be a huge success!"

While Mr. Sheng pondered this idea, Bowen let out a huge belch.

"This could work, this could actually work," replied Mr. Sheng excitedly. "But don't the women want the fetuses after aborting them?"

"Absolutely not! Once the operation is over, the women usually don't want to have anything to do with the aborted fetuses. Moreover, the fetuses are usually treated like medical waste, but in some cases, more like garbage."

Bowen added that he could sneak all the recently aborted female fetuses out of the hospital, and instead of disposing of them, he could have the fetuses secretly delivered right to Mr. Sheng's restaurant free of charge. Of course, Bowen would want a cut of the profits and would have to offer his boss some *renminbi* as hush money.

"This just might be one of your best ideas yet," Mr. Sheng exclaimed. "Don't tell anyone about this idea. Anyone!" he said and rushed home to devise an appropriate dish.

Bowen came over the following evening with a few fresh fetuses still covered in bits and bobs from their plight. Following a thorough inspection of the goods, Mr. Sheng set out to prepare an extremely spicy dish to cover up the rank odor that emanated naturally from the fetuses.

After a process of trial and error, he eventually hit upon the right combination of herbs and spices to make the soup taste delightful. To prepare the new dish, Mr. Sheng would shave the fine hair off the fetus, wash it in soap and water, boil it to kill off any bacteria, marinate it overnight in a special sauce in the fridge, and then serve her up in a super spicy hot broth with a nice array of vegetables. He called his creation *xiao nu la tang*, which meant "spicy little girl soup."

Once Mr. Sheng had secured enough female fetuses and was satisfied with the preparation of the dish, he began offering it to his most faithful customers. The first few people who were given the opportunity to try the new dish were initially hesitant, especially after they found out what it consisted of, but a few diehards gave the soup a shot and raved about the tender meat and the delectable brain.

Customers dug into the fetus with their chopsticks as it floated around in the thick, super spicy broth. They ate the flesh, the innards, and the surrounding vegetables; drank the soup; and chased it all down with a bowl of steamed white rice.

"Especially delicious," they all proclaimed, "was the meat on the cheeks and buttocks."

Word spread that eating fetuses was good for your health. Lines soon formed around the building with customers eager to try this new specialty. Consequently, Mr. Sheng worked overtime to fill all the orders and had to hire a few new chefs and install more tables in the restaurant to meet increased demand. Meanwhile, Bowen rapidly made deals with every hospital and abortion clinic in town, as well as with those in nearby cities.

Sure enough, copycats sprang up and began offering the exact same dish, all claiming to be the first, the originator. But what the competitors' customers didn't know was that Mr. Sheng and Bowen had cornered the market on fetuses in Guangzhou and the competitors were actually using cleverly disguised animal fetuses in their soups instead.

Once customers at other restaurants learned that they were not eating human fetuses, they fled to Mr. Sheng's. Faced with fewer customers, the competition fought back and began importing female fetuses from all over the vast country, but could not match Mr. Sheng's price for the locally made commodity. And Mr. Sheng was such a great chef that he could even make female fetuses taste fantastic!

After earning a lot of money in his new venture, Mr. Sheng decided to celebrate and cheer up his wife who had seemed down as of late. One night at home he prepared a special new dish for her: *xiao nan la tang*, which meant "spicy little male soup."

Upon hearing the name of the new dish, Mrs. Sheng looked at her husband curiously. "You have a male fetus, not a female?"

"Yes indeed," he proudly proclaimed. "This new dish is going to make us super rich," he said, then noticed that his wife seemed haggard. "Old Love, you look pale. What is wrong with you? Are you sick?"

"Oh, it's nothing, just a woman's problem," she said, as she slowly sat down to eat.

"This new dish will make you strong again," he exclaimed.

Mr. Sheng brought out a huge bowl of piping hot spicy red soup with a male fetus floating inside. The Shengs served themselves a bowl of white rice and began eating the hearty meal. Mr. Sheng dug into the floating fetus with his chopsticks and encouraged Mrs. Sheng to taste the cheeks and buttocks of the unborn child. In his own way, he was trying to reconcile with his wife. By offering her the best bits of the meal, Mr. Sheng was showing his wife a smidgen of respect.

Mrs. Sheng tore into the buttocks.

"Good, yes?" he asked his silent wife.

"Very tasty, my husband," she said, chewing slowly.

"Now try one of the cheeks, but dip it in sauce first," he said, pointing to a small side dish that he had prepared made primarily of soy sauce, garlic, hot sauce, lemon juice, and vinegar.

Mrs. Sheng tore off part of a cheek, dipped it in the sauce, and gingerly pushed it into her pouty little mouth.

Mr. Sheng pointed to the fetus's penis with his chopsticks and offered it to his wife. She simply shook her head and politely encouraged her husband to take it. A brief battle ensued over the fetal penis with each person rapidly gesturing to one another with their chopsticks trying to respectfully force the other person to consume the best part.

"You really outdid yourself," she said, pushing her husband's chopsticks towards the fetal penis. "This is exquisite! It will make you a fortune if you can only find enough women who are aborting male fetuses."

"We don't have to find them because we are very lucky. Ha, ha! A new doctor has arrived in town, and I offered him a lot of money to give me male fetuses because some of my very wealthy customers have specifically requested them. And get this, I can probably charge my customers five times, maybe ten times more than what I charge them for the female dish. We will soon be ridiculously rich!"

"But why does this doctor abort male fetuses?" she asked, as Mr. Sheng adroitly broke off the little fetus's uncircumcised penis and began dipping it in the sauce bowl.

"Well, that's just it," he said still dipping. "Apart from the occasional distressed teenager or whore, there aren't many women aborting male fetuses. So I told the new doctor to trick his patients into thinking that they are pregnant with a female fetus—not all of them, just the gullible ones—and then encourage those patients to abort their fetuses.

"The doctor makes his money both from the operation and from selling me the fetuses. He is newly married, just moved to town, and recently opened his own clinic. So he needs all the help he can get. It's actually a perfect situation! He makes money, we make money, and everybody's happy!"

Mrs. Sheng quickly reviewed the events of her busy day in her head. Once her husband had left their apartment that morning, she had secretly gone to visit Dr. Liang on Renmin South Road to have an abortion. She had been to see him once before, and he had assured her that she was pregnant with yet another female child.

Having argued with her pig-headed husband over the merits of raising a female child numerous times before, Mrs. Sheng knew that Mr. Sheng only wanted a male child and birthing a female child was out of the question. And since the government only allowed one child, Mrs. Sheng was well aware of what had to be done.

This was her fourth abortion; she knew the routine. However, she did not want to tell her husband about the pregnancy out of fear that he would call her stupid, complain about the cost of yet another abortion, or worse, want to cook it! So she borrowed the money from her best friend and unbeknownst to her husband, made an appointment with Dr. Liang.

She had carefully chosen Dr. Liang because he was new in town, had a nice clean new office, and she hoped and prayed that he had not been in business long enough to be in cahoots with her crafty husband.

When she checked in, Mrs. Sheng used a fake name so that the doctor would not have any inkling who she was. After all, she did not want anyone finding out what she had been up to. This was a very private matter and it was risky because sex-selection abortions were technically illegal. Due to this fact, she had to pay a lot more to get hers done.

In the small sterile clinic, Mrs. Sheng chatted with the nurse before the operation and learned that hers was the only abortion being performed that week by Dr. Liang.

Concerned, Mrs. Sheng asked, "The doctor has done this before, hasn't he?"

"Oh yes," the young nurse stated confidently.

After the operation, Mrs. Sheng's suspicions were aroused when she asked to see the fetus. The doctor became nervous and made excuses. Mrs. Sheng stood her ground and demanded to see it. She waited until the nurse finally came out carrying a rather large female fetus covered in blood.

"This fetus is ice cold," complained Mrs. Sheng, gingerly poking the lifeless child.

"Yes, yes, we put them on ice to preserve them," said Dr. Liang. "You see, after every abortion, we always turn the fetuses over to scientists to inspect them for abnormalities, but we put them on ice first before sending them out."

"Well, why is it so big? I've only been pregnant for fifteen weeks at the most."

"Don't worry, it's about normal size for fifteen weeks," the doctor assured her.

Trusting her gut, Mrs. Sheng ordered the nurse to put the fetus in a bag and hand it over to her. Afterwards, she was quickly shooed out of the office even though she complained that she wasn't feeling very well.

In the taxi ride home, she noticed that she was losing blood. She hurriedly made her way to a hospital and learned that she was permanently damaged from the abortion and could not conceive any more children. Dr. Liang had botched the operation. To make matters worse, Mrs. Sheng had another doctor inspect her aborted fetus and was told that it was probably at least twenty weeks along.

Burdened with this incredibly terrible news, she made her way home, afraid to tell her husband that she would not be able to conceive children anymore.

With all her might, she struggled to put the previous events out of her mind and appear as if nothing had happened, but in actuality she just wanted to cry out loud.

As she arrived home to their small, cluttered apartment nestled in an old building, her husband—unaware of her extreme agony—prepared his male fetal soup. She wanted to vomit when she saw it on the table, wanted to run and hide, but she had to appear as if everything was normal. She definitely could not let her husband know about her abortion or the fact that she was now infertile. He would only blame her again and might even want a divorce. Thus, she had to be strong and not let on.

Back at the Sheng's dining room table, Mr. Sheng sucked the fetal penis into his mouth as the couple's black cat sat expectantly in the corner. Mrs. Sheng summoned all of her strength to ask her husband the one question that was troubling her—a question that she really didn't want answered.

"You say that you now have a doctor giving you male fetuses?" she asked.

"Yes, it's pure genius!" said Mr. Sheng, slowly munching the penis while anticipating the vitality it would surely bring to him.

"What is the doctor's name?" Mrs. Sheng asked carefully, while clenching her fists tightly.

"Dr. Liang," he said, stuffing his mouth full of rice.

"Dr. Liang what?"

"Dr. Liang Rong," he said, licking a grain of rice from his lips.

"On Renmin South Road?"

"Yes, that's the one," he said, accidentally spitting out a few grains of rice as he spoke. "Do you know him?"

The realization abruptly hit her like a sledgehammer: She had been misled by Dr. Liang. Mrs. Sheng had thought that she was aborting yet another female fetus, while in reality, it had actually been a male fetus, the very one that the couple had just been consuming!

Attacked by a vision of extreme clarity, Mrs. Sheng projectile vomited all over the dining room table, threw her chopsticks at her husband, and then completely lost her mind. She quickly stood up and began yelling and screaming. She grabbed her head and started pulling out her hair. She spun around the room in circles, howling at the top of her lungs.

Mr. Sheng thought his wife had suddenly become possessed by an evil spirit.

"What are you doing?" he cried, standing up and trying to calm his wife down.

Mrs. Sheng continued screaming incessantly and spinning wildly. Eventually, she ran downstairs and out into the streets, wailing in agony. The neighbors tried, but they could not console her.

Because Mr. Sheng had no clue what his wife had been through that day, he was completely shocked by her erratic behavior.

"Women, they're so emotional," he muttered to himself, as he cleaned up Mrs. Sheng's mess. "She'll calm down once we become super rich from my new dish," he assured himself.

After clearing the table, Mr. Sheng tossed bits of the soft fetal tissue to his black cat who devoured it in seconds.

Neighbors quickly began coming over to his apartment wondering what had happened to his wife.

"She saw a ghost," he replied, simply to avoid conversation. In fact, he didn't know what had happened to his wife nor what he had just eaten, but once he finally found out that he inadvertently harmed his wife and to make matters worse, cooked and ate his own child, he became deeply distraught.

Later that same evening, Mrs. Sheng confided in some of her neighbors about how Dr. Liang had duped her. The news spread like wildfire. A mob quickly formed and completely demolished Dr. Liang's office and ran him out of town. He was lucky to escape with his life.

◇◇◇

Back at the restaurant, Lao Liu who was extremely drunk by this time said, "And that is why Mr. Sheng does not serve *xiao nu la tang* anymore. But you should try the boiled rat fetus, it's '*tamade hao*,'" which loosely translated means "it's fucking good!"

"Maybe next time," I said as the waiter brought out our main course. A big plate of black dog stared me right in the face. I was so disgusted by Lao Liu's story that I couldn't muster the energy to try the dish.

"Come on," said Lizard, attacking the meal enthusiastically. "You must try the black dog, it's unbelievably good!"

I apologized profusely and just nibbled on my white rice while chasing it down with more beer.

For more information, search online for "China fetus soup."

Totally Losing Face

It was Christmas Eve 1994 and I was on my own drinking away my misery in the Moxy, one of the few foreign hangouts in Taipei, Taiwan. The Moxy was an ancient two-storied bar complete with old rock posters, cobwebs and rats crawling on the rafters. I was sitting at the end of the downstairs' bar, keeping to myself and enjoying a quiet beer or two, when suddenly she slinked her way into the dingy, music-throbbing, light-twinkling, smoke-billowing bar, like a lioness on the prowl. I thought about ducking for cover, but instead stood my ground and ordered another beer. Watching the mirror on the wall behind the bar, I saw her sniff me out, before moving in for the kill. I was hopelessly perched on a barstool, alone in a foreign country, and bracing myself for the inevitable agony that she was surely about to inflict. Putting my beer to my mouth, I stared straight ahead, until someone tapped me on the shoulder. The attack had begun. Slowly, I turned around on my barstool and faced her.

"Hi," she said shyly, looking downwards, as if to apologize for her misgivings.

I wanted to act like one ferociously pissed off motherfucker, but civility prevailed. I said, "Hmmm," without emotion. Then I turned back towards the bar, as if I hadn't seen her. I was hoping she'd get the hint and LEAVE. But instead, she just waited, without saying a word. After a few minutes had passed, I finally spun around and said, "WHAT?"

"I want to say sorry for you," she said in a high-pitched little girl's voice. I hated that voice. I had heard that shrill whine many times before. She knew how to use it well to get what she wanted.

"Why," I asked, through clenched teeth. I stared her straight in the eyes for the longest time. Her glassy orbs were so dark that you couldn't see where her pupils began and ended; they just merged with her irises.

"You good boyfriend. I very, very bad girlfriend." She pouted her lips and lowered her head again.

I had been in Taiwan long enough to ignore the locals' English-speaking errors, much like I ignored everything else. But I couldn't ignore the pain I still felt towards her. "YES! WHY?" I angrily exploded.

"I telled you before. My before boyfriend very bad. He lie me. He tell me, I and he marry. Then he break. I very angry so I play many boy. I play you. I sorry to you."

Yeah, yeah. I'd heard all this shit before. I hadn't been able to make any sense of it then, and I sure as hell couldn't make any sense of it now. I leaned towards her ear and said quietly with force, my teeth grinding, "You tried to fuck my fucking friend! You were my girlfriend!" All the anger was starting to come back. "WHY," I screamed. That was all I wanted to know. After four months, you'd think I was entitled to a little truth. I just looked her in the eyes, searching for sense, trying to fucking understand what was going on in that little head of hers.

"Why don't I just take her home and fuck the shit out of her," I thought to myself. With her silky, shiny black hair, cut short into a bob, she seemed somewhat older now, not so innocent, but she still looked good, real good. All of a sudden, everything that had happened between us came back to me in tidal waves. The pain was still there, as if it had all just happened that morning.

When I initially moved to Taiwan four months ago, I was living in a traveler's hostel with thirteen other people, mostly males. We were all foreign travelers, who were at that moment sharing similar space in a strange foreign country, and, for the most part, teaching English. This hostel was actually a converted small two-bedroom, one-bathroom apartment. It wasn't much, but for someone who abruptly dropped into a completely different culture for the first time all by himself, it was information, communication, sanctuary and family all in one. We spent a lot of time together, huddling in the hostel, trying to get a grip on Taiwan, debating politics, talking about our travels, drinking Taiwan Beer and playing cards. I rarely ventured anywhere or did anything without thoroughly discussing it with my hostel mates first. We were a tight knit group. It was as if we had all been in a plane wreck together and were honor-bound to each other's survival in this backwards foreign land.

One day, I was out on my own, exploring *Shimending*—a trendy section of town, suggested by one of my hostel mates. Everything in Taipei was so new, different and exciting. I remember loving the challenge of it all. Out on my own in a strange land and slowly figuring out how it ticked. I couldn't speak a word of Mandarin, but that didn't matter. I was in Taiwan, learning about life in a different country: Living it, touching it, smelling it, right in the heart of it all. I was lost as usual, but that didn't bother me anymore. I was learning how to find my way back home.

Taipei is extremely difficult to get around in because very few street signs are in English, thus a map in English is practically useless. If you can't speak or read Mandarin, it's tough at first to get orientated. I actually enjoyed getting lost and then finding my way home. I called it "future face." I figured if I could get home from any point in Taipei by myself, I wouldn't have any problems in the future with directions, and I would then be able to get anywhere in this big, bad city by myself, on time and ready for whatever I had to do.

This was a new beginning for me. I wanted to do everything right. I wanted to get my shit together. I knew that integrating into the culture as fast as I could was key to being a success in this country, or any country. Being late or lost was a loss of face. Conversely, not being late or not getting lost meant gaining face. Not losing face had become a top priority, because Taipei is a big face town. Everybody wants a big face and nobody wants to lose face. This cultural safety tip is very evident from the moment you set foot in Taiwan.

At that time, I had the basic idea of "face," but I didn't completely understand the concept. I don't know if I completely understand it now. It seems to be everywhere. It's lurking under the surface in everything everyone does. It's in the way people do business, interact and socialize. It's there on the child's face when they give their teacher a big gift. When an employee kisses up to their boss. When a neighbor does you a favor. When somebody sets you up. Or when somebody takes you to dinner. And it's there when you full-on yell at someone. Or refuse an invitation. Or even pick your teeth on the street (A bad habit of the lower classes, a fact I discovered only after I'd been doing it repeatedly for several months). Mostly though, it's all about relationships. They start out as embryos. Then they slowly build into a web of trust and acceptance. Your face finally becomes very big, and you become a well-trusted person with a solid set of relationships.

Sometimes I got a little too lost in this jungle of meaningless pictures and pitch-friendly sounds, and I needed some assistance. Usually I would ask the prettiest girl I saw walking on the street to help me out. This is how I met my first local girlfriend. I was very lost and patiently waiting for a beautiful girl to walk by. Sure enough, after a few minutes I saw one coming out of a hotel. She seemed young and sweet. If I only knew then what I know now. Fate. I could have chosen half a dozen girls, but I chose her instead. Bad luck.

She was walking right by me, so I stepped in front of her and smiled. She paused and tried to skirt around me. I skirted with her and asked her in English how to get to the main train station, which was conveniently located right next to my hostel. She stopped and looked at me with a nervous smile. Immediately afterwards, she became completely red in the face and waved her hand repeatedly back and forth, crying, "No Englishy, no Englishy." And then she walked backwards in fright, like I was going to hit her, or worse yet, speak some more English.

"Wait," I said firmly. She kept backing up and looking around for help. "Train Station, where?" I made train noises, "Chugga, chugga, choo, choo." She backed up right into a wall, her right shoulder pinned under a pay phone and her left pinned under the bottom part of a window frame. I had her right where I wanted her.

"Train station. Choo, choo. Where?"

A perplexed look came over her face, so I repeated my train noises. I could see communication was beginning to take place. "There," she pointed, as she squirmed away from the phone and the wall.

"Oh, thank you so much," I said, grinning from ear to ear. Quickly, she began to leave. "Wait. What's your telephone number?" I said, putting my hand to my face and making a dialing gesture. I figured asking for her number was worth a shot.

Much to my surprise, she took out a pen and paper and scribbled something down. She handed me the piece of paper and again, tried to leave. "Wait. What's your name?" She quickly grabbed the paper and jotted down a Chinese name, which I couldn't read, followed by: B-U-N-N-Y. She had a Chinese name as well as an English name, as most of the younger locals did. "Oh, Bunny. Very pretty name. Hi, I'm Justin," I said, as if speaking to a young child. She nodded and tried to say it.

"Dustbin," she repeated. She waited for a second, as if I was going to say, "Wait," again, and then hurriedly walked away. It wasn't the most effective first meeting that I've ever had, but it was one of the most interesting.

A few days later, with the help of one of my Chinese-speaking hostel mates, I called Bunny and set up a meeting place and time.

She decided to meet me in front of a busy department store. I arrived on time with an English-to-Chinese/Chinese-to-English dictionary firmly clasped in my hand. I looked out into the fast-moving crowd of locals and realized that I couldn't have picked her out in a line up to save my life. I just wasn't used to recognizing Chinese faces yet. Plus there were a million girls running around who were medium height, slender, and who had long black hair. They all kind of blended in together. I sat beneath a big ceramic dog—it was 1994, The Year of the Dog—and began reading a newspaper, hoping she would see me first, the one foreigner in a sea of Chinese people.

Luckily, she found me, and we decided to go for a walk. We ventured to a park, sat down on a bench and tried to communicate. It was like "a chicken and a dog trying to communicate," as the Chinese say. At first, it was really tough. We spent about twenty minutes going over basic chitchat. She spent most of her time thumbing through my dictionary and occasionally pointing to a word. At the end of the evening I felt like the night was a success. "This communication stuff is highly overrated," I thought.

We started dating. It was difficult at times, but her English began to improve, and I began to study Chinese. Other than the obvious communication problems, everything seemed to be going smoothly. And did I mention that she was wild in the sack? Not only that, she wanted to have sex every-and-any-where. Who was I to refuse?

And then, for reasons still not clear to me, she was kicked out of her house by her loving mother and father and decided to move in with me into my lower bunk bed in the hostel. Kind-heartedly, I agreed. Of course,

I figured I was going to get laid every day and night. Little did I know that she had plans of her own.

Letting her move in was actually a pretty dumb idea. First of all, the room I lived in was very small and crammed with three bunk beds occupied by myself and five smelly guys. On top of that, the beds were poorly built and made a lot of noise every time anyone moved an inch.

One evening, a week after she moved in with me, my friend and hostel mate, Anders, was acting a little strange. I asked him what was up, and he explained that my innocent girlfriend had tried to rape him. "What," was my first response. It's not every day that you hear a guy say something like that. So I asked him about fifty times to clarify that sentence. "Raped?" I swear I thought he was joking.

According to him, one day when I was out teaching an English class, he was on his upper bunk bed reading. Bunny, out of the blue, jumped up and started grabbing his privates and kissing him. She wanted to go all the way, but he refused until he sorted everything out with me first. What a friend! I can't say that under similar circumstances, I would have done the same. He further stated that other guys in the hostel had said that Bunny had also come onto them, but in a less aggressive way. With one swing of the bat, my seemingly innocent girlfriend had somehow managed to seriously damage what little face I had. My mind raced. Could she really be that, that, psycho? That horny? What was she doing? Did she think that I wouldn't find out?

Or wait, was my friend lying? Naw. He was obviously flustered and troubled and not quite sure how to handle the situation. Neither was I. We did the only thing two men could do in this sort of predicament; we went out and got drunk together.

The next evening, very perplexed, I confronted my girlfriend. She emphatically denied all allegations like a frightened lamb. I gave her a burning stare while broken English jiggled out of her mouth. Even in broken English, a lie still sounds like a lie. It was hard not to believe those sad little doe eyes and that small pouting mouth on that cute round face. For a second, I believed the sugar-coated lies. She was telling me just what I wanted to hear.

"Okay, wait here," I said, as I pulled my friend aside and went over the story with him yet again, just in case.

Anders told me the same exact story, again. "Why would my friend say these things?" I thought to myself. "He must be lying!" But wait, why would he make this shit up?" He was visibly shaken and not quite sure what to do. Part of him wanted to go out with her, part of him knew she was a psycho, and another part of him was my friend. He was a mess. I was a mess. If I had been another man, I might have totally believed Bunny and my life would have been shit for being so stupid.

"Look, you can have her. I don't want her," I told Anders. Obviously, she didn't want me anymore, so why would I want her? Deep down I was hoping he'd say "No." I didn't want her to come between my friendship with him.

"I'm not sure," is all he said. He was going to take a wait-and-see stance. He was the only friend I had in town, and she had swooped down and tried to crush that. God, I hated her. Traveling makes you weary and confused. Cultural cues are constantly crushing your cranium with questions. But wait. Maybe it was just a communication problem? She couldn't read me and I couldn't read her. Fuck that. She tried to fuck my fucking friend!

During the following week, I broke up with Bunny, kicked her out and told her not to return, but she kept coming back to me like a faithful dog. I stood my ground and told her to leave each time. Only an idiot would go back to her now. But why would she want to come back to me? Didn't she hit on someone else? Doesn't that usually mean that you want to break up? Apparently not in Taiwan. I was so confused. I kept trying to tell her, "Look, I'm breaking up with you. You, me, break." I made a breaking-a-stick gesture for emphasis. "In my country" I said slowly, "that means you go bye-bye. Do you understand? Me, you, no more." But she kept saying "No," and coming back. What the hell was going on? Every day she'd be waiting outside the hostel for me when I returned from work. "What kind of sadistic chick is this?" I kept thinking. Finally, I had a Chinese-speaking hostel mate talk to her on my behalf. He relayed to me that all she wanted to say was, "Sorry."

I told him, "Okay, okay! Tell her that I accept her stupid apology, and then tell her to get the fuck out of my sight." He did just that, and amazingly, she left.

After seeing how she acted, Anders was completely disinterested in her and so was I. However, my other male hostel mates were a bit sad to see her go. The wankers!

Bunny stayed away for about a week. Then, just when I thought I wouldn't see her again, I found her waiting for me outside the hostel when I got back from a teaching lesson. She had flowers in one hand and said that she wanted to talk. She had cut her hair very short to show how serious she was. She was giving me the Chinese treatment: cause pain to yourself when you cause pain to others to show how sorry you are. I guess cutting her hair was the most painful wound she could inflict on herself. She looked so pathetic that I gave into her plea.

We went to a nearby teahouse and talked. She rambled on about how her old boyfriend had promised to marry her, and how he had played around on her. For some reason, she felt that by cheating on me, she could somehow avenge him. They weren't even dating anymore! It made no sense whatsoever to me. There had to be something else. She was holding out. She was just saying this to protect herself, maybe to save her face. She should have thought about her face before she got wet with excitement for my friend. I sipped my bitter oolong tea and listened and couldn't make heads or tail of anything spilling out of her mouth. She was just drooling and babbling for drooling's and babbling's sake. Definitely not for my sake. I didn't want to hear any more of her bullshit. I was about to storm out of there, happy never to see her again, when she boldly and totally unexpectedly said, "You, me, last sex?"

Whoa! Hold the phone! "Last sex." I repeated it in my mind. I pondered its implications for a moment. There was something intriguing and wild and crazy about that suggestion. Last sex? Hmm?

"Oh just do it," my libido cried. "What are you, a fool?" No chick had ever asked me for, "Last sex." What's the worst thing that could happen? I'd already fucked her before. I was almost going to fuck her "for the last time," just because of the novelty and finality of it all. Last sex? What, are we going to die afterwards or something? Then I suddenly remembered the pain and the shame that she had slapped on me. Pain and shame that I had never felt before. It had cut a fresh new hole in my heart and the wound was still gaping.

She sat there fluttering her chiseled eyelids, patiently awaiting my response. "No," I yelled in her face. What did she think I was, a toy for her to abuse at her beckoning? Was I some obedient slave who responded only to her needs? How fucking preposterous. Last sex my ass. "No," I repeated. She dejectedly feigned sadness. "You and me no more," I said. "I no want see you again. Okay?" She nodded her head sadly, and then I got up and walked away.

I was so pissed off. I started thinking about friendship, and what it meant to me. What is a friend? Someone you have the greatest respect for. Someone you're there for and who's there for you. A girlfriend, by definition, is a girl who fits the above description, but gets even closer to you than any member of the same sex can. She is someone who you entrust your soul to, someone who's always there for you, and you reciprocate. Bunny was only a girl and probably not even that. Whore came to mind. No, she wasn't smart enough to be a whore. But she definitely wasn't a friend, that was for sure.

A traveler must trust his instincts. People can be met quickly on the road. "Who to trust?" is always the question. It's difficult. Lies. Truth. They're all out there, but it's so hard to see through everyone's bullshit. You try your best to weed through it all. Your life is in a bag on your back. Your heart is on your sleeve. Who is my friend on the road? Who are my friends back home? What is a friend? You make friends. You miss a friend. You leave friends, and make new friends. But friends don't contrive. They don't slither behind your back and shoot you down. That's an enemy. How can a friend, a girlfriend, stab you with all her might and twist and turn the sharpened steel until you're lying on the floor in a pool of fluid, flopping for help and then as if nothing had happened, offer a hand? She was one hundred percent not a friend and I didn't want to have sex with non-friends. Goodbye and good riddance!

I felt I had definitely made the right decision. This is a big "face" town, and I finally realized what it meant to lose face. Unfortunately, I was on the losing end. She took what little face I had garnered and jumped all over it until it was nothing but a little piece of flesh and hair. After that brief encounter on the wrong end, I vowed never to lose face again.

That was four months ago. Four months of lonely nights. Four months of wondering what the fuck I was doing in Taiwan. Four months of wandering around these throbbingly crazy streets trying to make sense of this nutty place. Homesickness, culture shock and frustration had all settled in and lack of sex had loosened my loins. My love was the size of two bowling balls and a baseball bat by the time Bunny trapped me at the bar. She was no longer a friend; she was a nobody and sex was the enemy that had to be eradicated. Sex screamed from my being, begging to explode out of my skin. I was sure every woman in the bar could smell the lack of sex on my body. They could see the fullness in my eyes and the weight of my walk. I got aroused when someone opened the door and the cool breeze brushed across me just right.

Standing at the bar facing her again, I could only think of one problem separating the two of us. This problem had been haunting my brain. I had to know the answer as to why she tried to fuck my friend. "Just tell me the truth," I inquired. After four months, I was goddamned entitled. Fuck the lingering lies. The terrible unadulterated truth was the only thing that could soothe my burning inquisition. She stuttered and mumbled and fumbled and obviously tried to contrive another prefabricated-propaganda-laden-commercially-sugar-coated lie. The truth, I pleaded. "I know what you are," I thought, "Just say it! Treat me with some fucking respect for once." My mind was afire. I had to know the answer. I stared her down, trying to pry it out of her like a dentist trying to pull teeth with just his bare hands. She opened her mouth.

"I like." She paused for effect. "I like sex." Then she bowed her head down low, as if she had just admitted to a horrendous crime. "Don't you?" She added.

I closed my eyes and shook my head. Did I just hear her say, "I like sex, don't you?" Of course, don't we all? What kind of shit was that? "I like sex, don't you?" It was too simple, too basic. I just stared at her in disbelief. But somehow her explanation pacified my ears and burped my brain. It wasn't a lie, I knew that, but it was hardly any earth-shattering news either. I rolled her words around my brain. I let myself take the bait.

"Let's have sex. I pay you," she said with a calm businessy chill.

I was taken aback. What did she just say? She'll pay? Now what the hell was that supposed to mean? I was still trying to figure out her last sentence, and now she was hitting me with this. Like since I wouldn't have sex with her before, it would somehow impersonalize the situation if money was involved as an incentive to have sex. So now she was just a woman looking for sex and willing to pay. She was in the mood, and I could help. It was honest; I'd give her that. She set the boundaries: no love, just sex. We fuck and that's it, because money is involved. She wants sex and I want sex and instead of me paying a nameless, faceless prostitute, I can fuck her, and she'll pay me. What's wrong with that? What is sex anyway? It's just sex. Is it any different if I fuck her tonight or go find some bimbo and fuck her? I don't love either of them. I'm an adult and I just want to have sex, is that so bad? Who gives a fuck who I fuck? I'll just go in and have sex with her and then blow her off. That should do wonders for her face.

But it all seemed too simple. There had to be something more to this that I couldn't see, something evil lurking under the surface. No normal Chinese woman was going to pay an old boyfriend for sex, right? Maybe it was a face thing. She'd lost face when I denied her "last sex" four months ago. And she'd most certainly lost face when I broke up with her under such shameful circumstances. She'd gotten busted almost red-handed. She got the old double-dreaded-facial-whammy. She lost face big time. Now I was in the driver's seat: The curator of her face. She hadn't given a fuck about me from day one. She still didn't care about me or why else would she have offered to pay cash? She just wanted her face back, bigger than ever. She lost face to a lowly foreigner. It was all becoming clear.

"I pay you," she said again, as she started to unzip her purse for emphasis. I guess she wanted a few financially flavored lies to go with her large library of lies. It was as if she was saying, "It's simple. I pay you, or you pay me. No love is involved at all. It's just a sex purchase. I sex you, you sex me. It's nothing."

I was really tempted to say, "How much?" I wanted to know, out of curiosity, how much she was going to pay me. Honestly, I was very flattered by the whole notion of getting paid. How much was I worth? How much would I take for sex?

"I don't want your money," flew out of my mouth, instead. I pushed her purse away. I could see that she was willing to do anything to get her face back and this was her way of showing it. If she was willing to pay for me to have sex with her then she was very willing. And I was very willing to do anything to rid myself of the loud aching sorrow filling my loins. It was Christmas and I was far from home, all alone. It was Christmas, and I needed a big sexy present to make me feel whole again.

I looked around the lonely dark bar and tried to think clearly, but sex was clouding my mind. That was it in a nutshell: I just wanted to have sex so badly that nothing else mattered but sex. And here was sex on a hot Chinese platter. "Goddamnit," I yelled to myself. "Don't do it!" I tried to think clearly. I tried to contemplate the offer, but my head was zooming and good God, I wanted to fuck her so badly, right then and there.

"Give me a shot of tequila," I murmured to the bartender. I needed something to wake me up. I downed the shot and looked her up and down. What a cute face. What a hot body! You would never have guessed that she was a slutty psycho. I looked around for something normal, something to help me think straight, see straight, but all I could see were a bunch of drunks getting shitfaced on Christmas in a lonely bar in Taipei. "Let's go," I said reluctantly, and before I knew it, we were outside, together.

It was cold and wet. I zipped up my jacket, but I still felt cold, cold to the bone. We walked to a nearby sex hotel. The rates were posted by the hour. She insisted on paying for the room. Good, I wasn't about to spend a dime on her. She looked in her wallet at her money and gestured to me, as if she was going to pay me. I gave her a give-me-a-break glare.

We entered an old greasy, tiny elevator with mirrors all around the inside. She looked at herself in the mirror and tried to make herself look pretty, while I just looked at myself and shook my head. We exited the elevator into a narrow dimly lit hallway with crusty old wallpaper that was heavily stained, faded and peeling. We found our room and walked quietly in and closed the door.

The room was clean, but it smelt rotten. The bed was round. We took off our coats. Quiet. There was a slight awkwardness between us.

"Well, are you going to do it?" I thought to myself. "YES!" I just wanted to jump on top of her and rip her clothes off, enter her and squeeze her tits, bite her lip, suck her neck and cum on her face. I wanted my flesh moving rapidly inside her flesh. I wanted to work it all out of my system. I wanted to fuck her like I'd never fucked anyone before and then toss her away like a used condom. Fuck her. Fuck her hard. My whole body was focused on this one thought. I was like one taut penis from head to toe.

"Don't kiss her," I said to myself, "just fuck her, okay?"

She smells good. I take a good long whiff. We jump on the bed and kiss, urgggh. She's warm. Rip off clothes. Hold. Feel. Hug. Lick. Kiss. NO KISSING, JUST FUCKING, DAMN IT! Touch. Hot. Inside. Good. Now get in and get out. Don't waste time. Stay focused. NO KISSING! Get in, drop anchor, then shove off."

Grinding and sighing and moaning. Face mangled. Body taut, about to snap. Sweat pouring off my brow. Titties flappin'. Bodies smackin'. Hey, this sure beats jackin'!

"Wait! Uh-oh. What's going on? This is taking far too long. What happened to get in and get out? Too much alcohol? Oh no, too much alcohol! That shot of tequila; it's imprisoning my seed, blocking my barrage."

"Aghhghghghghgh," my soul screamed for some sort of justification, some answers, some understanding, some speed. Forced to feel her and be with her for longer than I had expected. I just wanted to get it over with. "Why am I here? Aye-ya! Why did I get hard? I hate this chick! Why won't I cum? God, she looks good. She feels good. This feels good. Cum! For fuck's sake. Cum for cum's sake. Cum for me. Cum for pain and agony. Cum, cu-cu-cum, CUM. It's so easy to cum, but my soul had trapped my semen and locked it in a cage in my gooey heart. It would take hell fire to break the chains on my vagina-worthy semen. But doesn't she look good? Doesn't this feel good? But, this, can't, go, on, for, much, lon, ger..."

> *I once saw two dogs sniffing in the night*
> *They whimpered and mingled with such delight*
> *Without a single thought of love or fright*
> *One climbed behind and slid in just so right*
> *They pumped and shook under the hot moonlight*
> *After grunting and groaning with all their might*
> *They calmly unwound, tired from their fight*
> *Then walked separate ways with cares oh so slight.*

I felt the rusty drawbridge slowly lower, while the chains rattled and the bridge slammed to the ground, dust flying everywhere. Then, like a gushing geyser, the organic glue of life came bursting out, like a volcanic blast from a dormant mountain. Poooooooooogh! It exploded out, along with all of my pain and hate and rage. It quenched the ache in my soul, pacified my penis, soothed my loins. And then the condom, thank God for the condom, snatched my seed back from the den of destruction.

I quickly pulled out and rolled over, just lying there in our juices, stabbed again by my mortal shortcomings, while she was there once more with the hallowed sword. The cavern of calamity. The crusader of Cain, triumphantly rising above her victim and callously discussing previous conquests with humor and pride. And I just lay there; limp and lifeless like a popped balloon.

"Just shut the fuck up," is all I wanted to say, but part of me wanted to hear, wanted to listen for any clues to her insanity. "La di da di da!" I could barely make sense of her fractured phrases. Who knew what the fuck she was saying? Who cared? Not me. She should have barked instead; it would have made more sense. I just wanted to escape, run, flee, vamoose. The deed was done, but I was sapped.

I heard an old woman bellowing loudly in the hall in an inaudible tongue. I queried my whore about what was being said. She laughingly stated that a very old woman in the hall was propositioning sex from a young man and telling him that she was only eighteen years old, hoping he would give in.

That's all it is, a proposition. You prop me and I prop you and if things are right like two dogs in the night, then we mingle and twist and entwine our bodies and exchange fluids. Let those fluids flow. The fluids have to flow. But our souls are alone, left to die on their own. Falling like a dried leaf at the end of the season, floating quietly and forcefully to the ground with all the other dead souls: Food for worm souls.

I lay in her dreadful presence, listening to her voice fluctuate rapidly and her hands gesticulate mesmerizingly, and I was unable to move. I was trapped by her spell. Suddenly, she flew to the shower, which was visible from my grave, and I watched as she mysteriously and beautifully bathed without remorse, reclamation, ramifications, resignations, reverberations or regurgitations. I needed respiration.

When she finished, I mustered enough energy to pry myself from my casket. I heard my bones creak. I stepped into the shower and washed myself, continually looking downward in disgust. "What were you thinking," I asked my shriveled member. "*Bu hao!*" I said in Mandarin, which means "not good," obviously thinking my cock understood Chinese now.

I dressed and she dressed. Once again, we were two separate people full of hate and pain and life and love. She seemed to know me and I her. The curtain was lifted and there was nothing behind it but a little naked woman scratching her vagina and a little naked man holding his dick.

The hallway light slapped me like a doctor hitting a newborn. She suddenly looked like a whore in a cheap dress, and I felt like a marionette. She tried to hold me, but I jerked away. She was no longer possessed of the power to control my cum. I was as empty as a man-made lake after a dam burst. I needed to repair the machine before it could be manipulated again on such a basic level. Sex for sex's sake. Pugh! I felt alone and arid as a desert. A lone dying soul splayed out on a dry, dusty plain. Her eyes were like two vultures perched on a dead cactus watching a pathetic jackass slowly die.

The elevator was filled with a nice pond of fresh vomit. It looked like hot, cheesy, vegetable soup. It was part of someone's essence spilled in vain. Forced to evacuate its comfortable home. Forced to venture alone and dry up in this cruel, crazy world. "Maybe a dog will give it a home," I thought.

Three merry-makers stumbled in, propped up on each other. One man and two whores. "Whoa," they shrieked, as they noticed the puke and tried to dance around it. "Merry Christmas," the proud man said in English and then burped loudly. Oh yeah, it was Christmas. He seemed to have given himself a nice present: The gift of sex. Sometimes it's not an easy gift to receive.

Outside was outside. It was the same—wet and cold. She dug into her purse and gave me her phone number, fluttered her eyelids and casually said, "Call me when you need sex." She shoved the piece of paper in my hand. I looked at it and noticed she had jotted down her home and work number. So now I can call her, day or night. She's just a phone call away. She's content to just have sex with me for sex's sake, for my sake and for hers. And is that what I'm content with? Do I really want to keep this lying, cheating Bimbina on the side, forcing myself to occasionally listen to her mad yappings, just so I can get a piece? Or do I just leave it alone?

Flesh is indeed truly weak, but my mind gave in before my body did. Had you told me four months ago that I'd be spending Christmas with her in a seedy hotel; I would have thought you were crazy. But it happened and how do I know it won't happen again? All I know is that I have to stop thinking about my dick and start thinking about my face. In the end, she got just what she wanted, and maybe I did too.

She glanced sweetly at me before she walked away. I tried to avoid looking into her eyes, but her face was so big that they couldn't be avoided. Her face had grown as large as a zeppelin and was shining bright with neon lights. It would take years for me to get a face that big in a town like this. There was nothing left of my face, it had changed zip codes. I stuffed her number in my jacket pocket and walked away, hoping desperately to never give in to her again.

Chris Versus the Succulent Pear

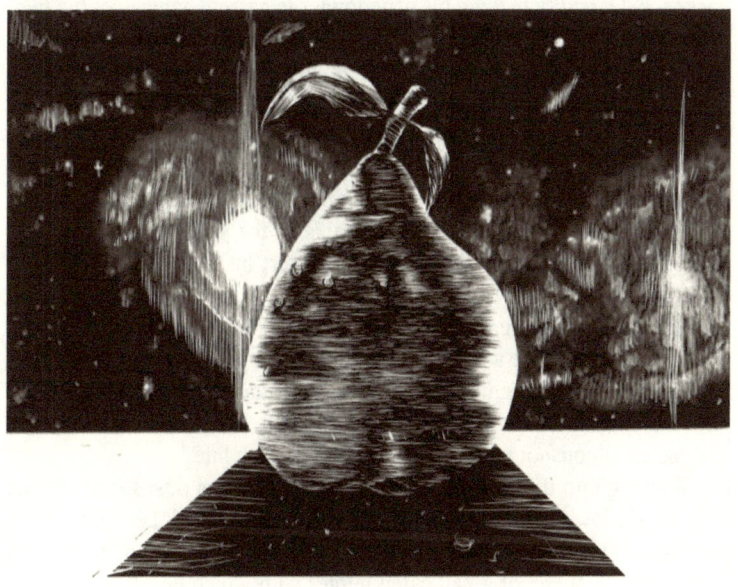

Chris, a fifth-year senior at Arizona State University, is passed out on his bed; his body splayed across his mattress like roadkill spread out across a barren expanse of pavement. The hot Arizona sun cuts through the holes in Chris's blinds, piercing his exposed skin, and triggering his sweat glands to form pools of liquid on his slumbering body.

Slowly spiraling out of a deep dream, he abruptly comes to and is initially aware of a slight ache in his head. Opening his eyelids is a struggle. With each nanometer of eyelid lifted, the pain in his noggin intensifies ten-fold.

"Eeeeyeowharghugh!" he squeals in agony.

Fighting to throw the bed covers off his sticky body and sit up, he teeters on the edge of his bed, looks at the clock on his desk, and rolls his eyes.

"2:00pm!" he says in frustration. "Shit, I wanted to get up early today."

Suddenly becoming dizzy and disoriented, he rests his arms on his knees and focuses on his breathing. When the cobwebs in his mind have cleared, he stands up, only to fall back on his bed.

Jerking himself up and trying to steady his swaying body, he steps over a pile of clothes and nearly slips on a notebook jutting out of his open backpack. Carefully making his way down the narrow hallway of the two-bedroom apartment, he slides his hands along the walls for support. Dick fully erect and sticking out of his boxers, it guides him to the toilet like a divining rod directing a farmer to water.

"Ahhhhh," he groans, after flicking on the lights.

Shading his eyes with one hand and steadying himself against the wall with the other, he takes a long, relieving piss, which mostly hits the mark.

Forgetting to flush the toilet, he walks to the sink, turns on the tap, and puts his head under the lukewarm water; his hair absorbs it like a sponge.

His reflection in the mirror is a bit shocking.

"Gawd, I look like a trauma patient," he complains.

Chunks of an unidentifiable substance are stuck to his long brown hair and his face is swollen with a blueish-green tint to it. His eyes are completely bloodshot and surrounded by a darkish hue.

Walking into the kitchen, he searches for a morsel of sustenance. The sink is overflowing with old dishes and the kitchen hasn't been cleaned in months. Lifting a few pans up from the kitchen counter, he hopes to find a crumb here or there, or a half-eaten burger with which he can squelch his hunger.

A large roach runs for cover. It's been in the apartment so long that Chris views it as a pet.

"Rufus, you start hanging out here much longer," says Chris to the roach, "I'm *gunna* start charging you rent!"

Seeing nothing edible, Chris opens the cabinets, hunting for any sign of food. An unopened bottle of Tequila stands alone in the corner, beckoning him.

Shaking his head, Chris continues his search.

Finding not one iota of nourishment in the cabinets—not even any canned products—he desperately opens the refrigerator: nothing in it except beer and sour milk. However, a small packet of ketchup has mysteriously adhered itself to the back inside wall. He contemplates opening the packet and oozing the contents down his neck, but decides against it.

He opens the small freezer door on top of the refrigerator; a gust of cold air slaps his face. Gazing across the frozen landscape like an arctic hunter in search of food, he only finds two ice trays, a pair of dirty socks, and a rusty crescent wrench.

"Denied, but wait, what's this mound of chunky ice in the corner?"

A frozen container of Margarita mix is locked in an icy tomb. After being pried free with the crescent wrench and inspected, the object is tossed back into the freezer without much consideration.

Chris roams into the living room which is sparsely decorated with old, mismatched furniture; but heavily littered with ancient pizza boxes, empty soda cans, and beer bottles full of spent cigarettes and chewing tobacco spittle. Spotting a box of crackers under the couch, he makes a beeline for it, then opens the container and squints deep inside.

"Not one damn cracker!"

He turns the box upside down and drops the measly portion of crumbs lollygagging at the bottom into his mouth. A minuscule amount of cracker dust rests on his dry tongue and latches on unwilling to hop off and descend down his arid throat.

Swallowing hard, Chris returns to the kitchen and luckily finds a used green teabag in the trashcan and dusts it off. A not-so-dirty cup is grabbed from the sink and briefly cleaned. Hoping to wash down the cracker bits and mute the chorus of growls emitting from his stomach, he heats up a kettle of water to make some green tea.

After quieting the screaming kettle, he sits down and slowly sips his tea while gazing curiously at the afternoon sun forcing its way through his kitchen window. The sun's rays spread out across the kitchen like a fan. Each individual ray produces different shades of white and yellow.

Chris glances at the beer calendar hanging on the wall to his right displaying a gorgeous, sparsely clad woman holding up a large mug of brew and smiling lovingly. She seems to truly want him to consume the amber-colored beverage.

"Sorry honey, I'm too hungover to start drinking again," he says to the model.

His mind wanders as the wind blows gently outside. Meanwhile, loud rumblings continue to emit from his stomach and sharp pains continue to pulsate from his forehead. Too hungry and too hungover to think clearly, he stares back at the sun's rays which have become more intense.

His attention turns back to the calendar, it's on the wrong month. Slowly rising, he flips the calendar pages forward two months to April where a different girl in equally scantily clad clothing is promoting the same brand of beer. She's pouting and seems to be thinking sexual thoughts as she bends over the product which is creatively displayed on an oak barrel. Her bulging bosom is threatening to break out of her tight blue blouse at any second while her tight, bare torso invitingly entices him.

"Sorry honey, I'll tell you what I told Ms. February, I'm too damn hungover to start drinking again. And I'm starving like Marvin!"

Chris re-contemplates what he'll do for food while staring intensely at the calendar model.

Leaves rustle on the trees outside.

He sluggishly arises and flips the calendar pages back to February.

"Sorry Ms. April, but Ms. February has you beat," he says.

Wishing his hunger pangs and hangover would suddenly disappear, a thought drifts across his mind.

"Didn't I buy a pear a few days back and not eat it?"

Awkwardly running to his bedroom, he locates his backpack and digs around to find the fruit.

"A pear!" he yells.

After kissing the fruit, he carries it carefully into the kitchen. Slowly dancing, he washes a dirty plate and a knife, then dries both of them on his underwear. He washes the pear as well for good measure. All clean, the multi-orbed fruit is dried on Chris's boxers and then polished with Chris's breath and his hairy forearms to give it a good shine.

Chris walks over to the table and places the oblong greenish pear upright on the plate and lays the long, shiny knife close by. The knife is arranged so it's perfectly perpendicular to a point exactly tangent to the plate at 3 o'clock. The pear's light green skin, only slightly bruised, seems to glisten. It's almost begging to be eaten.

Sliding the plate forward so that it's bathing in sunlight, Chris notices that the sun's rays slicing through the window are striking the pear in such a way that it looks like it's glowing.

Knife in hand, he eyes the plump fruit hungrily.

"Wait a second, this would make a great still life picture, if I only had some apples, grapes, and kumquats to adorn it with."

With his stomach rumbling even louder, he decides to skip the still life and instead slice the juicy fruit into small pieces and chew each one slowly while enjoying his warm cup of green tea.

"Eating this delectable pear and sipping this refreshing brew would be the most perfect start to this most glorious afternoon!"

Chris raises the moist knife above his head and pauses to consider the best angle in which to slash the defenseless fruit.

"What are you doing?" a voice says clearly from inside his head.

"What do you mean, 'What am I doing'?" Chris replies to the voice. "I'm going to eat a pear, isn't it obvious?"

"You can't eat me, I'm not a pear," says the voice.

"What? You, the Pear, are talking to me right now?"

"Yes, I'm using mental telepathy."

"Hey, that's pretty cool! Okay, quick, what am I thinking about right now?"

"You're thinking about having sex with Jenny in a Jacuzzi," says the Pear.

Jenny is the hot girlfriend of Chris's roommate, Kyle.

"Hey, you're pretty good," says Chris, lowering the knife. "Let's do it again. What am I thinking about now?"

"You're thinking about scoring the winning touchdown at the Rose Bowl and then having sex with the entire cheerleading squad on the football field while the fans in the packed stadium cheer you on."

"Holy shit!" thinks Chris, shaking the knife at the Pear. "You're really good! So wait, who are you and why are you inside *my* pear?"

"I'm not inside it; I'm actually a pear-shaped being from outer space."

"No way!" says Chris.

"It's completely true; and the story of how I arrived here on your table is very long and drawn out."

"Go ahead, out with it. I'd really like to hear it," he says, slurping his tea.

"Okay, but I'll try to be brief." The Pear stares at Chris, then continues. "I soared through space for ages, zipping from solar system to solar system in my spacecraft. By chance I happened upon your planet. I did a normal scan of the surroundings—as I usually do—and then, much to my surprise, I noticed a huge section of land covered with gourd-shaped beings just like myself—not knowing at the time that they were all just ordinary fruit you call 'pears'.

"I incorrectly assumed that they were beings like myself because they had almost the exact same chemical makeup as the inhabitants of my planet. Curious, I tried to contact the pears on the trees through mental telepathy and through various channels on my spacecraft, to no avail. After all my communication attempts had failed, I concluded that the pears were either imprisoned by the people of your planet or that your people were conducting an evil experiment and growing the people of my planet on trees and somehow blocking their telepathic powers."

"Like some kind of weird genetic experiment?" asks Chris.

"Exactly. So you can imagine how shocked I was to come across this horrendous scene. Furthermore, if *your* people were growing *my* people genetically on trees, then this would have to be documented immediately and reported to the authorities on my planet."

"I'm following what you're saying," says Chris, squinting as he looks out the window at the bright sun. "However, it sounds like you've got a very warped imagination, don't you? And if you are indeed an alien, I suspect you've been out in space a long time, possibly a tad too long?"

"Perhaps I've flown too close to large suns, once too often. But I assure you, this is all completely true."

"All right, please continue."

"So, I landed my space machine near the pear grove and went outside to take a look around."

"Ah-ha! Gotta call bullshit on that one, buddy! Let it be noted that you, Mr. Pear, do not have any arms or legs. So how the hell do you get around?"

"Simple, I have a mechanical body which is like a spacesuit. My people have evolved to the point where we just have brains and no longer need any external extremities. We command machines via telepathy and wear mechanical bodies as you would wear clothing; and those mechanical bodies help us to work and move around and interact with the world around us."

"Cool. So you're actually just one pear-shaped brain?"

"Bingo."

Chris rubs his scruffy chin and peers deeply at the Pear.

"So, like, uh, how do you have sex, make babies, and shit?" asks Chris.

"Well, you might find this a challenge to understand, but we actually use our mental powers to please one another sexually. And we replicate additional beings artificially when the need arises. Moreover, let it be noted that we do not defecate. I actually find the process quite repulsive."

"Freaky," Chris says, as he looks out the window at a bird flying by. "But you don't know what you're missing. Let me tell you, offloading a giant turd is one of the best feelings on the planet!"

"Maybe so, but my people do not routinely release such disgusting objects out of our hindquarters. However, we do release waste through our skin much like you humans sweat."

"Trippy!"

Still not sure if he completely believes the Pear, Chris adds, "So, you've got otherworldly mental powers, eh? Let's put these powers to the test. Hmm. I've got it, can you make any of the machines in this kitchen work using only your mind?"

"Of course."

"Okay, turn on my toaster."

Chris looks up and the red toaster light abruptly turns on.

"Whoa, that was interesting, but could've been a coincidence or a random electrical surge. All right, turn it off and then turn on the lights in the kitchen."

The red toaster light turns off and then the kitchen lights turn on.

"Not bad, Pear man, but can you turn off the kitchen lights, they're too bright."

Believing the Pear a bit more after the lights turn off, Chris decides to probe deeper. "So what does this mechanical suit of yours look like?"

"It's metallic with two arms and helps me fly about and interact with planetary surroundings when I'm not in my spacecraft. Inside my ship, I sit beneath a solid dome and telepathically control the entire vehicle."

"Rad! So, like, you use the spacesuit to fly around outside of your spacecraft and get a closer look at the planets you're visiting and collect samples of cool stuff, right?"

"Precisely. While out of my spacecraft, I always put on my mechanical body and usually turn on its cloaking function so no one or no thing can notice me. However, I had a rough landing the last time I used the suit. Long story short, I had been cooped up in my spaceship for ages and desperately needed some external entertainment. Spotting an interesting planet far from here, I landed, donned my suit, and went out to explore. It was a gorgeous day, brilliant pumpkin-, rich mustard-, and dark ketchup-colored clouds painted the sky. A fast-flowing liquid nitrogen river with an incredibly long fall caught my attention. Of course, I jumped in for a swim.

"On a whim, I thought it would be fun to go down the nitrogen fall in my mechanical body. However, I underestimated the power of the roaring fall and somehow the liquid nitrogen seemed to hamper my ability to mentally communicate effectively with my suit. Sailing down the fall at a rapid descent, I told my suit to shoot through the nitrogen fall to safety before pummeling into the river below. Sadly, the suit did not respond fast enough, and I slammed into the river with full force. Other than a few bumps and bruises, I was fine; but my mechanical flying suit hasn't been the same ever since. You might say it's on the fritz; and no matter what I tried, I couldn't seem to repair it back to normal."

"Ouch! I once jumped into a lake and cut my leg on a rock, got a wicked scar. My leg hasn't been the same since either."

"Exactly! Your skin is very soft, as is mine. That is why I must always wear my protective suit when venturing outside of my spacecraft."

"So what happened to your suit?" asks Chris.

"As I said, my mechanical body wasn't working that well and neither was its cloaking feature which keeps my suit invisible to potential predators.

"Before using the suit this last time, I descended to earth, flew into the pear groves, and closely examined the pears via my spacecraft which also had its cloaking feature on. As I stated earlier, the pears in the groves looked nearly identical to the beings from my planet with only a slight variation in genetic makeup. It was a truly eye-opening discovery!

"After observing the pears, I landed my spaceship in the groves to obtain a closer look. All situated in my mechanical body, I exited my spacecraft and then flew in to inspect the pears hanging from the trees. Before long, I extracted some tissue samples from a few of the pears and was ready to return to my spaceship.

"However, not far from me, one of your earth beings was picking pears on a tree and putting them into a basket while standing on a ladder. All at once, the picker's hand started coming towards me. Having forgotten that my mechanical suit did not work properly, I naturally assumed that I was cloaked. The picker looked right at me and was about to grab me. I tried to communicate with my suit mentally by telling it to stun the picker. Alas, the signal was crossed, and I was abruptly ejected from the suit and shot up into the clear blue sky. Flying high into the air, I was helpless. To make matters worse, I abruptly came down right into the picker's wicker basket."

"Wow! That must have totally freaked you out! What are the odds?"

"Yes, it did; and the odds are about one in four hundred trillion."

"Whoa!" Chris exclaims, trying to fathom the odds. "Okay, so what happened to your suit?"

"I don't know," the Pear sighs.

"Come on. Don't you have protection on those things, like lasers, or trackers, or transport devices, or something? I mean, how can that thing just shoot you out and leave you hanging?"

"Of course, we have very sophisticated equipment installed along with numerous defense mechanisms. Anyway, to continue, I immediately told my suit to come get me, but it was not responding. Instead, it shot up into the clouds and, regrettably, my ship followed it! Please recall that I stated numerous times that my suit was a bit defective."

"Okay, okay, chill," says Chris, his stomach rumblings reaching a crescendo. "Man, that's some bad luck!"

"Indeed," says the Pear, still glistening on the table. "After numerous excruciatingly mundane days, I ended up together with a pile of pears in a grocery store and that is where you bought me. I chose you because I thought you could help."

"Wait, what? You chose me?"

"Yes, I directed you to pick me from the numerous other pears in the pile."

"Huh? Let me see if I get this straight: My hand might have been going towards another pear, but you used your superior mind-altering skills to guide my hand towards you?"

"Correct."

"Hold it! I'm honestly having trouble believing all this," says Chris, struggling to picture the entire story in his foggy hungover head. "But wait, why is it that you can't have your ship come rescue you?"

"Well, as you can imagine, I'm quite helpless without my suit or my ship. If I had my suit on, I could easily send a message to my ship to come get me, or I could fly to my ship; but I'm not wearing my mechanical body now, am I? And my range of telepathy without it is very limited."

"Can't you call it using phone lines or computer lines or something?"

"No, unfortunately not. There's too much chatter on those lines for my ship to be able to locate my distant cry for help. Believe me, I've tried to contact my ship for days, but nothing seems to work. And I'm sure it's out there at this very moment, scanning the globe looking for me, but I just can't seem to contact it."

"Sounds like a conundrum: Without that suit, you can't get to your ship; and without that ship, you can't leave."

"Right on the button, old boy. So I leave it to you, Chris, to help me find my ship."

"Whoa! You know my name! You're good! This mental telepathy is the shits! Okay, right, gotta find your ship."

Chris notices a few thin clouds dotting the afternoon sky and then glances briefly at the beer calendar hanging on the wall. The model gives him a wink. He winks back and then says, "Hmm. Dude, Pear man, I'm a busy guy, finals are coming up. I've gotta graduate. Plus, I can't simply give up school and trounce all over the planet looking for your ship."

"Chris, I don't think you'd need to travel far. Certainly there aren't many pear groves that supply the grocery store from which you purchased me."

"That's true, but how do we know your ship is even close by; and more importantly, how do I know you aren't some sort of evil pear out to destroy my planet?"

"Do I look like an evil pear out to destroy your planet?" asks the Pear innocently.

Chris looks carefully at the succulent Pear. "No, you don't. But, you do look very tasty, and let me tell you something: The last thing I ate was a rancid burrito twenty-four hours ago. It upset my stomach and gave me the shits! So, for your information, I didn't eat anything last night. Then I went out and partied like a man possessed. You can't begin to imagine. I'm actually amazed I'm still alive now. Then, on top of all that, I got laid late last night and still managed to stumble home early this morning! So to say that I'm weak and in need of a pick-me-up is an understatement."

"Sounds like a bit of a conundrum."

"Yes, I suppose it does."

"You could always go outside and buy some food. It's a beautiful day. Or order some food to be delivered," says the Pear.

"Well now, aren't we the smart one! Yes, those are viable options. However, they both require A) energy, of which I have none and B) time, of which I have, but do not want to wait.

"Do you hear that?" Chris says, pointing to his midsection. "It's my stomach screaming for food. And I really, really want to eat you, like right now! I paid for you fair and square. Furthermore, it's false advertising—don't you think—me buying you, and you being a space Pear that doesn't want to be eaten," he explains, while squeezing his stomach.

"You could take me back and exchange me," says the Pear. "Or you could help me find my ship and I could manufacture millions of tons of gold and jewels on my ship and give them to you as a reward. However, if you eat me, you would not only give up all those riches, but also would only be satisfying yourself and your selfish need for a hunger stopper, while I would be no better off. In fact, I'd be worse off, for sure."

"Oh, nice try with the guilt trip," Chris says, noticing the girl on the calendar smiling at him. He smiles back. "Hey, speaking of food, how do you eat?"

"I have evolved to create energy much like your plants do by performing photosynthesis."

"No shit! Truly fascinating! You're one incredibly advanced fruit," he says, then carefully ponders the situation. A violent chorus of grumblings emits from his stomach. "Okay, let's do this. You try with all of your might to stop me from eating you. If you succeed, I'll help you find your ship. However, if you don't succeed, I'll eat you with extreme pleasure."

"That doesn't sound like such a positive opportunity for me, Chris. Can't we play Chess or Go?"

"Naw, I suck at both of those games."

"Yahtzee?"

"Nope, simply use your powers to stop me from eating you. If you win, I'll help you. That's my deal, take it or leave it; my mind's made up."

"Can't we play something a bit less violent? Is this the only choice you are going to offer me?"

"Look, Pear dude, if you can really stop me from eating you, it will shatter my entire belief framework and force me to come up with a whole new paradigm of life and an entire new way of seeing the world." Cracking his knuckles, Chris continues, "Having said that, I do have a question that I have not posed yet."

"What's that Chris?"

"Do you taste exactly the same as a regular pear?"

"Well, my physical make-up is extremely close to that of a normal pear. In fact—I probably shouldn't say this under the circumstances—but you might actually find me even tastier than your average pear."

"Oh my God!" Chris says, as a long stream of drool glides down his chin. "That makes me even hungrier to eat you. So, let the games begin!"

"Wait..."

Chris reaches for the Pear, but cannot seem to grip it even though he's using all of his strength. A force field emanating from the Pear becomes more and more intense until Chris is thrown against the wall opposite the table and slams into it with a loud thud.

Rufus runs for cover behind a salt shaker on the counter.

Chris yells, "Okay, you want to play?" He stands up, loosens his neck muscles, and begins plowing through the Pear's mighty force field like a fish swimming upstream in a river of mercury.

Fighting his way forward, he eventually lunges for the knife that lies shining brightly on the table. After a long struggle, he manages to grab the knife and raises it above his head, intent on stabbing the Pear with one quick movement. Suddenly, the hand holding the knife turns on him and begins angling for his thigh.

Chris fights his hand for control of the knife. It gets close enough to his thigh to graze several leg hairs. Both hands wrestle to inch the knife away from his leg. Fighting with all his might, he manages to fling the knife at the wall where it imbeds itself deeply into the sheetrock narrowly missing the calendar.

Ms. February looks greatly concerned.

Chris runs to the sink and begins flinging dirty plates at the Pear hoping to distract it just long enough so he can rip it apart.

Take this! And that!

Unfortunately, each plate that Chris chucks is successfully deflected against the wall where it shatters into numerous pieces and showers to the ground.

"Fuck!" Chris yells in frustration. "What would Captain Kurt from the original *Star Trek* do in this sort of situation? He'd outsmart this crazy Pear. Yes, of course he would! Okay, think quickly. Got-to-think-quickly. I can nuke him in the microwave. Nah, that won't work, I can't touch him. Think! I just have to outwit it! But how?"

"Chris, I can hear everything you're thinking," says the Pear. "I suggest you quit now; you don't stand a chance."

Chris charges forward again and tries with every ounce of energy in his body to plow through the force field and get close to the Pear.

Chris's roommate, Kyle, abruptly walks in sporting a torn up old T-Shirt and holey boxers, his curly blonde hair looks like it's been subjected to an electrical experiment. He scratches his nuts and yawns as he strolls to the refrigerator, oblivious to the titanic struggle that is occurring in the kitchen. Opening the fridge door, he bends down and scans the terrain.

"Who the fuck ate my burrito?" he yells.

Kyle slams the refrigerator door shut, turns around, and notices the mess on the floor. "You'd best be cleaning this up," he says, shaking his head. "Christoble, did one get hungry, venture into our fridge, grab-ith that which is not his-ith, and consume mine cheesy burro with excessive malice?"

"Kai," Chris says, as the Pear's force field suddenly releases him, and he falls flat onto the ground.

Kyle watches Chris's strange movements with a smirk and asks, "Well now, is one a bit drunk-ith?"

Chris quickly stands up, brushing off a few plate shards and says, "Listen, that burrito gave me the shits!"

"Good, you deserve it!"

"It's not like you don't drink my beer all the time."

"And I don't get you high all the time?" asks Kyle.

"I buy toilet paper all the time, and I've never once seen you buy it."

"I pulled you out of the bushes late last night, passed out in your own juices," says Kyle.

"Really? I vaguely recall trying to relieve myself on a bush last night. But anyway, what does that have to do with what we're talking about?"

"It's just one example of what a great guy I am. You want something more financially oriented? Okay, let's see...I buy pizza all the time and you always snag a slice or two or three."

"All right. I, I, I cleaned the bathroom," says Chris, grasping for straws.

"That was like three months ago! Dude, dude, dude. I don't consume your food, period! Roommates don't consume-ith that which is not theirs-ith unless invited to do so-ith. That is a sacred, secret oath we as roommates take and never should we cross-ith that path, or else it will lead-ith to anarchy or worse, thermal nuclear war!"

"I was fucking starving, man! I'll buy you another one. You know I'm good for it. Chill!"

"That's not the point," says Kyle. "I'm hungry now. One might even say that I'm in need of some serious nourishment. I dreamt about eating that lovely bean-and-cheese burrito all night long and now when I try to find it, it's nowhere to be found, *comprende*? You have robbed me of my happiness this beautiful Sunday morn."

"It's after morn," says Chris.

"Whatever! I'm greatly disappointed in you. Greatly!" Kyle turns his head towards the table and notices the alien fruit standing erect on a plate. "Hold the phone. I am suddenly eying a beautiful, uncut pear lying ever so sweetly on that *thar* table. And whose pear may that-ith be, lying so availably on yonder wooden apparatus?"

"Kai man, don't even go near it; it's an alien!" says Chris, as serious as a heart attack.

"My-my, did we devour a plethora of mind-altering consumables recently and forget to share-ith?"

"Listen, I'm telling you, yonder is a fucking alien Pear hellbent on killing me. I have to outwit it! Must use all my mental resources to overcome its incredible telekinetic powers."

Looking around the room at the shattered plates, Kyle says, "Right, and I assume this mess came from the Pear?"

"Yeah! Like, I was fucking having a full-on galactic war with it. I flung the entire contents of the kitchen sink at it and let me tell you, that there alien life form deflected each and everything I sent its way. I kid you not! And dude, it can read my mind!"

Looking carefully at the unassuming Pear basking in bright sunlight, Kyle says, "Really? Well then, do tell me how you communicate with it?"

"Mentally. Telepathy or some shit like that. But get this, he's been talking to me all afternoon begging me to scour the globe for his lost spaceship."

"Really! Well, Chris, as farfetched as this all sounds, I'll grant you a minutiea benefactora of doubtage. Just a fractito. If said green fruit-ith can communicate mentally, then by all means, let it communicate with me. Please, let it display its awesome powers of telepathy," says Kyle, closing his eyes and placing his fingers firmly on his temples.

"Okay, hold your horses. I'll tell it to use telepathy with you and you, uh, clear your head. All right?"

"Okay, I'm ready when you are."

Chris eyeballs the Pear. "I'm telling it to talk to you. Do you hear it?"

"Naw."

"Concentrate," says Chris.

Kyle closes his eyes tighter, rotates his fingers on his temples, and concentrates as hard as he can.

"Anything?"

"Nope," says Kyle, then a loud fart comes out.

"Dude, uncalled for," Chris says, holding his breath and waving his hands around frantically.

"It was the Pear!"

"Come on, try harder, but with less gas."

"Okay. Wait, I see something! No. Wait! Yeah, I see something. No way! It's you and Jenny, my girlfriend, kissing each other in a Jacuzzi," says Kyle, looking accusingly at Chris.

"Oh, that was so unfair! That didn't happen! You fucking psycho Pear! He did that to piss me off. He's playing games now."

"Eating my burro and going after my girl! Can you ever be trusted again?"

"Come on, that was so uncalled for. I told you, I'll get you another burrito, ten if you want! And nothing's going on between me and Jenny! Listen, you gotta believe me! That there thing resting so innocently on the table is an evil, mind-manipulating alien Pear that's putting thoughts into your head and into my own. I'm absolutely not hitting on your girl! Come on!"

"Well, whatever," says Kyle, unconvinced. "I've played your little game long enough-age, and now, one is going to glide-ith right on over to the luscious green edible virgin Pear and consummate our relationship, orally."

"No, don't! It'll kill you! Dude man, I'm not fucking around!"

"That, *droogie*, is a chance I'll have to take."

Kyle walks over to the table, touches the Pear, then turns and smiles at Chris. "Its force field is amazingly powerful, not!"

"Don't do it!" screams Chris. "Look, I've been battling this thing for ages. It's a fucking alien, I tell you. It's got unbelievable powers. Back off, before it destroys us both!"

Kyle picks up the Pear, places it close to his mouth, and opens wide.

Chris lunges for his roommate. Kyle quickly tosses the Pear back on the table and begins fighting Chris. They wrestle to the floor, struggling back and forth on top of the plate shards bespeckling the floor.

"You don't want to do this Kai; I've been working out."

"So have I! And tell me the truth, have you been with my girl?" he asks, lying astride of Chris's back trying to administer a half nelson.

"No! No, I just think about her sometimes. And I dreamt of her last night, but it was only a dream, nothing happened in real life, I swear."

"Now you're dreaming of her! And if you're dreaming of her, you're guilty of dream cheating."

"Come on, that's not the real thing," Chris says, flipping over onto his back to face Kyle.

"It could lead to the real thing," says Kyle, shaking his finger at Chris. They both start choking each other.

"Wait! It's the Pear," grunts Chris. "He's making us do this. Free will! Free will! Refuse to be controlled by the Pear," he says, loosening his grip on Kyle's throat. "Clear your mind, get up, and walk right on out of here. I know you can do it. Go. Now. Just, go!"

They both simultaneously release each other.

Kyle rests on his knees above Chris and takes a long hard look at the Pear.

"Did you really pull me out of the bushes last night?" asks Chris, trying to catch his breath.

"Yeah, you're lucky I didn't hose you down first, you reeked!"

"Thanks man," Chris says sincerely.

"No problem, you'd probably do the same for me, if I was passed out on some shrubbery in the middle of the evening, snoring so loudly I was waking up the neighbors and every little critter for miles around," Kyle says, admiring the Pear on the table.

"Look," says Chris, getting up onto his knees and dusting off the plate shards on his stomach. "If you eat my Pear, you'll be guilty of the same crime I'm guilty of: eating your food. How can you commit the same crime you're accusing me of?"

"Hmm," says Kyle. "You're right. I cannot eat your Pear because I would be guilty of the same low-life behavior that you exhibited. I'm better than that. But I want you to hear me out.

"One day, in the not-to-distant future, someone, somewhere, somehow will discover that electrons move in a predictable manner, like the moons of planets. The electrons orbiting the atoms must move in a predictable way as normal moons move in a predictable orbit or else the electrons would slam into each other. Sure, some planets do have so many moons that the moons ram into each other. A planet like a multi-electron boosted atom can only hold so many stable orbitals. But planets must have moons that move in a predictable pattern or else the planets, will become unstable.

"And atoms as well must have electrons that move in a predictable pattern or else the atoms will become too excitable and unstable. And if planets and atoms become unstable because of irregular orbitals, that's chaos! Thus, atoms must have electron orbits that are predictable or else the whole shithouse will explode on itself. Are you with me? Will you grant me that one iota of explain-atude?"

"Does that mean that you won't eat my alienic fruictoid?" asks Chris.

"Yes, that would be beneath me, although, I am very tempted. I do, however, have free will. I *will* walk away from said luscious green fruit. And, I *will not* allow that measly Pear to warp my morals."

"But wait! Can you really compare electrons and moons? Aren't electrons negatively charged particles? Unlike moons, electrons can't run into each other because one negatively charged particle would naturally repel another, like two negatively charged magnets. That negative charge would act like a buffer. So theoretically, an atom with a bunch of electrons wouldn't have to worry much because the electrons wouldn't ram into each other even if their orbits were totally random. And since they have that external buffer, they can revolve any damn way they'd like and not worry about hitting anything. And planets, unlike atoms, have gravity that would suck moons with funky orbits right up into the planet and gobble up those badass moons without becoming excitable or unstable."

"Yes, planets can clean up bad-moon orbits by sucking them into the planet, but you gotta think-age that atoms have some sort of gravity as well, to keep the electrons in orbit; and in order for the atoms to be stable, the electrons must be stable, in a stable orbit. You just can't have all the electrons bumping around like bumper cars. They must all be contained in a stable, predictable orbit, or they'll jump away to the next attractive atom that zooms right on by. And if they do that, all the atoms would constantly be changing their chemical makeup; and we couldn't have that, or there'd be anarchy in the atomic system, which would lead to anarchy in our system. Think about it! Imagine grabbing a glass of water, and it suddenly changes into salt. It's nutty, but it could happen if electrons weren't stable and weren't in a stable orbit."

"I'll have to think about it more, but I'm pretty sure you've just re-invented physics to suit your own delusional way of thinking."

"I did not!"

"Anyway, since we're having this discussion, I'd like *you* to grant *me* one nano of understanding-o," says Chris. "Yes, I did dream about your girl. Yes, I did have sexual thoughts about your girl. She's hot, what do you expect? However, I did *not* act on any of those thoughts. That's all they are, just thoughts. And we all have thoughts, right? But good people filter out bad thoughts and try to act decently.

"I assure you, I have not acted on my bad thoughts and have only acted righteously. And we cannot as a society start condemning people for having impure thoughts. We cannot exist in such a paranoid environment. If we did, everyone would be dead or in jail or both. And believe me, I've had much worse thoughts than just giving it to Jenny, oh yeah, I have! And I'm sure you have too, but at the end of the day, they're just thoughts."

"Bad actions start with bad thoughts, my friend. Those bad thoughts revolve around your brain like a moon or an electron. Once your brain picks up enough of them, they gain speed and eventually implode onto the center of your brain, thereby causing you to act out the bad thoughts. So by having this bad thought about my girlfriend, you're going to carry it with you until you act on it or it fades away or till you die."

"But I'm going to keep all my bad thoughts locked up in a stable orbit, so they don't implode on me. Yes, I may get drunk and impede my sense of right or wrong, but even then, I won't act on my bad thoughts. Well, not on my truly bad thoughts. But as I said, I can contain those thoughts. Have you ever known me to do anything really bad? No—the burrito doesn't count—but I, like most good people, contain my bad thoughts in a tight brain-ual orbit. When you go crazy, that's when you lose grip of your bad thoughts, and they zoom away into some weird orbit causing all types of strange things to happen in your noggin. But my bad thoughts are contained, and remember, they are only thoughts. Believe me, I haven't done anything with Jenny! Nothing!"

Kyle takes a deep breath and gazes out the window. A distant plane glides by. "Your theory needs work, broham, but I'll accept your explanation like the gentleman that I am. Now, I'm going to show you that I'm a better person than you. I don't eat other people's food. Period. You owe me!"

He stands up and brushes the plate shrapnel clinging to his shirt and underwear. As he walks towards the living room, he takes a long, cold hard look at the Pear on the table. He pauses and licks his lips, but decides to leave it be.

Chris, who is still kneeling on the floor, begins to formulate a plan. After brushing off the remaining plate particles sticking to his chest and thighs, he grabs the window seal and pulls himself upright. Looking out the window, Chris pauses to take in the scenery. A big beautiful yellow orb is spewing sunlight directly at him.

Glancing at the calendar, Chris sees Ms. February cheering him on.

He takes a deep breath, then rushes the Pear.

It puts up its force field again.

Undaunted, Chris fights his way through the force field like a halfback rushing through a solid defensive line.

The Pear's force field repels him once again and pushes him back towards the kitchen entryway.

Extremely frustrated, Chris decides to venture into the living room to regroup and construct an awesome plan that will crush the diabolical Pear.

Kyle sits on the sofa lighting a long bong.

"Dude, I've got an idea," says Chris. "Give me the worst song you've got. I'm going to play it for the alien and hopefully interfere with its thought-waves just long enough so I can get close to it and destroy it with extreme prejudice. You got any Babette Morganstein?"

Kyle exhales a large cloud of smoke which billows throughout the room. "Hey, come on," he says. "Babette's hot and all, but she can't destroy an alien Pear. What you need is some metal." He takes another hit of the bong, breathes in deeply, holds it, and then exhales an enormous stream of white smoke. "I've got it! Pink Floyd. Yeah, Pink Floyd's got an album called *Meddle* which has a song called, 'One of These Days'. That song should do the trick. Guarandamnteed to annihilate any mutated alienic fruit or vegetable."

He offers Chris a bong hit.

"That song will definitely do it," Kyle says, and then sifts through his phone's music collection for the song.

Chris lights the bong and takes a long fluid draw.

Kyle opens a newfangled music mixer app on his phone, selects a number of hardcore beats, and layers them into "One of These Days". "Now, that *oughta* do the tricket," he says, extremely satisfied with himself.

Chris holds the bong hit in and grunts, "Thanks man, I knew you'd come through for me." He exhales and tries to clear his head.

Handing Chris his phone, Kyle says, "Just press play, but be very careful, this is potent stuff."

"I will," Chris says, standing up.

Grabbing two large speakers and hauling them towards the kitchen, Chris hums loudly as he stacks the speakers on top of each other at the kitchen entryway.

"Chris, let's call a truce," says the Pear.

Chris hums even louder.

"Chris, perhaps we started out on the wrong foot. Let's begin again, shall we? My name is ~^~`~-~^~'-, but you can call me Burt."

Chris continues humming as he carefully arranges the speakers so that an optimum amount of sound is aimed directly at the Pear. He returns to the living room and then presses play on Kyle's music player.

After cranking up the volume and returning Kyle's phone, Chris confidently walks back towards the kitchen. As the music amps up, it slowly fills the kitchen with streaming waves of throbbing sound.

"Chris, let's be friends," urges the Pear.

Swaying back and forth with a broad smile on his face, Chris stands in front of the speakers as he feels the amplified current of music emitting outwards, penetrating his body.

Ms. February begins to dance erotically.

"Sorry Burt, I can't hear you," he says, pointing to the speakers.

The music builds as Chris saunters over to the kitchen counter.

"Chris, I just need your help," says Burt. "If I offended you, I must apologize deeply."

The music starts to rattle the plate on which the Pear rests.

Chris grabs something on the kitchen counter and walks backwards towards the table carefully concealing from Burt what he's holding in his hands.

The entire kitchen vibrates from the continuous flow of sound.

The music reaches a pulsating crescendo and begins to confuse Burt. "Chris, I, just, want, to, say…"

"One of these days," bellows from the speakers.

"Can't hear you, Burt," says Chris, still backing up.

In one motion Chris spins around and slams the open end of a blender jug on top of the helpless Pear.

"Aha!"

"Chris," the trapped Pear mutters.

"I can't hear you, Burt baby!" says Chris, sliding the jug off the table and quickly flipping everything upright, thereby capturing the Pear inside. "Gotcha!"

Chris runs to the mixer, slams the jug on top of its base unit, swiftly pops the blender's lid on, and holds it in place with both hands.

"Ah-fucking-ha!" he screams.

After jumping to the freezer for ice and the frozen margarita mix, he spots an old packet of lemon juice on top of the refrigerator and tosses it on the counter for good measure. Jumping back to the blender, he pops off the lid, rapidly pours in the ice and margarita mix, and then squirts the entire contents of the lemon juice packet into the formula. Lunging for the tequila in the cupboard, he instantly snags the bottle and unscrews the lid practically all in one motion. Jumping back to his creation, he pours an ample amount of alcohol into the mixture and then successfully slams the lid back on the blender jug.

"Soak it up, Burt! And get ready for a big surprise!"

Chris thinks about pressing the *puree* button on the blender, but hesitates before running over to the living room and cranking the music even louder. The blender pulsates wildly due to the loud music.

Quickly returning to the kitchen, Chris puts his hand on top of the blender jug to steady it and then presses *puree* with intense force.

Nothing happens.

"Cock fart!" yells Chris, thinking the Pear is mind-blocking the blender. Frustrated, he looks behind the blender and notices that the machine is unplugged. He rams the plug into the socket and the blender begins to whine.

"Take that you neuron-numbing, force-field-emitting fructoid!" shouts Chris in triumph.

After the mixture is completely blended, Chris salts two freshly cleaned glasses, fills them to the brim, and walks towards the living room where Kyle is vegging out in front of the tube.

Curious and thirsty, Rufus ventures over to the blender, sips some of the mixture dripping down the jug, and then scurries away.

As Chris walks past the calendar, Ms. February raises her mug of beer to honor Chris's gargantuan victory. Chris nods proudly and then ventures into the living room.

After setting the margaritas on the coffee table, Chris jumps up and down on the couch and says, "Dude man, I did it! I defeated Burt the evil mind-altering, force-field-emitting, spacesuit-and-spacecraft-searching Pear from outer space!"

Kyle reaches up and gives Chris a high five.

"Well done," says Kyle. "The world is now safe until we are invaded by man-eating watermelons."

"Right you are, and I must say, I feel better prepared now for if and when any alien melons arrive. But honestly, I could not have defeated Burt without your help. That music was the clincher. You are the master."

"Thank you, kind sir, and if you need some tunes to make out to, you know who to call."

Chris raises his margarita.

"What shall we drink to?" asks Kyle, raising his glass.

"Here's to knowing that life will be just a little better from here on out."

"Well, that's awfully tame. I'll drink to that, but I was hoping you'd put a bit of a sexual slant to it."

"Okay, here's to knowing that sex with super-hot women will be just a little better from here on out."

"I'll drink to that!"

They clink glasses and both sip the frosty froth.

"Oo," says Kyle. "Quite tasty."

"It's the lemon and maybe the alien Pear that gives it the extra zest."

"Not too shab-dab-dabby."

"Why thank you," says Chris, sitting down. "And thanks again for saving me from the shrubbage last night and dude, seriously, sorry about the burro."

"There'll be none of that! Listen, if that burrito gave you the most runniest of shits, then you actually saved me from a serious anal infestation of the dreaded diarrhea bug. The way I see it, you pounced on that burro like a soldier sacrificing his body on a grenade to protect his buddies from the blast. To that, I salute you," says Kyle, and then offers Chris the bong again.

After taking a long slow drag and exhaling a steady stream of bong exhaust, Chris says in a raspy voice, "You know what would make this setting perfect?"

"A hot blonde with a shaved pussy and a pierced navel sucking my throbbing member?" asks Kyle.

"Nope, a massively greasy pizza burning our wanting palates!"

"Oh lordy! Make it so, number one!"

"Aye-aye, captain!"

To be continued...

Pinching Zits

My workmate, Sven, confidently announced his presence at my house party, downed a few drinks and began mingling by my wet bar. Instantly, everyone within shouting distance noticed the incredibly large bandage he had draped on the side of his head, to the right of his temple.

I was tending bar, acting as DJ, introducing people and trying not to gawk at the right side of Sven's face. Eventually, someone got up enough nerve, pointed to Sven's bandage and uttered, "Sven what happened?" We all intently listened in for Sven's reply.

"I don't know, I was on vacation in the tropics, just got back today, and all of a sudden I developed this thang on the side of my head," he said, shrugging his shoulders.

"Thang? What kind of thang?" we inquired.

"It's kind of a big zit," he said casually.

Well, that piqued everyone's curiosity. "Wanna have a look?" he asked. Sven wasn't shy, so he carefully peeled back the bandage carpeting half his face, as our jaws dropped in utter amazement. I had a good selection of music going and everyone seemed to be having a good time. Then Sven wanted to go and show his big zit!

"Good gawd Sven, look at the size of that thang," someone said, as Sven peeled back the protective covering. I almost choked on my drink when I had a gander at it. I mean, it was large! And it was bulging out of the side of his head like a balloon that was about to burst.

"Why don't you squeeze that thang and let the puss out?" someone asked.

"I tried, but it really, really hurts. I mean it *fucking* hurts like the devil!" Sven explained.

"Well, it hurts me to look at it," said my longtime friend and coworker, Fred Wrangler, an engineer who fit the bill. He was a bit inebriated, we all were—I don't play around when it comes to mixing drinks. "Why don't you let me have a go at it?" Fred added. He's the type of guy who's reserved most of the time, but get a few drinks in him, and he's the life of the party. Earlier on, I had seen him contemplating wearing one of my lampshades for shiggles.

We all thought Fred was nuts for offering to help out.

"Well, okay," Sven said pleasantly surprised.

Actually, if it had been me, I would have told Fred to fuck right off! I mean, there is something inherently odd about a friend pinching your zit in front of a crowd at a house party. But Sven's the type of guy who'd whip out his dick and slap it on the table if you dared him to.

Unfortunately for us, since he'd already uttered his approval, Sven was obligated to release custody of his massive zit to Fred, while the rest of us could do nothing but look on with intense curiosity. Sven tore off the protective bandage and placed that greasy, gooey patch on the bar right near my drink. I wasn't going to touch that nasty looking thing. It really grossed me out!

Fred rolled up his sleeves and dramatically loosened up his fingers and neck while Sven bent over, laid his head—zit-side up—on the bar, and braced himself for the pain.

Fred moved in for the kill.

Jeanie from HR yelled out, "Maybe you should get some tissue first."

"Like a tissue sample," Fred quipped.

"No, like some tissue paper Fredrick!" Jeanie yelled, rolling her eyes. She gets loud and bossy when she drinks.

"Here, we can use this," someone said, holding up a heavily stained bar rag.

"I don't think so; here, use this," Sven said, pulling out a clean, red-checkered handkerchief from his pocket and handing it to Fred, who quickly stuffed it into his shirt pocket behind his pocket protector.

Satisfied, Fred pounced on his prey, put his thumbs across an ample amount of real estate on the side of Sven's face, and began to squeeze with great force.

Sven's eyes almost shot out of their sockets as Fred began to wrench his elbows. Everyone in the audience was cringing, as Fred seemed to be applying way too much pressure.

"I can see something making its way to the surface! Hang in there Svenny," said Fred, as he struggled to gain leverage on Sven's gigantic growth.

It was almost too much to bear. I had been cutting limes with a knife and seriously contemplated stabbing that zit to put Sven out of his misery. Then I thought twice about it and decided not to. It's best to just let these things run their course. I figured Fred would tire quickly, or Sven would throw in the towel, and we could get back to the party. I had not planned on this circus act, but it was amazing how entertaining it was, and everybody was thoroughly enthralled. I had invited a few friends and a few coworkers over and they all brought a few friends with them and the party naturally swelled. The drinks loosened everyone up and now everybody was peering in at Fred bisecting Sven's face! What next, a live appendectomy? I sat patiently through the exorcism. I looked around and didn't even know half the people at the party. But that didn't matter; they all seemed to be having fun, except for Sven of course.

The crowd had slowly closed in on the two men. Mouths were agape, eyes bulging. The tension was as thick as oatmeal. Then all the straining forced Fred to let out a massive fart, but the gaseous stench didn't stop him from continuing to pinch Sven's ginormous zit.

"Holy smokes Fred! You're suffocating us," yelled someone in the crowd. "I'd check your shorts if I were you," said someone else. I grabbed the crusty bar rag and tried to twirl it around a bit to dissipate the odor. Someone else lit a match.

Sven's head repeatedly slapped on the bar as Fred wrestled that humungous zit with all his might. The vibrations caused Fred's glasses to fall right off of his face and onto the ground. While Sven's face was mangled with pain, he began to moan softly until it became a loud, steady squeal, almost peeling the paint from the walls. Not to be out done, Fred began to moan in harmony and managed to grunt out, "This is hurting me more than you buddy!"

"Come on Fred, it's not funny anymore," screamed Jeanie. I flashed her an it'll-be-all-right look as she glanced at me for some sort of guidance. I probably should have stepped in and put an end to it then and there, but unfortunately, I didn't.

The struggle seemed to last for a millennium, when finally: POP! The zit exploded, sounding like a champagne cork flying off of a freshly opened bottle of bubbly.

A good proportion of the white, bloody, gelatinous substance shot right into Fred's eyes, temporarily blinding him. The rest shot all over the crowd, who responded with a unanimous, "Ohhhhhh!" I damn near ate a glob of it as a specimen shot right into my open mouth. I immediately spat it out, and gargled a bottle of tequila to rid myself of the disgusting taste.

The pinching left Sven speechless and in need of some serious medical attention, because blood was gushing out of his zit hole like a geyser.

There was utter confusion as people tried simultaneously to hurriedly wipe off the zitty mess from their faces, to make room for Fred spinning around in pain clasping his eyes screaming in agony, and to help Sven whose head continued to bleed profusely like that of a gunshot victim.

The grimy bar rag was used to sop up the blood on Sven's face and to create pressure on the wound because Fred was using Sven's handkerchief on his own eyes as he clenched them and whirled around like a crazed tornado.

An ambulance finally arrived to take both Sven and Fred to the house of the learned medical community. I wanted to accompany them to the hospital, but I was pretty drunk by that time and wasn't sure I would be much help. Jeanie, bless her heart, went instead, shouting at both Sven and Fred to stay calm as she boarded the ambulance. "Don't worry Calvin," she belched at me, "everything will be all right." Famous last words.

I tried to kick start the party again, but we had somehow lost the mood. The previously happy-go-lucky crowd filed out one after another, making excuses. After everyone had left, I finished off a large proportion of the alcohol single handedly and passed out on my couch.

For the next few days, doctors ran test after test on Sven and scratched their heads. Eventually, they unanimously agreed that Sven had been suffering from some strange new viral tumor. It wasn't a real zit after all. Instead, it was a flesh-devouring tumor that ate away at whatever internal organ or protein-rich cellular substance it could find, bulged out of the skin disguising itself as a zit, and then like a spore-shooting fungus, shot its spawn on whoever or whatever was within close distance, before finally spreading like a rampaging virus. It was the damndest thing I'd ever heard of.

Shortly afterwards, we all learned what we had feared most: Sven had expired. The tumor had eaten clean through his brain. The trauma of the squeezing, the dirty bar rag, and fresh air getting to the wound all might have contributed to its rapid growth while he was in the hospital. The voracious tumor quickly overcame Sven's natural defenses and turned out his lights once and for all.

Poor Fred fared no better. Sven's zit juice quickly fed off of Fred's delicate eye tissue, worked its way back to Fred's brain, bred like a whore on navy pay day, and then completely ravaged his brain as well. He too passed away months later, after an abominable stay in the hospital.

The rest of us are still under temporary quarantine until the authorities see fit to release us with a clean bill of health. So we wait in our own quarantined little hovels and continue to wait, not able to make physical contact with the outside world. To this day, nobody knows where the hell Sven got that nutty viral tumor from! According to the powers that be, if that virus gets out into the local populous and spreads like the common cold, then we're all in for it.

As for me, well, I'm fucked! I really am. I'm so bored with my quarantine. Armed guards are positioned outside my door, day and night. I tried to preoccupy my time by getting some personal stuff done at home in my quarantined little prison zone, doing things I've put off for ages. I've painted the living room, read a lot of books, repaired the kitchen sink, and got caught up on emails.

Unfortunately, I seem to have developed a wicked case of testicular elephantiasis. In other words, my balls have swollen to the size of giant beach balls. I have to bounce all over my house like a five-year-old just to get around. The doctor gave me a small tube of salve to put on my nuts. One small tube. Really? Worthless!

I can't do much real work at home on account of my huge balls. I'm a Quality Assurance guy and I can't really inspect much of our products from home either. The company I work for, PharmaSide, makes advanced pharmaceuticals. I get samples in the mail every day and do my best to inspect them, but it's not the same as being there in the office working with a team and advanced equipment.

And this strange virus has practically decimated the entire company. We might as well close shop. Nobody wants to work for PharmaSide anymore and we're hemorrhaging money.

I started putting two and two together and figured out that our main competitor, Konichiwa Happy Golden Lucky 8 Dragon Pills Company Ltd., is more than likely behind this virus. Who benefits the most if everyone in PharmaSide is dead or disabled: Konichiwa Happy Golden Lucky 8 Dragon Pills Company Ltd.!

Thus, with all this free time, I've concocted an ingenious plan! I mean, it really is something! I know, it sounds a bit wild and dangerous at first, but if I can pull it off, it will be amazing! I mean, like the best thang ever!

So here's the deal. I'm going to pump my balls full of helium, put a large supply of food, oxygen, and water in a backpack, float up to the stratosphere, and wait till Japan spins around. Then I'm going to slowly ease out the helium in my nuts and dive bomb Konichiwa Happy Golden Lucky 8 Dragon Pills Company Ltd.'s HQ with extreme pleasure and spread the love!

The Fecal Anomaly

Many years ago while I was still in high school, my folks were planning on going away for the weekend, leaving my younger brother, Gus, and myself to fend for ourselves. He was a freshman in high school, and I was a junior. We were definitely old enough to be left alone and were happy for a bit of freedom. We had been anticipating my parent's departure the whole week and had planned many things to do while we had the house to ourselves.

On Monday, four days before my parents were to leave for the weekend, my mother took my younger brother to the doctor's office, because he had been complaining of stomach problems. This was nothing new; my brother had been complaining all his life about stomach problems. However, this time he was experiencing more pain than usual, so my mother reluctantly took him in to see yet another specialist.

This was to be the first of several visits to the stomach doctor that week. During the initial visit, the doctor ran a full battery of tests and then decided to administer a thick bluish, chalky shake comprised mostly of the chemical barium, which is an element that isn't easily digested by the stomach. After a patient drinks it, the barium will slowly coat the digestive tract and show up on an x-ray. The doctor can then gaze inside the patient's digestive tract and determine what is causing the patient's stomach pain. Before the doctor could administer the barium shake, he had to wait until my brother's stomach and digestive tract were completely empty. The doctor explicitly told my brother not to eat anything for an entire day, which was easier said than done, and then return on Tuesday for the barium shake and the examination.

Unfortunately, my brother failed to resist a late-night leftover pepperoni pizza on Monday and failed to disclose this crucial fact to our mother and more importantly, to the doctor. The following day at the specialist's office, the doctor gave my brother the barium shake. My brother winced as he forced the super thick substance down his throat. Afterwards, Gus stood naked behind an x-ray machine as the doctor peered deep into Gus's stomach and digestive tract. Big gobs of partially digested pizza showed up clearly on the x-ray. When he discovered that his instructions had been disobeyed, the doctor removed his glasses and said sternly, "You are going to follow instructions this time or there won't be another time. Is that understood?" The test was postponed for two days.

My mother and brother came home that Tuesday night, and she allowed my brother to eat whatever he wanted for one night, followed by a day of not eating. Thinking he might starve if he didn't eat for an entire day, my brother ate like an ogre that night. He gorged himself, knowing that he could not eat for twenty-four hours after the following morning. He woke up, had a huge breakfast and then somehow made it through the rest of the day, Wednesday, without eating. The following morning, they went back to the doctor's office for the second heaping helping of barium. Thankfully, this time the doctor was satisfied with Gus's empty digestive tract and completed his examination without incident. Afterwards, the doctor informed my mother that Gus might be suffering from an ulcer and prescribed the appropriate medicine. The doctor warned Gus that the barium might cause constipation. Thus, the doctor advised Gus to consume ample amounts of fluids and foods high in fiber. Gus interpreted those words to mean: Eat a lot of food.

On Friday, we said goodbye to our parents and felt free. Gus and I were ecstatic. We were going to stay up late, order pizza, drink my parents' liquor and watch movies all night long. We were also planning on throwing a small house party on Saturday night, even though we had been explicitly warned not to.

A strange thing happened that Friday evening. While watching one of the rented movies, my brother started to complain about severe stomach cramps. I naturally administered some stomach medicine, hoping it would ease the pain. Sadly, it seemed to have no effect. All night long, Gus groaned miserably. Being the older sibling, I felt responsible for him, but didn't feel his pain justified medical attention. I had heard his stomach complaints all my life and knew they would subside, as did he, so I wasn't overly concerned.

The next morning, I checked in on Gus and he hadn't slept a wink. His sheets were soaking wet from his sweaty body and he was in excruciating pain. "Dude man," I said, "you want me to take you to the hospital or what?"

"No more doctors," he eked out. "I'm fine. Really. I just think I need to take a shit. But I don't think I can make it to the shitter. Can you help me?"

"What? Get up you wimp!" I commanded.

"I can't, come on," he whimpered.

Reluctantly, I jerked him out of bed. He was sticky like a glob of glue and could barely stand, so I grabbed both of his arms and dragged him to the bathroom, while he moaned in pain. I tossed him on the commode and left him to his own defenses. What else was I supposed to do: Wait until he was finished and then wipe his ass? Fuck that!

I ventured into the kitchen and heated up some of last night's pizza and then crashed in front of the tube to watch some more flicks. After the first movie was over, I checked in on my younger brother like an expectant father. "Dude man, any luck?" I said through the bathroom door.

"No," he grunted, "but I can feel it coming. Give me some more time."

I made some popcorn, poured myself some soda and then eased back into the sofa for another movie. After the second movie ended, I checked back in on him.

"Gustav, what the fuck? Are you dead?" I said as I listened through the door and heard loud wailings. "Are you giving birth in there or what?"

"Twins," he said. "Sebastian, come in here!"

"What?"

"Dude, get your ass in here, now!" he yelled back.

That's one phrase no one wants to hear from their brother. I mean, I am his older brother, but there are only so many things I would do for him. "I ain't going in there," I yelled back. "What are you, nuts?"

"Come in now!" he yelped.

I can't say that I was the least bit happy about what I was about to do, but I took a deep breath and went on in regardless. He was in serious pain; maybe I could help.

I eased open the door and the grossest smell I've ever sucked into my nostrils hit me like an uppercut from a prizefighter. My eyes were squinted and my right arm was covering my nose because the stench was overpowering. "Holy shit, you reek! What the hell's the matter with your anus?" I asked. I stared up through watery eyes and saw my brother bent over the crapper, his boxers hanging around his ankles.

"It won't come out," he cried.

"What?"

"It won't come out and it's hella huge!"

I squeamishly fought my way through a gaseous wall of stench and quickly looked down at his ass and, holy shit, it looked like he was giving birth to a football! I mean, the thing was massive! Gigantic! And it was stuck half way out of his gaping hole. I rapidly turned away and ran outside for a breath of fresh air.

"Get back in here, you wuss!" he grunted at me.

I took a deep breath and went back in waving my arms rapidly to try to dissipate the rank odor. "You've got an alien coming out of your ass!" I exclaimed as I rummaged around for some air freshener. Luckily, I found a can and fumigated the entire bathroom.

"Look, you gotta help me," he said, gagging from the air freshener.

"What am I supposed to do?" I said, waving the air around with one hand while wiping my tearing eyes with the other.

"Fucking help me!"

"And do what?"

"Get it out!"

I looked down there again and could see that his shit had a queer bluish-white tint to it. "It's the barium," I said.

"What?"

"It's the barium that's coming out. It must have formed a super shit inside of you and now it's forcing its way out."

"Well do something," he begged.

"Like what? Call the cops and tell them my brother's taking a massive shit and it won't come out?"

"No dick wad, pull it out!"

"What?"

"You heard me, pull it out!"

His face was turning blue, and he was completely exhausted! It was clearly evident that something had to be done, and I was the only one that could do it. "Okay, listen, first and foremost, you best not be telling anyone about this," I said. "Secondly, I will do this, but you're cleaning my room until I leave to college, got it? And you're doing my laundry, and, and, and anything else I can think of!"

"Okay, okay, just hurry the fuck up," he squealed.

"I'm going to hold you to it, you know I am," I said as I ran out, inhaled some fresh air and tried to formulate a plan.

"Believe me, I ain't going nowhere," he said.

I made my way into the kitchen hoping mom would have some stool extracting tools to help me out. I snagged some big yellow dishwashing gloves from below the sink and ran back into the bathroom.

"Okay," I said, trying to hold my breath. "I'm going to yank that hairy bitch right out of you!" I said, suddenly charged up. My eyes were watering from the gasses seeping off the steamy conglobulation. I was about to puke at any second. "But first I'm going to open the window, because your goliath shit fucking stinks to high heaven!"

I opened the window and then helped him lay on his stomach on top of a shaggy white rug, which my mom had bought to beautify the bathroom.

I cautiously approached his blocked orifice and gently prodded the movement, which was as solid as a rock and had bits of skin and blood on it. What a masterpiece! He was lying on the rug face down, ass end up, with a ridiculously Jovian-sized turd hanging halfway out of his butthole, and I swear I didn't know if I should kick a field goal, or spank it and give it a name.

"All right," I said, trying to move him so that the massive mound hanging out of his ass wouldn't touch the white throw rug. "I'm going to grab that piece of shit and yank it right out of you. When I say 'go' you push, I'll pull, and that should do it."

I knelt in front of the beast and loosened up a bit.

"Hurry up," he said.

"Cool your jets, this is delicate surgery, and might I add that I am literally saving your ass," I said as I grabbed hold of that gigantic chunk of blue-white chocolate with both gloved hands. "GO!" I yelled.

I squeezed and pulled at the same time, but that fecal anomaly was solid all the way through. I pulled and pulled and finally, lost my grip as my gloved hands slid off the shit and right into my face! I can't tell you how fucking gross that was! I had shit all over my face. My brother heard me yell, looked up and laughed.

I peered at that festering football jutting out of his ass and realized I hadn't even made a dent in it. "I need some better equipment," I said while rubbing my gloved hands all over my brother's back. "Stay put, I'll be right back!" I added as I ran out of the bathroom.

"You're going to pay for that one," he yelled.

I ran back to the kitchen and washed my face and gloves in the sink. Then I grabbed some tongs from a drawer and ran back to the bathroom.

"Tongs," my brother grunted. "If gloves won't work, what makes you think tongs will?"

"Sit tight, this is plan B. If this doesn't work, then I'm moving on to plan C."

I cranked the tongs open as far as I could and placed them next to his ass. I stood over him peering straight down at that disgusting fecal abortion: time for surgery. I could barely get the tongs around the rancid loaf, it was so huge, but finally I managed to get a grip on it. I squeezed with both hands and tried to pull it out. "Push," I screamed.

"I am," he fired back.

I pulled and pulled, but that noxious abomination wasn't even budging. It was as if it was permanently adhered to his ass. "That didn't work, so now I'm not holding back. I'm going in for the heavy equipment," I said.

"What are you going to do?" he asked.

"Sit tight, I'm going to dad's tool shed, I'll be right back."

I returned with a hand drill, some WD-40, some rope and an old army gas mask. I put on the gas mask and rolled my brother over onto his side.

"What the hell are you going to do?" he repeated.

Unfortunately, I couldn't breathe with the gas mask on, so I ripped it off my face and gagged as the odor hit me again. "Okay, first I'm going to squirt some lubricant on your ass pipe, then I'm going to drill a hole through the turd, put some rope through the drilled hole, tie a knot around it and pull with all my might."

"Do you think it'll work?" he said nervously.

"Hell if I know, but it's our only hope." I said. "If it doesn't work, I'm calling in the fire department, or the marines, or both!"

I sprayed some WD-40 all around his crusty a-hole. That WD-40 is amazing stuff! I once used it on an old rusty wrench that had been outside all winter long and got it to work again.

Gus squealed as the cold fluid attached itself to its target. My next move was to find the right sized bit for the drill. I didn't want one that was too big, because then I risked breaking the humongous hemorrhaging sphere in two and that would be bad. Too small a bit, and I wouldn't be able to get the rope through the hole. This was a delicate maneuver, so I studied my equipment carefully.

"Hurry up," he said breathlessly.

"Okay, okay!" I put in what I thought was the correct sized bit and locked it in place. I went outside for a quick breather. I pulled my T-shirt over my mouth and nose and then fought my way back in. He was lying on the cold tile shivering. The white rug was next to him covered in brown goo. Oops. "Now whatever you do, don't fart!"

"Ain't nothing squeaking out of me till I'm freed of this abortion," he grunted.

I began to drill right in the center of the menagerie, which was bespeckled with pieces of corn and pepperoni. I used all my force and cranked that bit as far as it would go.

"Okay, I'm halfway through, now I'm going to drill from the other side," I said.

I pulled out the bit, it was caked in gunk. I flipped him over and said, "Whatever you do, don't move." I stepped over to the other side and again drilled with extreme force. My aim was true and the two holes met somewhere in the middle of his incredible log.

I ran to the kitchen and snagged a long skewer. As I made my way back to the bathroom, a festering wall of offensive odor hit me. The drilling had somehow unlocked the gasses residing at the turd's core. I jumped to the sink and hurled.

Still gagging, I tried to work as rapidly as I could. I tied one end of the rope to the skewer, slipped the skewer through the hole and pulled the rope through. I used his underwear to grab the skewer because my yellow dish gloves were caked in greasy grime and were very slippery.

I tied the rope into a wide variety of knots. Once the rope was taut, I said, "Okay, grab hold of something, anything!"

He wiggled to the toilet and put both arms around its base.

"I'm going to pull and give it all I got, so hang on!" I commanded. Before moving back into jerking position, I sprayed some more WD-40 around his ass pipe.

He braced himself by gripping the shitter with all his might.

"Here I go," I said, as I started to pull and heave.

My socks were making me slip about on the glossy tile, so I flicked them off and then slipped the rope through the metal towel rack screwed into the wall, to give myself extra leverage. I pulled using every ounce of energy in my body, as my brother screamed in extreme agony.

I gave it all I had. The metal towel rack suddenly flew off the wall and slammed into the bathroom mirror, breaking it into a hundred pieces. I stopped to quickly clear a path and then hurried outside to catch my breath.

Now I was really pissed off! I made my way back in and applied some more WD-40. I walked out to the doorway and put one foot on one side of the doorway and the other foot on the other side. "When I say push, you push like you mean it!" I said. "Okay? Push! PUSH!!!" I wrapped the rope around my hands, pushed with my feet on the doorway and simultaneously yanked on the rope with extreme intensity.

I was literally standing perpendicularly on the doorway and pulling Gus up off of the floor. I pulled and pulled and pulled. He yelled, and screamed and cried. We were suspended in midair for what seemed like hours. Something had to give.

"POPPPPPPPPPPPP!"

That super-sized shit shot out of his ass like a bullet, hit the ceiling, ricocheted around the room and finally fell to rest near the sink, all in one piece.

He crashed to the ground, and I sailed backwards slamming my head and body on the wall across from the bathroom doorway and landing with a thud on the ground.

We lay there panting. "That was one tough piece of shit," I cried. I slowly got up and went to administer aid to my brother, who was still clenching the commode.

"We did it. We fucking did it!" I yelled. I helped him up while gas and odds-and-ends seeped out of his swollen orifice.

After he'd wiped his crater clean, I helped my brother to bed, placing another white throw rug under his ass, so he wouldn't soil his sheets if he farted in his sleep or if some excess happened to seep out. He immediately fell asleep, the moment his head hit the pillow. Then I went into the bathroom and cleaned up as best as I could.

When our parents arrived the following evening, we recounted our little adventure to them. They seemed more amused than anything. I tried to tell them how scared I'd been and how difficult it had been to get that crazy turd out of Gus's swollen ass, but they just laughed and laughed.

As a family reminder, we laminated the barium shit and turned it into a lamp, where it stands today in our living room, like a trophy to mark our tumultuous ordeal.

Years later, my brother discovered he was allergic to pepperoni. After he stopped eating it, his stomach pangs mysteriously disappeared.

GoMo BoMo

In the near future.

Sitting at his desk in a remote genetic research lab somewhere in North Central Queensland, Australia, Wallace Hummel peered diligently over several printouts from a recent gene-splicing experiment. He leaned back in his squeaky lab chair and looked down at his raging erection which was struggling to break through the zipper of his tight khaki pants. He shook his head at his crotch, then gazed up to the ceiling and twisted his face as he tried to stretch the skin around his tired eyes.

Mitesh Chinkara, Wallace's coworker, walked into the main lab room and began to place feed into the cages of numerous test subjects.

"Hey Mitesh, the little guy is at it again. Every time I sit in this damn lab chair, I can't help but get aroused."

"Perhaps you shouldn't sit in the lab chair," said Mitesh with a grin, as he stood by a long row of cages.

"Mitesh, that's what I like about you, you have the uncanny ability to state the obvious."

"Why beat around the bush?"

"Hey, I'm horny enough, stop talking about bushes!"

"Ha! Perhaps we've been working too hard. Maybe we should take a break."

Wallace swiveled his chair around and directed his attention to Mitesh. "What do you have in mind?" he said curiously, as he scratched his balls.

"I believe in two hours it will officially be considered 'the weekend', at least on the outside, beyond the walls of this lab. What do you say to having a few beers at that bar in town next to the big hotel? The last time I drove by, the bar seemed fairly vibrant."

"'Vibrant' sounds good, especially after being cooped up in the lab all day and all night. Sometimes I feel like one of our test subjects, like a caged animal."

"Exactly and a tall cold glass of fine Aussie brew usually takes the bite out of researching endlessly."

"Yes, it sure does," said Wallace.

"Great. When do you think you'll be ready?"

"Give me a few minutes to close up, then I'll be raring to go."

"Super! I should be through feeding the test subjects in about ten minutes."

Forty minutes later, casually dressed and fully doused in cheap cologne, the two American scientists drove a beat-up jeep down the main street of Winton, a small town in the outback of North Central Queensland.

"There she blows," said Wallace, as he slowed down to park the jeep in front of an old dusty Western-styled bar.

"Banjo's Last Stop," said Mitesh. "What kind of name is that for a bar?"

"Doesn't sound too hip, but one must never judge a bar by its name or something to that effect," said Wallace. He hopped out of his jeep and glanced over at a few large motorcycles parked out front. "Looks like a biker bar."

Wallace and Mitesh entered the sparsely populated bar and sat down near an occupied pool table. The two researchers ordered a few appetizers along with a few cold brews.

"Hey Wallace, what do you call a group of scientists?" asked Mitesh.

"I don't know, what do you call a group of scientists?"

"This isn't a joke. You know, you always hear people saying 'a group of scientists' or 'a team of scientists' and I think we need a better, more attractive word to define our people."

"Okay, how about 'a throng of scientists'? That sounds tough and manly. No one would mess with us if we were announced as such."

"Nah, I was thinking more along the lines of something that sounds intelligent," said Mitesh. "Something that really represents who we are as a profession."

"Okay, how 'bout a nerd herd of scientists'?" Wallace said jokingly.

"No! Come on," Mitesh said, picking up his beer. "How about something like 'a super intellect of scientists'?"

"That's a bit too modest, don't you think?" Wallace quipped. "Hold it. I think I have it. Yes! 'A noodle of scientists'! You know, scientists noodle around and use their noodle so why not use 'noodle'?"

"I like mine better."

"Hey, need another beer?" Wallace asked, looking around for their waitress. "I'll giddy up to the bar and get us some."

Wallace leaned over a long wooden bar and asked the bartender for two glasses of *Four X* beer. A youngish, slightly inebriated female customer perched at the bar leaned over to Wallace and said, "Hey, you a Yank?"

"Well, if you're referring to the fact that I come from America, then yes, you are correct."

"I like the way you talk. Hey, Linda," she said, elbowing her friend standing at the bar beside her, "ask this guy if he's a Yank."

Linda stuck her blonde head across her redheaded friend's shoulder and shouted, "Hey, you a Yank?"

"Why yes, I am," Wallace said, not quite sure if it was the desired response.

"Oo, I like Yanks," said Linda, as she pushed her friend aside and looked Wallace up and down. "And Shell," she said, leaning back and shouting in her friend's ear, "this one's good for the bush!" After nearly shattering all the glass in the bar, Linda directed her full attention to Wallace. "Hi, I'm Linda, what's your name?" she asked in a smooth voice, and then almost tripped over her high heels.

"My name would be Wallace."

"Hello Wallace, I'm Linda, oh sorry, I just said that. Ha, ha. And this here is Shell," she said, putting her arm around Shell who by this time had had already struck up a conversation with someone else.

"Oh hi," said Shell, turning back to Wallace. "You better be careful; I think Linda likes you!"

"Well, what's not to like," said Wallace. "Say, would you two ladies like to join me and my friend for a round of drinks?"

"Hey, who you calling a lady?" asked Shell seriously. "Ha, just joking!"

Two hours later, the inebriated foursome was in the jeep heading back to the remote research lab. The radio was blasting as Wallace drove erratically down a deserted dirt road. Mitesh was in the back making time with Shell while Linda was licking Wallace's ear and grabbing his crotch as he drove.

Mitesh pried himself from Shell's lips and tapped Wallace on the shoulder. "Do you think it's okay to bring them back to the lab?" he said loudly.

"We want to see the lab!" The girls screamed in unison. "We want to see the lab!"

"Calm down," Wallace replied, as he turned down the music. He shushed the girls and then said in a serious tone of voice as he slowed down, "Ladies, we are taking you to a top-secret laboratory. You are to tell no one about the location or what you see inside. Do you promise?"

"We promise," they yelled in unison.

"It sounds so exciting," said Shell.

"Okay, and under no circumstances can you play with the electronic microscopes and absolutely no gene splicing," he said, tongue in cheek.

"But I want to play on your microscope," begged Linda.

"And I want to splice your jeans," pouted Shell, as she dove back onto Mitesh's lips.

A brilliant flash of lightning followed by an ear-shattering clasp of thunder made the two women jump.

"Don't worry ladies," said Wallace. "Just a bit of a storm heading our way."

"You twose really are remote out here," said Shell, looking around at the desert landscape. "Who's going to protect us if we get flooded?"

"Don't worry my dear," said Mitesh, snuggling closer to Shell. "We're trained to handle most any unusual situation, including but not limited to natural disasters."

"I feel safer already," said Linda, as the rain began to pour.

Wallace stopped the jeep a few miles from the lab. "Okay ladies, now we must blindfold you before we get to the lab. Remember, our research here is very top, top secret! We also must ask that you hide in back under a blanket so the cameras do not detect you."

"Oo, what are you guys, kinky or something?" asked Linda.

"No, just very careful," said Wallace. "We are working on some very important research, and we cannot reveal any of it to you. In fact, if anyone found out that you two were in the lab, we would be fired immediately."

"Sounds risky, I don't know if I can be counted on not to spill the beans," said Shell. "I might tell if someone beats it out of me," she said, winking at Mitesh.

With the girls safely crouched down underneath a blanket in the gap between the front and back seats, Wallace drove the jeep up to a large metal gate, inserted his ID badge into a slot, pressed his thumb on a fingerprint scanner, and entered a code on a keypad. The gate opened slowly and Wallace drove the jeep up to a parking space near the front door of a large nondescript building.

Wallace jumped out of the jeep into the pouring rain, entered another set of digits on a keypad, and then quickly opened the front doors of the research lab with a set of keys. He shook off the rain, strutted into a large sparsely decorated lobby, and then stood in front of a thick glass door. After he inserted his employee ID badge into a slot, an electronic device scanned his face. The door slid open and he entered a small-enclosed containment area. A red light above a second set of glass doors blinked directly in front of him. The door behind him closed. Large jets of air immediately streamed over his entire body and then a suction device below the grate he was standing on sucked up all the dust particles from his clothing.

A green light appeared and a second door opened. After passing the security check, he sauntered down a narrow hallway, entered the main lab, sat down at a computer, and brought the surveillance and security systems down. To cover his ass, he sent a message to Headquarters in America stating that he was simply running a routine test on the security system.

He walked to an intercom and informed the others that it was safe to enter. Mitesh held the front doors open as the ladies stumbled into the remote research building, still blindfolded and shaking from the cold rain. Shell nervously walked into the containment area and giggled as streams of air brushed across her body.

Linda entered next. Wallace purposely sent a sustained jet of air straight up her small blue jean skirt. Linda squealed as Wallace laughed heartily. "I've always wanted to do that," he chuckled to himself.

Once Mitesh passed through the containment area he said, "Okay ladies, follow me."

The group walked into the slightly cluttered main research room which housed numerous animal research subjects and a variety of sophisticated equipment.

"Okay, we will now remove your blindfolds, but you must swear that you will not touch a thing!" warned Mitesh.

"I solemnly swear that I will not, under any circumstances, touch your thing," said Linda with a loud cackle.

"I promise not to let Linda touch your thingy," said Shell, hiding her grin with her hand.

Mitesh removed the ladies' blindfolds. They immediately took in the research lab and were slightly disappointed.

"This is it? This is your big secret?" asked Linda.

"It looks like a big, boring lab," said Shell.

"Well, let me show you where I do my research," said Mitesh, as he escorted Shell out of the central lab.

"I'm going to let you into our advanced research room, but you have to agree not to look at anything along the way," said Mitesh to Shell, as they swayed down the narrow hallway arm-in-arm. "Close your eyes until I say it's okay."

"What are you, some kind of secret spies or something?" asked Shell.

"Better, we're a super intellect of scientists. Now close your eyes," he said while standing at the door to a small research room.

"Okay," she said, putting her hands over her eyes. "Closed tight as a koala's bum. Tell me when I can open them," she said, peaking through her fingers.

Mitesh carefully opened the door to his research office and guided Shell in. He purposely left the lights off, but several computer monitors were on, giving the room a slightly romantic, yet oddly eerie feel. "Okay, you can open your eyes."

She looked over the room complete with desks along one wall, a huge table in the center, and rows of wire cages lining the back wall. "Hey, I've never done it in a real lab before," she said, as she removed Mitesh's glasses and lunged for his lips.

Shell threw her open purse down on the ground, right next to one of the cages and began undressing Mitesh.

Shell heard something rattling in the cages and listened briefly, "Hey, what's in those cages?"

"Wild animals, don't get too close," said Mitesh, as he pulled her near to his lips and reached under her blouse for her bra clasp.

"What kind of wild animals?" she asked nervously.

"Toads."

"Toads? Really? That's disgusting. Here I thought you were putting together a nuclear bomb or something exciting like that. Toads? My gosh, how, how utterly boring," she said, laughing hysterically. "Toads! Ha, ha, ha!"

After the two had completed a particularly wild act of fornication, Shell got dressed, picked up her purse, and wobbled down the hall to a small bathroom to fix herself up. As she reached into her purse for some lipstick, she touched some weird squishy substance covering everything inside. She quickly pulled out her hand; it was covered in a thick warm brownish jelly. "Disgusting!"

She emptied the contents of her purse into the sink and cleaned the jelly off each affected item and watched the goo all go down the drain.

She waddled back into the lab room, nearly tripping several times over her high heels. "Somebody put jelly in my purse. Can you believe it? What kind of sicko puts jelly in a woman's purse?" she said to Mitesh, who was washing his face in the lab's sink.

"Jelly," he said curiously. "What kind of jelly was it?"

"Dunno, just some gooey brown jelly."

"Hmm," he said, walking to her purse. "Can I see?"

"I already cleaned it up," she said, as she threw her arms around his neck and kissed him passionately.

"Hey Shell," Linda screamed down the hall, "you ready to go?"

One year earlier.

As darkness fell, Oliver Dendracopus drove his scooter to his apartment complex in Sacramento, California. He was wearing a thick jacket to prevent the cool March winds from piercing his skin while he drove. He walked up to his door and entered his dark two-bedroom flat. As Oliver flicked on the light switch, his roommate Marco Columba lifted his head up from the couch. Oliver could clearly identify two small female hands firmly wrapped around Marco's neck.

"Dude," said Marco, smiling embarrassingly and pointing to his female companion. "Could you, uh, give us a few minutes?"

A female voice shouted, "A few minutes! I think we'll need more than that!"

Oliver spun himself around, scampered outside, and closed the door. He drove to a fast food restaurant to eat. After receiving his order, he carried his tray to an open booth and grabbed a used newspaper resting on top of a dirty garbage can. He stuffed his mouth full of fries and began to read. One article entitled *"Decamate to Acquire Poultry Company"* attracted his attention.

"Oh great," he said to himself, "what are they up to now? First, they buy a cosmetic company and now a chicken farm. Can somebody please tell me where this company is headed?" he said, shaking his head.

Large business conglomerate, Decamate, Corporate Headquarters, Sacramento, California.

A group of high-powered executives sat in a gigantic, expensively decorated boardroom discussing their latest top-secret project. Chief Executive Officer Wharton Lionsgate sat at the head of the table. At fifty years of age and well over six-feet-five inches tall with grey hair and deep voice, Lionsgate was an imposing figure who ruled his company with an iron first

Two research assistants, James Hu and Jack Brudstein, stood in front of a huge projector screen addressing the executives sitting around a large rectangular, hand-carved table. Brudstein and Hu were scientists who had been hired to crossbread chickens with toads. The brass at Decamate were hoping to develop and then market an inexpensive chicken replacement. Still in its early stages, the project was slightly behind schedule. The purpose of this meeting was for Brudstein and Hu to update Decamate's upper management on the progress of the project.

"We've finally selected the subject to conduct our research on," said Brudstein.

"And the winner is?" said Lionsgate.

"Bufo Marinus," said Hu.

"Who's he?" said Lionsgate.

"Uh, Bufo Marinus, the toad," said Brudstein.

"Bufo Marinus, the toad?" said Lionsgate, twisting his brow. "It sounds like a clown's name."

"Or a hitman: Bufo the toad," joked Chief Operating Officer Alan Tourterellie.

"It's a type of toad, sir," said Hu, "A very hearty type."

"And?" said Lionsgate.

"And he's quite possibly the ugliest toad on the planet," said Hu.

"Yes, very ugly, but very hearty," said Brudstein.

"I'm still listening," said Lionsgate.

"This toad is a gutsy survivor," said Hu, "and while frogs and toads all over the world are rapidly dying out, BM is expanding exponentially in Australia. It has actually taken root and is not leaving any time soon."

"BM?" asked Tourterellie.

"BM is short for Bufo Marinus," said Brudstein.

"Oh, I thought you were talking about a bowel movement," joked Tourterellie.

"Uh, no sir," said Brudstein.

"People," barked Lionsgate as he peered coldly as Tourterellie, "let's keep the joking to a minimum."

Tourterellie nodded.

"Okay," said Brudstein tentatively. "Might I, uh add, that if we can properly genetically engineer BM, then we might possibly be ready for human tests in two years' time."

"Fantastic!" said Lionsgate. "Tell me more about this BM."

"Well, sir," said Brudstein, "BM mates all year round. They clutch each other in an embrace called an amplexus that lasts as long as a day."

"A day!" said Tourterellie. "That's some serious love making!"

Lionsgate stared briefly at Tourterellie.

"What are the results of this daylong love fest?" asked Lionsgate unimpressed.

"From 3,000-20,000 eggs are laid in a jelly-like chain in fresh water," said Brudstein.

"Hot-damn!" said Lionsgate. "Now we're talking! Go on, what else can you tell us about this BM?"

"Well, it's a nocturnal creature, so we might have to look into breeding out their love of the evening," said Brudstein. "But that's not important at the moment."

"Our only real concern is keeping a tight lid on our research so that our competition doesn't find out," said Hu.

"Absolutely," said Lionsgate. "People, listen up. Secrecy is job one on this project. We cannot afford any leaks at this stage of the game."

"Absolutely, that's why we thought of moving the program to Australia where they kind of have a Bufo infestation."

"Go on," said Lionsgate.

"Yes, sir," said Brudstein. "Bufo Marinus, more commonly known as the Cane Toad, was actually brought into Australia in the early 1930s. Once introduced, the Bufo Marinus population quickly grew out of control and remains a growing concern to this very day."

"And might I add that if we conduct research in Australia under the guise of attempting to control the BM population," said Hu, "the Australian government might actually give us a research grant."

"I see," said Lionsgate approvingly.

"Plus, we will be far away from our competitors, and thus be able to keep a tighter lid on our research," said Brudstein.

"Sounds very plausible," said Lionsgate. "All right. Let's do this thing. Let's get our marketing research team on this as well to start digging up whatever they can about this Bluto Mariner."

"Uh, Bufo Marinus," said Brudstein.

"Yeah, whatever," said Lionsgate, preparing to leave.

"We'll get on the research right away," said Barbara Beaver, Chief Marketing Officer.

"Fantastic. Okay, are we done here?" said Lionsgate about to stand up.

"Uh, not yet sir, we have some research of our own to show you," said Brudstein, gesturing towards Hu.

"Okay, what we've prepared for you today is a little background documentary on BM or the Cane Toad as it's popularly called," said Hu, picking up a remote control. "Remember this is just a lighthearted look at our test subject."

Hu started the documentary as Brudstein turned off the lights.

"Frogs and toads, some of the most diverse and adaptable creatures on the face of the earth," said the narrator, Rafe McCory, in a thick Australian accent. "From rain forests to deserts they have learned to thrive and survive on most any terrain and can be found in almost any corner of the earth. Consider this, they were around long before the dinosaurs ruled the planet 165 million years ago. Sadly, due to habitat destruction, chemicals such as pesticides, the greenhouse effect, disease, invasive species, and deficient environmental controls, the world is quickly witnessing the largest destruction of the species in the history of the planet. Of the over 4,000 known varieties, all are facing extreme population reductions. All but one: The Mighty Cane Toad, King of Beasts."

A Cane Toad appeared on screen and croaked loudly.

"Wait a minute," yelled Lionsgate. "What the hell is all this crap?"

Brudstein paused the video and said, "Give it a minute, sir. It'll get to the meat of the matter shortly."

"This documentary guy, Rafe McCory, is the foremost expert on Cane Toads in Australia," added Hu.

"And might I just say, sir, it's an incredibly interesting documentary," stated Brudstein.

"Thanks for that Brudstein," said Lionsgate sarcastically. "Start it up again."

"Ah Australia," said McCory, "land to some of the most diverse species of life on earth. And unfortunately, land of some of the most ruthless creatures the world has ever known. And believe it or not, the Cane Toad is on the top of the list!

"The Cane Toad was brought into Australia in the early 1930s from America to solve the Cane Beetle problem plaguing the Australian sugarcane growers. Once the Cane Toads were transplanted and much to the dismay of the Aussie people, it quickly became apparent that the

Cane Toad had and never will have an appetite for Cane Beetles. They loathe them, but loathe practically nothing else.

"You'd think that the Aussie Government would have spent a few days or even hours to see what the Cane Toad actually liked to eat. It seems only natural. Do they like bees? Crocs? Steak and lobster with butter sauce? Human flesh? What are their culinary habits? One thing is smashingly obvious; the Cane Toad does not like, and never has liked Cane Beetles! But in the intermittent years between introduction to Australia—BC (Before Cane) and AC (After Cane)—the Governmental wankers have bungled over and over again and are directly responsible for introducing Australia's numero uno unwelcome guest to this great land of ours: The Cane Toad. Pommies rank a close second."

"Pommies?" asked Lionsgate.

"Uh, it's Australian slang for a British person," said Brudstein.

Rafe McCory continues his lecture on the video.

"Ooops," said the Government, "that was a horrible mistake. No worries. We'll just round 'em all up and ship 'em back to the Yanks.

"Right! Easier said than done. The Cane Toad settled into Australia faster than a Pommy tourist and started breeding faster than rabbits. We began with 500 of the horrible hoppers, now there are more than 3 million of the little buggers scattered all over Australia. And now we can't get rid of the things. Even if every man, woman and child spent the rest of their lives trying to kill the beast; there's no way to rid Australia of the Cane menace.

"Not only was it revealed that the Cane Toad did not consume Cane Beetles, it was also discovered that the Cane Toad had no natural predators in Australia. To make matters worse, once firmly planted on Aussie soil, the Cane Toad population exploded! We didn't need the Cane Toad in the first place, but we were stuck with 'em. Worse yet, four years later, a pesticide was developed to control the Cane Beetle. But the pesticide unfortunately had no ill effect on Cane Toads or on Pommies.

"The government quickly tried to gloss over the entire ordeal and created an 'Eat Cane Campaign'. The older brainwashed segment of society quickly went along with the ridiculous suggestion from the Government that we try to integrate Cane Toad into our 'culinary diets'. So you had the inevitable Cane Toad cook-offs and fresh new recipe contests. The newspapers were awash with gray-hairs consuming Cane with joy and satiation written all over their lip-smacking faces. From the posh bowling green of Sydney to the dry outbacks of the territories, the old folks were creating new ways to serve up the belching baritone.

"You had Cane Pie, Barbied Toad, as well as Cane and Maple on toast. They were getting creative; I'll give that to 'em. However, a slightly overlooked fact was only sparsely reported to our great trusting compatriots: If the Cane Toad's twin sacks of poison aren't removed before cooking and Mr. Cane isn't boiled for 48 hours prior to eating it, then consuming the bewarted fat lizard will cause cramping, diarrhea, and yes, even death. Henceforth, the government quietly ended its Cane cooking campaign; much to the chagrin of the Pommies.

"To make matters even worse, a rare documentary I discovered, created a few years after the Cane Toad arrived, revealed shocking footage of exactly how ferocious this Cane Toad actually is. Here's a glimpse of the amazing footage.

"Test subject number 1, the mighty Taipan, the deadliest snake in the world, mind you, in action versus the mighty Cane Toad, King of Beasts.

"Okay, watch the Taipan slowly slither up to the Cane Toad. He's thinking 'lunch'. Boom! There's the snake's strike, directly to the skin of the Cane. Now watch what happens. Nothing! Seems the Cane Toad's armor-like skin is impenetrable to even the most poisonous snake in the world. Sadly, as the Cane Toad prospers in numbers, the population of the once mighty Taipan, King of Snakes, is now dwindling and is on the brink of extinction.

"Test subject number two, the Tasmanian Devil, the most ferocious hunter for its size in all the world. Okay, the Tazzie sees the Cane Toad. He's thinking, *nice little froggie snack to tide me over till din-din.* He's licking his lips; he's moving in for the kill. The unsuspecting Cane sits quietly meditating; almost impervious that imminent danger is approaching. Wham-O! The Tazzie bites down and starts to chew. (The camera zooms in on the Tazzie). How does he taste Mr. Devil? Scrumptious? Delicious? Uh-oh, what's this? Seems our friend Mr. Devil didn't quite like the flavor of the Cane Toad. He's spitting him out. Incredible, the Cane is actually taunting the Tazzie, hopping up-and-down in front of the frothing hunter, unscathed.

"Let's check in with Mr. Devil. What's this? He's rolling over. Sick? Nearly dead? No, completely dead! The Cane Toad's twin sacks of poison located directly behind his eye sockets secrete a milky, lethal poison when attacked. This poison is only slightly less poisonous than the Taipan's poison. Sadly, the Tazzie Devil population too is rapidly declining due to the Cane Toad infestation.

"This test unequivocally shows how ridiculously powerful our little hopping toad is. Listen, letting the Cane Toad into Australia was one of the biggest fuck-ups in modern times. So who's to blame? Well, as you can imagine, documents concerning this case have been conveniently lost.

"Having said that, I was luck enough to obtain an interview conducted by gonzo journalist Harold Kinghorn with one of the Governmental wankers responsible for this whole Cane Toad infestation and his name is Retired Brigadier General Sir Roystin Smyth-Wesson. Word has it that he was directly involved in the Cane Toad scandal shortly before he keeled over. He ran the office of Animal Control right into the ground from 1925 right up till his death in 1984. Here's the interview from the early '80s."

An old scratchy video starts to play.

Kinghorn: Harold Kinghorn here standing outside Sir Roystin Smyth-Wesson's gaudy multi-storied mansion. The general has agreed to meet with me today to discuss his involvement pertaining to the introduction of the Cane Toad in Australia. Here we are in his posh living room. He is wheelchair bound and has a full butler and maid staff at his beck and call, all paid for by our tax dollars. Not wanting to waste any time, I decided to play the tough guy and get right to the point.

Kinghorn: Sir, Roy, you don't mind if I call you Roy, do you?

Smyth-Wesson: What, speak up!

Kinghorn: ROY, after researching this CTD, Cane Toad Debacle, it is clearly evident that the government did not have a clue what it was doing. Are you following?

Smyth-Wesson: Yes, STD.

Kinghorn: No, CTD, Cane Toad Debacle.

Smyth-Wesson: Oh, is that what you're here for? Right.

Kinghorn: Sir, I have never heard of such a serious cock up in all my days. The country is now infested with Cane Toads and I hold you directly responsible! What were you thinking?

Smyth-Wesson: Listen here. If you're going to sit there and blame me for this whole Cane thing, then you've got another thing coming.

Kinghorn: Come on Roy, ya old Digger, out with it.

Smyth-Wesson: Listen here you snot-nosed bastard. I've been all through this before. I begged them to research it first? Did they listen? No! And did I sign the papers to let them in? Hell no, I was against it from the start.

Kinghorn: Uh Roy, you did sign the papers, you lying dickhead.

Smyth-Wesson: Listen up, I'm not going to sit here and let you recreate history. Perkins, roll me home.

Kinghorn: Roy, you are home.

Smyth-Wesson: Oh, right. Well then, Perkins, get this filth outta my house.

Kinghorn: Roy, come-on matey. I was just having a go.

Rafe McCory appears back on screen.

"So as you can see it's very difficult to get to the bottom of this whole mess. That was about as far as I got into uncovering how and why the Cane Toad arrived on Aussie shores. I personally bet that the U.S. sent the Cane Toad here to destroy us.

"Meanwhile, the mighty Aussie youth, who were up in arms at the extreme lack of intelligence shown by our elders, decided to take things into their own hands: They declared war on the Cane Toad and found other more productive uses for Mr. Cane. From golfing matches using Cane Toads as golf balls, to squish rallies where two lanes are lined with Cane Toads and then two trucks tear down the road trying to squish as many fat hoppers as possible.

"And don't forget the Cane shredder. The object is to fill an ordinary wood shredder up with as many Cane Toads as you can and then turn the shredder on to high to see how many toads the machine can take before it clogs up. What's spewed out can be directed at a canvas, then mounted on a frame and hung in your living room. Interestingly, a thriving underground art scene has emerged. Some shredders are actually in talks with the government to set a new standard. If they have their way, the shredding companies will stamp all passed shredders with a CTT stamp which means the device is certifiably "Cane Toad Tested" and can shred up to 10,000 Cane Toads before it needs servicing."

"Stop the video! What the hell is this crap?" screamed Lionsgate.

"Well, sir," said Hu, turning on the lights, "you asked us to put together some background information on the Cane Toad and this is all that's out there."

"This outdated, green, profanity-laden piece of junk?"

"Well, we felt the video summed up the love-hate relationship Aussies have for the Cane Toad. It showed BM in a light few people in the States have noticed or even cared to notice."

"And, might I add, the Cane Toad is one hearty beast," said Brudstein.

"I asked you two idiots to come up with something to help me sell my idea, not ruin it before it even gets started! Squish-a-thons, golf matches, and toads on canvas are not what I'm interested in. I want to paint a rosy picture, not this crap!"

"Well it depends on what you mean by rosy," said Hu. "Obviously, the Aussies hate the Cane Toad, and thus it will be easy for us to go in there and take advantage of that hate."

"We are not taking advantage of anyone or anything!" yelled Lionsgate. "We're saving the goddamn world from starvation and this documentary does not come anywhere near presenting our primary test subject in any conceivably positive light!"

"I see what you're saying," said Brudstein. "You bring up a very valid point."

"In our defense, we were just trying to set the scene for this project, sir," said Hu.

"Well thank you for that! Now, get your team together and get on this project pronto. I just read that Hemalux is entering the commercial crossbreeding market. It won't be long till we have more competitors to deal with. What is it, March already? We need results before the market is flooded!" he said, pounding his fist on the table. "I want a weekly update and a quarterly meeting."

"Yes sir," said Hu, "we'll get right on it."

"ASAP!" screamed Lionsgate, before storming out of the conference room.

Three months later.

Decamate's Global Marketing Director, Peter Gulovski, hammered away on his computer's keyboard in his large, brightly lit office as Oliver Dendracopus knocked on the open door.

Gulovski acknowledged Oliver, held up his index finger, and returned to his computer. After entering, Oliver sat down on a comfortable chair across from his boss's desk. He looked outside the window and noticed an early summer rain gently falling outside. "Shoot," he said to himself. "I forgot to bring my scooter's rain jacket; I may have to hitch a ride home with Marco."

"Hello Oliver," said Gulovski abruptly, "I was just going over some notes for a new project that I'd like you to be involved with."

"New project?"

"Yes, I've been asked to create a new spin on an old toad. An ugly toad, in fact." Oliver rolled his eyes at Peter. "Don't look at me like that," said Gulovski, "I just got handed this, okay? Don't give me a hard time before you even know what I'm about to say." He took a deep breath and cleared his throat. "So here's the deal, basically, we've been assigned the task of researching a toad called Bufo Marinus or the Cane Toad."

"Why?" asked Oliver.

"I don't know why, they didn't say," said Gulovski, as he placed the project notes down in front of Oliver.

Oliver glanced at the paper and said, "There must be a reason."

"I'm sure there is Oliver. I'm sure there's a very good reason, but we are not privy to that bit of information at the moment. I'm sure it will all become crystal clear one day. In the meantime, I have come up with a few ideas, and I'd like you, Oliver, to help me with the research."

"I can't do it."

"Why not?" asked Gulovski, trying to hold back his anger.

"I can't work like that. I have to know why we're doing something before I can do it."

"Okay, how's this: We are doing it because the big boss says so. You know the CEO, the guy who signs your check?"

"And never comes into work," said Oliver.

"Yeah, that guy."

"Sorry, I can't do it. I'd tell it to his face if he ever gets off the golf course."

"Come on Oliver. Work with me here. I just need some research on this toad thing."

"Why?"

"I just told you, I don't know," Gulovski said, raising his voice.

"Well, I'm not going to do it. The last time I did research on something they told me to research 'just because', it ended up causing cancer."

"That was a long time ago, and it was never definitively proven to cause cancer. Look, Oliver, you're overreacting, as usual. Now listen, I'm not asking you to do it, I'm asking you to head the project."

"Oo, I feel so honored," he said sarcastically.

"Oliver, don't give me that attitude! You are going to do it because I said so," said Gulovski, slamming his hands on his desk and staring directly into Oliver's eyes.

"I know nothing about toads. In addition, I've probably got six rare forms of cancer brewing in me right now from working on these weird, top-secret projects that you keep handing to me, and I'm not going to take any more of them. Period! Where in my job description does it say I HAVE to research toads? Where? Show me!"

"Oliver! Look, all I know is we need to research the Cane Toad because we're going to test a new type of skin cream on it."

"I thought we were a shampoo and soap company. What's with the sudden shift to skin cream?" said Oliver.

"Dunno."

"Why don't we just buy out a skin cream company like we bought out the chicken company, the butter company, and the dozen others?"

"I don't know!"

"Talk about deworsifying the company. Look Peter, I can't research this toad. I simply can't do it; I'm too busy with all the other crap you want me to do."

"Well, find time! End of discussion," Gulovski said, as he pounded the table. Oliver clenched his teeth and glared at his boss. "Don't give me that stare, Oliver." Gulovski took a deep breath. "Look, the word I have is we're inventing some sort of skin cream and this toad is covered in warts and living under the ozone hole in Australia, and it is a very hearty toad, so we're going to test the cream on them. And yes, we're reinventing ourselves as a skin cream company."

"Oh great! Now we're using animals as test subjects for the lethal poisons we're creating. Look Peter, I can't do this."

"You're a marketing researcher, aren't you?"

"Yeah, but I can't do this. I know nothing about frogs," said Oliver.

"Toads, and neither do I."

"Exactly."

"Oliver! Just get on it. And might I recommend, and this comes from the top, that you focus your research on Australia."

"Australia?"

"You bet," said Gulovski.

"How big is this thing?"

"We just got a huge budget approval for this project."

"Oo, like what's the code name?" Oliver said sarcastically.

"Um. Let's call it, Project Wart."

"Really? That's the name?"

"Get moving, time's a-wasting."

"Yeah, yeah."

"Thank you, Oliver! I'll mention you in my will," said Gulovski.

"You better or I swear I'll dig up your corpse," Oliver said, as he grabbed the project printout from Gulovski's desk and marched out the door.

"I want a detailed report on how you're going to approach this project with clear deliverables and achievable timeframes," yelled Gulovski.

"Sure thing," Oliver said, followed by a muffeled, "God I hate that guy."

"I heard that," screamed Gulovski.

A month later, Oliver called marketing assistant, Zabra Moineau, at Decamate's Australian branch office in Brisbane, Australia.

"Hey Zabra, this is Oliver at HQ. My boss, Peter Gulovski, told me to contact you, do you have a moment?"

"Sure, how's it going?"

"Good, I guess, until I got put in charge of a crazy new project."

"I like crazy projects."

"Well then you'd like this one. Listen, I need you to do me a big, big favor."

"How big? Does it involve espionage? Torture?" joked Zabra.

"No, nothing that exciting, unfortunately," said Oliver.

"You're heavily disappointing me, Oliver."

"Well, prepare to get even more disappointed as this project isn't really that interesting."

"Boo-hoo."

"Don't cry just yet. If you've got a thing for amphibians, then this might wet your whistle."

"Nope, sorry, I don't like bugs or strange creatures that crawl around at night. But what is it that you need help with?"

"I need some information on a toad called the Cane Toad. Can you dig up any info for me in Australia on it?"

"Ick, the Cane Toad! What on bloody earth for?"

"I really don't know. HQ wants to do some research on this toad, and they want me to find some background data on it before they begin the research."

"I hate those things!" said Zabra.

"Really, you've heard of them?"

"Yes, they're all over Queensland, we can't get rid of them."

"Well, anything you could dig up for me would be greatly appreciated," said Oliver.

"Okay, I'll see what I can do. No promises. But if I do find something, you'll owe me big time!"

"How big?"

"Very!" said Zabra.

"How very?"

"You'll see."

"Hmm. You have the sexiest Australian accent!"

"Well, that's not even the sexiest part of me."

"Really, what is?"

"I'm not at liberty to say. I don't give out that kind of information to strange men calling me on the phone going on about toads," said Zabra.

"I am anything but strange. I'm a gentleman. A coworker! A gentleman coworker."

"Sure, you all say that."

"How can I prove it to you?"

"For starters you can send me a picture of yourself; I don't even know what you look like. Then write me a beautiful poem."

"A poem?" asked Oliver.

"Yes, I'm good at judging the intellect of men by their ability to scribe poetry," said Zabra. "Look, I gotta run, I've got a meeting in a few minutes. I'll try to send you some info on Cane Toads shortly. Talk to youse later, bye."

"Bye," Oliver said, and hung up the phone. "That was interesting," he said to himself. "I do believe she was flirting with me."

Oliver picked up the phone and dialed his roommate, Marco Colomba, who was part of Decamate's Management Information Services (MIS) team. "Marco, I have a top-secret assignment for you," said Oliver.

"Doing what?" asked Marco, staring over a computer workstation.

"I need you to find a picture of Zabra in our Australian Branch's marketing department and send it to me."

"What for?"

"I just got off the phone with her; she sounds smoking hot," said Oliver.

"That should be easy enough. Hey, by the way, we're going to do a little on-line video gaming after work tonight in the MIS department.

Care to join in?"

"Fuck yeah!"

"All right, come over around seven and be prepared to battle," said Marco.

"Will do."

That evening, Oliver walked into the MIS department with a backpack full of beer, holding a large pizza in one hand, and an elaborate video game joystick in the other. Four MIS members sat behind large computer monitors discussing what game they were going to play.

"Pizza and beer, you stud," Marco yelled at Oliver and then sat him down at a large computer screen. Marco put the pizza on a table and popped open a beer for himself and one for Oliver. "Oh, did you get the picture I sent you of that Australian chick?"

"Yeah, she's pretty hot, isn't she?" said Oliver.

"Damn straight!"

"I may have a chance to go over to our Aussie branch office one day."

"No way! You lucky dog! When?"

"I don't know yet, it's all up in the air at the moment, but there's an outside chance. And if I do go, maybe I can work some magic on Zabra."

"Outstanding!" said Marco while typing on the computer. "Okay, you ready to play?"

"Abso-fucking-lutely!" Oliver yelled.

Marco loaded the game and quickly returned to his computer.

A week later Oliver received a phone call from Zabra. "Okay, I dug up a comedy and an old documentary about the Cane Toad," she said.

"All right can you send me the documentary; I don't think I'll need the comedy."

"My pleasure, but don't forget, you owe me big time."

"Like how big?" asked Oliver.

"Oo, well, let's just say to be determined," said Zabra.

"Can I do the determining?"

"Only if it's creative and involves whips and chains."

"Whips and chains?" asked Oliver. "I'm delicate. How 'bout whipped cream and chain letters?"

"Naw, you'll have to do better than that!"

"Okay, give me some time to think about it. If and when they let me out of my cage and send me to Australia, I'll return the favor. Or better yet, if and when you come to the States, I can return the favor then."

"Actually, they're sending me to the States in January for training," said Zabra.

"Really! Where?"

"At the global HQ, of course."

"Well, that's interesting because I happen to be located at the global HQ," said Oliver.

"Well, I happen to know that, so when I arrive, I not only expect you to return the favor, but I expect the red-carpet treatment."

"I won't spare any expense."

"I'm going to hold ya to that."

"I hope you do."

"We'll see," said Zabra. "In the meantime, mark your calendar from January 15th to the 22nd, that's when I'll be in Sacramento. So don't schedule anything that doesn't involve me."

"That's like six months away!"

"I know, it's such an abearably long time! Can you wait till then to see me?"

"God, I hope so," he said sarcastically. "But wait; tell me something more about you. What do you like to do? And more importantly, is your husband coming?"

"Husband, ha! Show me around town, Oliver. Wine me, dine me, and show me the time of my life," she said.

"Wow, talk about pressure," said Oliver.

"Is that all you can say? You're letting me down, mate. Look, I'm giving you plenty of warning and I expect a detailed report as to what we are going to do when I get into town. I want that in my in-box ASAP."

"Yes, ma'am!"

"Okay, gotta run, bye," said Zabra.

"Bye."

Oliver hung up the phone, eased his seat back, and let his mind wander. "Did that just happen?" he said to himself. "Holy shit, I think she was coming on to me. Yes, she was definitely coming on to me! But six months! She's coming in six months. Why does it have to be so long?"

A few days later Oliver received the documentary from Zabra. He ordered some flowers online to be sent directly to Zabra's desk to thank her for sending him the video. The attached note read:

Roses are red

> Violets are blue
> Cane Toads belch sweetly
> And so do you!

Three months later.

It was a warm October day when Lionsgate burst into Decamate's boardroom as his high-level team sat nervously. It had been six months since their initial meeting concerning the top-secret Cane Toad project. Brudstein and Hu appeared on a large video screen beamed in directly from their remote Australian research lab.

"Now you two," said Lionsgate to Brudstein and Hu, "I would like a thorough update on the progress of this toad project, but first I want to remind you all why we're here doing this," he said, as he gazed around the room. "We are going to be pioneers in crossbreeding. Pioneers! Look people, we are on the cutting edge of science here! Okay? Now, I've spoken to you each individually about this project, but let me take this time to review. And let me remind you that no one ever accomplished anything by taking the easy road. We are attempting this because it is difficult and if done right, could garner us enormous revenue growth, huge market share, and the respect of the entire world.

"All right now, what we are attempting to do is to genetically merge two species: a toad and a chicken. I hope you can all see how gigantic the potential benefits are. Once we create a commercially viable product, we'll be able to corner the chicken market. Think of it. We take the best of both breeds. With the non-feathered amphibian, we have thousands of eggs from one creature to play with. The yet-to-be-named creature won't be territorial, so they won't fight in their cages. They won't have beaks to cut or claws to remove. And best of all, they'll be stackable. We can put up to ten in one cage. Think of the space we'll save. Plus, we'll be able to make them taste exactly like chicken. Hell, even better than chicken! We'll also be able to genetically increase the rate of growth, breed out diseases, breed in healthy nutrients, and save production time.

"This little project could wind up making us a fortune as well as the *de facto* leaders in this new industry. And let me remind you all, no one, and I mean NO ONE outside of this room is to find out a thing about this project. We are going to refer to it as 'Project Skin Cream' from here on out. If anyone outside of this room stumbles upon this project or asks questions, tell them that we are conducting research in Australia on a new form of skin cream. Are we all on the same page?" He looked sternly around the room of high-level executives and eyeballed each and every one of them until he received a nod or a verbal agreement. "All right then, let's hear the preliminary results."

Everyone in the meeting room gazed at the big video screen. Beamed in directly from Australia, the live feed of Hu and Brudstein loomed bigger than life. Standing in their remote lab, Hu looked at Brudstein and encouraged him to go first. Brudstein stepped forward a bit, cleared his throat a few times and adjusted his thick black glasses. "I'd just like to mention," said Brudstein, "that I recently read an article stating that a female cow was successfully crossbred in France with a turkey!"

"A female cow?" asked Lionsgate.

"Yes."

"A female cow is called a cow," said Lionsgate. "A male is called a bull, you idiot!"

"Oh, yes! You're absolutely correct sir, my mistake. A male cow is a bull. A female cow is a cow. I knew that."

"Let's try to focus on this chicken and toad crossbreed," said Lionsgate irritably.

"Uh, okay, will do. Regarding the results, we are now on our second test subject. First off, I'd like to add that this is a daunting task. No one has ever successfully bred an amphibian with a bird. It just has never been successfully done before. However, we feel we now have the technology to achieve this lofty goal. And, might I add, the process is a journey, a journey of failure, learning, making changes, and eventually leading to success. Only through failure, do we learn and proceed in the right direction."

"On with it Brudstein," said Lionsgate impatiently.

"Yes, yes. Our first test subject was a complete failure. By failure, I mean we did not reach our desired result, but we took one of potentially many steps in the right direction." Brudstein said, eying Hu who quickly displayed an image on screen. "Here is a picture of version one." What resembled a large, feathered toad was displayed on the screen. "We were successful creating a cross, but the subject died shortly after reaching maturity. As you can see it is feathered, has webbed feet, a soft membranous beak, and unfortunately lays sterile, gooey eggs."

"What were you aiming for?" asked Tourterellie.

The image disappeared and the two scientists reappeared on screen.

"Ultimately," said Hu, "we'd like to come up with a docile creature that is as large as a chicken, featherless, lays a large number of frog-like eggs, matures very quickly, maintains the amphibian life cycle, and of course, is very tasty."

"Won't that be a bit costly and labor intensive?" asked Tourterellie. "I'm just thinking of the end product. The ranchers will have to provide a large pond for this crossbreed and then will have to catch them and put them in cages until they reach maturity. So why don't you breed in the chicken life cycle instead of the amphibian one?"

"That's an excellent point," said Hu. "We've put a lot of thought into this exact issue. The main point is that chickens cannot lay as many eggs as amphibians can. That's why we are favoring the amphibian life cycle. We feel we can boost this crossbreed to lay somewhere near one hundred thousand eggs. And they'll be laying them all year round. Thus, we could have a plethora of product ready for market quickly and cost effectively. Another factor is, adult Cane Toads burrow in the soil and do not live in ponds. So once our adults emerge from farming ponds, they would be easily caught and then put into cages before they take to the soil."

"Essentially," said Brudstein, "to answer your question, by maintaining the amphibian life cycle, we can produce a greater number of subjects in much less time."

"And people, that translates to more products in the hands of our suppliers and it gives us a leg up on the competition," said Lionsgate. "And it will surely fatten up our bottom line!"

"I'd like to add that we have hired on a number of new researchers to help us out here in the lab," said Hu. "We are planning on developing more variants to speed up the process."

"Good," said Lionsgate. "I want something ready for human consumption ASAP."

"I have a question," said Roberta Warren, Vice-President of Production. "What about the eggs?"

"Eggs?" said Lionsgate.

"You know, chicken eggs? Are we going to get rid of them or will the new, yet-to-be-named crossbreed species be bred to produce regular chicken eggs too?"

"Weren't you paying attention?" yelled Lionsgate. "The crossbreed will produce amphibian-like eggs only! However, we are simultaneously working on creating synthetic chicken eggs at another research site in California. In addition, our Europen team has developed a super-booster which can get real chickens to lay ten times the amount of eggs that a chicken usually lays, the only problem is the egg-layers die relatively quickly and taste like shit."

"The chickens or the eggs taste terrible?" asked Warren.

"The chickens," said Lionsgate agitatedly. "People! If you don't have the bandwidth to comprehend the earth-shattering results we are about to achieve, then leave now!"

A brief silence fell over the room.

"I have a quick question," asked Tourterellie trying to change the subject. "What are we calling the said unnamed-crossbreed species?"

"We're looking into that," said Hu. "So far we've come up with 'Teack,' 'Tweak' or 'Token?' But nothing's finalized."

"How about 'Freak'?" joked Brudstein. "Ha, ha, ha, uh, excuse me, it was just a joke, sir," he said, adjusting his glasses and attempting to look serious.

"Not funny Brudstein," said Lionsgate. "I want to remind you all that the Cane Toad is the heartiest of all toads, and it's a gutsy survivor. That's why we like it. And if you two can't see the amazing benefits to this thing, if you don't comprehend the sheer goodness of this project, then maybe I should get someone else onboard."

"No sir, we understand," said Hu.

"Absolutely," said Brudstein.

Turning to Tourterellie, Lionsgate said, "Where did you find these two?"

"They come highly recommended," said Tourterellie.

"Well, I want a close watch to be put on these two and a very close watch placed on the entire project. If any information is leaked out prematurely, it could ruin everything," he said, grinding his fist into the table.

"People," said Lionsgate to the entire room. "Again, this is a highly top-secret project." Directing his attention to Brudstein and Hu, "And you two, spare no expense protecting the secrecy of this project. You are on the forefront of this technology and it cannot get out to anyone what you are working on, is that understood?"

"Yes sir, we understand," said Hu.

"My lips are sealed," said Brudstein, as he mimed sealing his lips with a key.

"I expect another update meeting in three months," said Lionsgate, getting up to leave the room.

Three months later.

After the second week of January, the weather turned cold and rainy. Zabra, Decamate's Australian marketing assistant, arrived in Sacramento to visit Decamate's corporate headquarters for training. That evening Oliver took Zabra to dinner at a fancy Italian restaurant. Tony Bennett's music filled the air with romance.

"So, I forgot to ask you, do you have a boyfriend?" said Oliver, stabbing a meatball.

"I did. He was drop-dead gorgeous, kind, funny, and came from a good family," said Zabra, buttering a piece of bread.

"And, what happened?"

"He couldn't seem to keep his hands off my friends, or they couldn't keep their hands off him."

"Were you in the same bed at that time?" joked Oliver.

"What?" she said laughing.

"You know, were you having a three-some or something?"

"No! I'm not that type of girl."

"Too bad," he joked.

"Hey, that wasn't funny. So anyway, now, I'm looking for an ugly, unkind, unfunny guy from a bad family. Maybe I'll find true love there."

"Come on, that's a bit drastic," said Oliver. "That guy was a jerk; we're not all like that."

"I know. It's just hard when you think you've found the perfect guy; then he goes and cheats on you," she said, running her finger slowly around the rim of her wine glass. "What about you? Are you seeing anyone and more importantly have you ever cheated on your girlfriend?"

"No and no, but I've had a girlfriend cheat on me and a friend's girlfriend try to come on to me."

"Why don't you have a girlfriend?" asked Zabra. "You seem like a nice guy."

"I am! I really don't know. It's not from lack of trying. It's weird. In some cities, I'm a babe magnet; in others it's just the opposite. Like every time I go to San Francisco it seems like I meet someone cool, but I'm having the worst luck here in Sacramento. However, it was relatively easy for me to find a job here. I wonder if there's a connection. I mean in cities where I find work easily, I never seem to have much success finding a girlfriend and vice versa. Do you have that problem?"

"Nope. Maybe it's just you. Maybe you can only focus on finding a

Sheila when you're not working."

"A Sheila?"

"That's Aussie slang for 'a girl'," said Zabra.

"Oh, you've got your own slang down under, doncha?"

"Yep, I'll do my best to avoid using too much of it in the beginning so you can follow me."

"Thank you, much appreciated. By the way, what's the most common slang word in Australia?"

"Hmm, maybe 'dickhead'. We seem to use that one a lot for some reason."

"Maybe you just have a lot of dickheads."

"Naw, they're everywhere really. I've seen some here in the short time that I've been in Sacramento or 'Sac' as you call it. What a terrible nickname! We tend to add a 'y' or 'ie' to make cute nicknames like 'Bundy' for Bundaberg, 'Tassie' for Tasmania, and 'Sydney' for, well, Sydney."

Oliver laughed and suddenly realized how comfortable he felt with Zabra. He actually hadn't felt this relaxed on a date in years. After wiping his mouth with his napkin, he decided it was time to take the date to the next level. "Hey, do you know how to snowboard?" he blurted out.

"You betcha."

"If you're not doing anything this weekend, I just heard that Lake Tahoe has tons of snow. It's only two hours away. Would you like to go snowboarding this weekend?"

"Sure, that sounds great!"

Later that same night, Oliver jumped out of a taxi alone and entered his apartment.

Marco was wrapped up in a quilt, lying on the couch watching TV.

"How'd the date with Zipper go?" Marco asked, as Oliver put his coat in the closet.

"Zabra, her name is Zabra!" said Oliver, sinking down into an old imitation leather loveseat next to the couch. "It went okay, I guess. Actually, it probably could have gone better. I'm just taking things slow in the beginning because I just met her."

"Come on, you've been talking to her for months on the phone. You just met her, my ass! Is she as hot as her picture?"

"Let me clarify, I just met her in person. And yes, she's hot and I love her accent."

"When's she outta here?" asked Marco.

"Early next week."

"All right, you got some time. Play it cool for a few days and then introduce her to your little friend."

"To you?" he said jokingly.

"Shit, you know me; I'd be all over her by now. You and I wouldn't even be having this conversation; we'd be talking about the color of her nipples and what her pussy smelled like."

"Shut up!"

"I ain't playing! Sometimes you gotta be the man, Holmes!"

"I just met her; give me some time."

"Okay, here's an incentive for you. If you don't fuck her by this weekend, you owe me twenty bucks."

"What if I do fuck her?"

"Then you *da* man."

"What kind of fucked up bet is that?" asked Oliver.

"I'm just saying that you should be penalized if you don't fuck this chick. You're telling me she's hot and available and crazy as it sounds, she seems into you. Thus, if you don't bang her, then there's something wrong with you."

"Dude, have faith. I'm not going to maul her the first night I meet her."

"Did you kiss her? Did you even try?"

"I was going to, but...," said Oliver.

"But what? Look, if she's into you, then you gotta give her a sign that you're into her!"

"It will happen; I'm just patient."

"Patient my ass, you're scared, scared of the pussy!"

"Fuck you! What are you, the pussy expert?"

"Damn straight. Got a PhD in Pussyology," said Marco. Oliver immediately grabbed a cushion and threw it at Marco. "You know it's true," Marco said, throwing the cushion back at Oliver.

Oliver borrowed a car and drove Zabra up to South Lake Tahoe on a crisp, overcast Friday evening. The streets of Tahoe were lined with five feet of snow. They checked into a nice cabin overlooking the lake and then went out for dinner at one of the casinos in town. Afterwards, they watched a show, gambled a bit, and then went to a club and danced until the wee hours of the morning.

The next day they took a bus to Squaw Valley ski resort and

snowboarded the entire day. At sundown, they went to a nice quiet Italian restaurant. After piggy out, they headed back to the cabin and immediately jumped into a hot tub located on their big snow-covered balcony. Huge Ponderosa Pine trees draped in snow stretched out around their cabin as the picturesque lake quietly rippled below.

Oliver jumped out, opened a bottle of wine, and quickly eased back into the hot tub. They sipped the wine while listening to romantic music that Oliver had specifically programmed into his music player.

"It was a perfect day for snowboarding," said Zabra, as she splashed hot water on her exposed skin. "The sun was out and the snow was soft and powdery." Inhaling deeply, she continued, "And it smells incredible up here!"

"Yeah, Tahoe's awesome, but I would have been happier had I not fallen so much on the slopes!" said Oliver.

"You did fine, but I have to tell ya, I'm sore as hell."

"Me too," laughed Oliver. "I gotta get up here more often, it's fantastic. And I'm so glad you came with me, I really enjoy your company," he said, easing over to give her a massage.

"Oo, Oliver, I didn't know you were so talented," she said, as Oliver worked the kinks out of her neck. "This is so romantic," she said softly, as she eased herself in between his legs.

A slow gentle snow began to fall.

"It's snowing," said Zabra. "This is so perfect!" She turned around to look at Oliver. "Thank you so much," she said, looking directly into his eyes and then at his lips.

Oliver gingerly leaned his head in towards her lips and looked deep into her eyes. Zabra grabbed his head and planted a long smoldering kiss on his lips. As she guided her tongue into Oliver's mouth, she wrapped her legs around his waist. She pulled free of his lips and looked into his eyes and played with his short red hair.

"Oliver," she said, "I think I'm becoming attracted to you."

"And I to you," he said, kissing her again and removing her top.

They made love in the hot tub and then collapsed on the bed exhausted.

After the romantic Tahoe weekend was over, Oliver drove Zabra back to Sacramento. They spent their last evening together in Zabra's hotel bed.

The following evening, Oliver accompanied Zabra to the airport and watched her plane take off and fly away into the distance. Part of him wanted to be on that plane with her.

When Oliver arrived home, he found Marco firmly planted on the couch watching TV and eating a burrito.

"Hey, hey," said Marco. "How was the trip?"

"Good, real good," said Oliver. "And thanks for lending me your car."

"No problem. Did you get some?"

Oliver smiled brightly, grabbed his crotch and said, "Oh yeah."

"Score city! Talk to me," Marco said, wiping his mouth.

"After an amazingly great day snowboarding, we went back to the cabin and fucked like rabbits in a hot tub."

"That's what I'm talking about! Oliver getting some action in Tahoe! My man!"

"It felt good, real good. She's a very cool chick. Only problem is, she left today for Australia."

"That's okay, gives you an excuse to go visit her."

"Believe me, that's in the works."

"Sweet."

"There was only one thing I didn't like about her."

"What's that?" asked Marco.

"She wore green underwear, like, pea green. You know, that color rotten fruit gets. She wore them to bed one night, and I got grossed out immediately. I tried to hide them, so she wouldn't wear them again, but she's got like ten pairs, all varying shades of green and yellow, piss yellow."

"Damn dude, I didn't know you were so hung up on underwear. Shit man, just buy her a few pairs of sexy underwear the next time you meet her."

"Rule number one when it comes to women's underware, they should only come in four colors: red, black, pink, and white. Period."

"Did she complain about your crusty, holey, shit-stained underwear?"

"Dude, I think you have me confused with yourself."

"Hey, I wash my underwear; you wear yours until they stick to your ass."

"How would you know?"

"I've seen the tracks on your drawers before. I've pulled out your disgusting shit-stained drawers from the dryer countless times because you never remove them yourself. Even after washing them; they're still crusty!"

"You're so full of shit!" said Oliver. "Maybe once or twice after a diarrhea fest, have my drawers been stained, but I always toss those."

"All right, show me your drawers right now, and I'll give you twenty bucks if they aren't shit stained."

"Fuck off! I'm not going to show you my underwear."

"I rest my case."

"You don't have a case. At least my feet don't reek," said Oliver.

"Hey, my feet sweat, okay?"

"Yeah, they do! And they smell like shit and stink up the house for days!"

"You're one to talk, your shits stink up the house for days!" said Marco.

"So what, your shits don't stink?"

"It's a matter of degree. My shit reeks around the toilet bowl. I flush and the stench goes down the drain. Your stench sticks to the walls and grows fungi."

"You know what I say to that?" asked Oliver.

"What?"

Oliver let out a long, loud and pulsating fart just as Marco took a bite of his burrito.

"Fuck me," yelled Marco, as he instantly dropped his burrito onto his plate, covered his nose, and waved a cushion around hysterically. "You sick fuck," he screamed, and ran out of the living room.

"I rest your case," yelled Oliver, chuckling.

Six months later.

June's summer heat brutally arrived in Sacramento as Decamate's quarterly top-secret meeting rolled around. The research scientists, Brudstein and Hu, emerged on the videoconferencing screen in Decamate's boardroom beamed in from Australia. A picture of a large, toad-like being appeared as a small insert on the video screen. The two scientists nervously awaited as Decamate's top brass poured in.

"What the hell is that monstrosity?" barked CEO Lionsgate, as he barged into the room and glanced up at the video screen.

"That's our latest test subject," said Hu.

"We have been trying to combine different attributes of both the Cane Toad and the chicken in order to come up with the most optimum crossbreed," said Brudstein. "This is a picture of our thirteenth test subject. It has a beak, reaches maturity twice as fast as a chicken, has chicken-like claws, and at twenty-five pounds, is quite large. It also has retained the Cane Toad's poison sacks, amphibian life cycle and amphibian-like body. And boy can it jump! In the lab, it has actually jumped up to fifteen feet at a time."

"So what's the verdict, can we use it?" asked Lionsgate.

"Not exactly," said Hu. "It is very territorial, has more potent poison sacks than the Cane Toad and is not very tasty."

"We were trying to suppress the beak and poison gene, and express a chicken-esque flavor, but, well, I guess we pressed the wrong buttons," said Brudstein.

"The wrong buttons!" shouted Lionsgate. "You're not playing a video game, damn it! You're scientists, *be* scientific!"

"We are, believe me, we are," said Brudstein. "It's a long process. Picture a car. This is one of our first test models. It crashed, so now we have to go back to the drawing board."

"Well, you'd better come up with something usable soon, or we'll be crashing cars into your head, at high speed!"

COO Tourterellie chuckled under his breath, cleared his throat, and said, "Can you describe what you're working on now?"

"Can do," said Brudstein, as he fumbled to display a picture of their next test subject. "We're working on GoMo BoMo version fourteen."

"Gumbo what?" asked Lionsgate.

"GoMo BoMo," said Hu. "We are now calling the test subject GoMo BoMo. That's short for 'Genetically Modified Bufo Marinus'. Catchy, isn't it?"

"And?" said Lionsgate.

"And it's looking good," said Brudstein. "This version of GoMo BoMo is weighing in at a hearty fifteen pounds. We've suppressed the beak gene and the poison gene and were successful altering the taste of the subject. Additionally, we've managed to maintained its amphibian characteristics and life cycle: egg, tadpole, and toad. And it doesn't seem to display any of the territorial characteristics of a chicken. Although, its feet do have claw-like protrusions, and it displays some light feathering."

"How many more test subjects before we get a prototype?" asked Chief Marketing Officer, Barbara Beaver.

"You mean until we get something workable?" asked Hu. "It's hard to say. It could be as few as two or as many as two hundred."

"Two hundred!" yelled Lionsgate. "I'm not paying you morons to test every possible combination. We don't have forever. It's already been a year! I want a marketable product soon!"

"Well, two hundred is a very pessimistic projection," said Hu. "We do have a lot of fine-tuning to do, but we do expect positive results soon. Very soon."

"Something better come to fruition in a hurry!" said Lionsgate. "Remember, we're trying to change the world, change the entire chicken industry, flip it on its head, time's a-wasting!"

Three months later in the Australian outback.

Rafe McCory lay quietly in the brush overlooking a mob of kangaroos congregating at a remote watering hole as the sun slowly began to rise. Rafe carefully rose to his knees, pulled back his boomerang, and prepared to launch it at an unsuspecting roo. He took aim as a gentle breeze blew across the dry plain.

"Steady," he said to himself. "Steady." He calmed his breathing and cocked his arm back.

His mobile phone abruptly rang just as he launched his boomerang. The kangaroos immediately fled as his boomerang sailed past the watering hole and off into the distance.

"Buggar!" yelled Rafe, as he reached for his mobile phone. "Oi," he said, turning his back to the watering hole.

"Hi," said Oliver. "May I speak to Rafe McCory?"

"You got him," said Rafe in a gruff voice on the other end of the line.

"Hi, I'm Oliver Dendracopus with Decamate, one of the world's largest consumer goods conglomerates. I've viewed one of your documentaries."

"You have! Which one? Girls with Skirts? Ginny and the Shetland?" joked Rafe.

"What?"

"Oh, just having a go," said Rafe. Afterwards, his boomerang suddenly returned and hit him directly on the head. "Son-of-a..." he yelled to himself as he bent over and rubbed his head. He put his phone down and tried to regain his composure.

"A what? Hello? What did you say?"

"I'm just putting you on, mate," he said, pounding his head.

"Oh. Well, I saw a documentary you made about the Cane Toad," said Oliver.

"Right."

"Well, it's very interesting."

"Indeed it is," said Rafe, raising his eyebrows.

"Do you happen to have any more information on the Cane Toad?"

"Actually I do. I'm currently working on a second documentary that will blow the lid off of a lot of peoples' heads. It's state-of-the-art, cutting-edge stuff!"

"So it's not out yet?" asked Oliver.

"Not quite."

"Well, can I get an advance copy?"

"For what purposes?"

"I'm just doing some research here on the Cane Toad. I'm not going to go public with it or anything."

"How much money are you going to pay me?" asked Rafe.

"Whoa, I just want to view it and that's it."

"Listen mate, this new documentary is top-notch journalism," said Rafe. "Journalism at its finest. Once this docy goes public, believe me, the world will never be the same."

"Okay, having said that, how much do you want for a viewing?"

"Make me an offer I can't refuse."

"Hold on a second." Oliver put the phone down and looked over his budget. "Plenty of money left," he said to himself. "Do I pay for this thing or not? If I do and it sucks, maybe I can talk my way into hiring a crew to film something worthwhile. And maybe there's an outside chance that I'll get to go to Australia to see Zabra."

"Look, how about a hundred?" said Oliver.

"U.S.?"

"Yes."

"You're gonna have to do better than that."

"Two-fifty?"

"You're heading in the right direction. Listen, I'm only offering you advanced viewing rights. You cannot, under any circumstances show it to any members of the press or academia, or I'll sue your ass."

"As I said, we just want to see it, that's it."

"Okay, let me first have my lawyer send your lawyer some paperwork."

"Come on," complained Oliver. "Do we have to get that formal?"

"You're damn straight we do! Mate, this documentary will change the world! There are events happening out there at this very moment that will blow your mind! And if you just sit tight, in due time, I will bring it all into focus."

"We are talking about Cane Toads, right?"

"Bloody oath I am! Matey, the Cane Toad is just the tip of the iceberg. Something very diabolical is happening, I'm talking something down right evil is happening right here in Australia, and I'm on the verge of uncovering it."

"Well, that sounds fantastic," said Oliver, shaking his head in doubt.

After haggling over the details and the price, Rafe finally agreed to send out the video once he received the money.

Two weeks later after a long day of work, Oliver ventured up the walkway to his apartment with a bag of fast food in one hand and a video case under his other arm. He opened the door and noticed Marco on the couch with a brunette. Seeing Oliver walk in, Marco immediately removed his arm from around the woman's back as she sat up straight. Oliver thought about turning around and going somewhere else to eat his dinner, but then decided against it and walked over to his loveseat and sat down.

"What's up?" Oliver said, as he tossed the video case on the cluttered coffee table and began to take his food out of its bag without even looking at the couple on the sofa next to him.

"Not much," said Marco a bit miffed that Oliver was interrupting him. Marco stared at Oliver, trying to attract his attention and hopefully get him to leave. Oliver quickly glanced at the woman beside Marco and noticed that she was much older than Marco's typical girlfriends. She had to be in her forties. She seemed to look familiar as well. He did a doubletake and immediately knew who she was.

"Oliver, do you know Barbara Beaver? She works at Decamate. You're the head of what again?" Marco asked Barbara.

"Marketing," she said. "Hi Oliver."

"Hi Barb, how's it going?" Oliver said, suddenly embarrassed and at a loss for words. Barbara Beaver was Oliver's big boss at Decamate.

"Good," she said.

"I didn't know you and Marco knew each other," said Oliver

"Marco is my savior," said Barbara glowingly. "He comes over and fixes my computer once or twice a month. I have the worst luck with computers."

"You really do," said Marco. "I think your body produces some kind of weird magnetic current that magically locks up hard drives."

"I'm just hot blooded," said Barbara.

"That ain't no lie," said Marco, picking up the video case that Oliver had set on the table. "What do you have here Oliver, a porn video?"

"No, it's just something I need to watch for work," said Oliver.

"We're making you watch videos now for work?" Barbara said curiously.

"Yeah, well, you know my boss, Peter Gulovski, he's having me do research on some toad we're testing for some new skin cream and this video just came in."

"What kind of toad?" asked Marco.

"A big, ugly toad called Bufo Marinus or more commonly known as the Cane Toad," said Oliver.

Barbara reached for the video case, looked it over, and then said, "You've got a Cane Toad video?"

"Yes."

"Are there any more videos?" asked Barbara.

"Yes, this is the second of two. The first one was from an Australian documentarian named Rafe McCory and it just kind of gave some background information on the Cane Toad. I called him up the other day and asked him if he had any more data on the Cane Toad, and he just sent me this video today. I haven't even had time to view it yet."

"I see. Would you mind playing it for us? I'm sure I'll have to watch it eventually," said Barbara. "I mean, I am working with a team on developing a marketing plan for this toad project once it takes off," she added.

"Sure, sure," Oliver said, trying not to seem tentative. "But it may be very rough because it hasn't been broadcast yet," he said, walking over to the video player and popping in the disk.

A title screen appeared with the words: **The Ravenous Mutant Cane Toad or Cane Mutated!**

"Cool title," said Marco.

McCory: "We all know what a royal pain in the arse the Cane Toad has become for Australians," said Rafe McCory. "Ever since being introduced in the early 1900s, their numbers have grown exponentially and there seems to be no end in sight to their ever-increasing numbers.

"In Australia, the Cane Toad has no predators. In Central and South America, its native homeland, they are kept in check by certain snakes and other creatures, ones which we lack in Australia. Very few Australian animals have a stomach for Mr. Cane. Hence, its numbers have skyrocketed out of control. The government has spent loads of money trying to stop this pest, but to date, nothing has worked. And now we have become infested with the bloody things.

"But the story doesn't end there. This reporter has recently uncovered something so utterly weird, so mind boggling that I don't know how to quite describe what has happened. Mutants come to mind. Yes, mutants. The Cane Toad has mutated!

"I currently have no proof, no physical evidence of these mutant Cane Toads, just a bunch of hunches and an intriguing trail of developing evidence and that's what I'm following now. But I will not stop until I have uncovered physical proof of the mutant Cane Toads in Australia. All I have now is this one testimonial.

"We're about a thousand kilometers outside of Townsville with famed crocodile trapper, fingerless Jackie Rattel. Now, tell us Jackie about your recent sighting of these mutants.

"Yes," said Rattel, "I've seen them sons of bitches. They ate up Missy, my oldest and sweetest croc. She was minding her own business in my crocodile pool," said a teary-eyed Rattel, overlooking an enclosed croc infested swamp. "At any one time I'd have up to fifty crocs in there," he said, pointing to the swamp. "One day I was down to twenty or so, so I knew something was up. I thought the kids down the road were catching 'em, and making boots and ladies handbags out of 'em so I kept a close watch on the pond. One night I was awoken by some loud chirping. It was like a chorus. Like a group of something was singing. I ran down here and couldn't believe my eyes. There was about one hundred of these weird looking creatures standing on two legs like mini-T-Rex's. They circled the lake looking, hopping, and chirping in some eerie harmony, just hungry for a victim. The crocs were noticeably frightened. The creatures closed in on Missy. One of them things is jumping in and out of me swamp trying to get Missy to munch on him, the cocky bastard. Missy ran out of the swamp after him. The next thing I know, old Missy's down, swarmed by those critters and being consumed by those things." Rattel cried uncontrollably. "They just massacred her. Poor old girl. I couldn't believe what I was seeing. I thought I was dreaming. But let me be the first to tell you, those damn creatures are fierce. They took down a full-grown croc and ate her to the bone!"

"Blimey! It's bloody frightening," said Rafe, leaning against Rattel's fenced swamp. "These new toads are a lethal bunch! They're crafty! They attacked and ate a full-grown crocodile!

"So what in bloody blazes is going on here? Where did these mutants come from? Did they mutate here on Aussie shores? Is it some sort of government plot? Ozone hole induced? Pesticide pumped? Alien introduced? Things don't just mutate, or do they?

"Any of these options are plausible. The only way to know for certain and make the world really believe me is to get a sample and that's where I'm headed next. I need proof; I need a smoking gun! So I'm off to find these Ravenous Mutant Cane Toads, and I'm focusing my attention on North Central Queensland where the majority of mutant rumors are occurring! And please let me remind you all, these things are real, very real!"

The video ended abruptly.

"That's it?" said Marco. "Pretty freaky."

"It smells distinctly like BS to me," said Oliver.

"What's not to believe," asked Marco.

"Come on, don't tell me you buy this? Mutant toads?" said Oliver.

"Why not? Every animal mutates! Hell, they've got frogs with three and four hind legs right here in America, and they can't explain it."

"Yes they can, they say a virus causes that."

"Whatever. If a virus can cause a frog to have four hind legs, what can pesticides and increased solar radiation do?"

"Come on, it's gotta be bullshit," said Oliver. "Things just don't mutate to that degree. I mean a normal Cane Toad doesn't run around on two feet and attack crocodiles."

"What if it isn't bullshit?" said Marco seriously.

"Whatever the case, Oliver," Barbara interrupted, "I'd like a copy of that video on my desk first thing tomorrow morning. And please, don't show anyone else that video."

"Sure," said Oliver. "Do you believe it?"

"I don't know what to believe right now, but just get that video to me tomorrow." She grabbed her purse and stood up. "Gentlemen," she said, "I have to be going. Toodles."

Marco stood up and walked her out. He came back to the couch a few minutes later. Oliver leaned back, crossed his arms and stared directly at Marco shaking his head.

"What?" asked Marco.

"What the hell are you doing with my big boss?"

"She's a cool lady."

"She's almost twice your age!" shrieked Oliver.

"She is not, but what if she were? Hey, let me tell you something, I may never go back to younger chicks. She gave me the ride of my life the other night."

"Stop! You're grossing me out."

"Don't knock it till you've tried it," said Marco. "Have you ever played basketball with a beginner? They barely know how to dribble, how to shoot, how to do anything. You just spend your time clowning around, and you don't really get a thrill out of the game. But when you play with someone your equal or better than you, you learn, you get challenged, you have a good workout. That's what older women are like."

"Man, I am so totally grossed out!"

"How old was the oldest woman you ever had sex with?"

"I don't know," said Oliver. "Twenty-five?"

"And wasn't she better than any nineteen-year-old?"

"I don't know, it depends on the person."

"The older you are, the better you get at sex," said Marco. "How can you not get better, the more you do it?"

"I'll stick to people my own age, thank you."

"You just don't know what you're missing. You need to start spreading your wings, sow your seed and not weed out older women."

"I'm happy where I'm at," said Oliver.

"You're happy whacking in the bathroom?"

"I'd rather whack it than sleep with an octogenarian."

"She's in her early forties! Why whack? Why not have sex? Why not explore your sexual horizons?"

"Why not hit on hot, nubile young chicks?" asked Oliver.

"Why not hit on hot, knowledgeable older chicks?"

"Let's agree to disagree. You hit on whomever you want to, and I'll hit on whomever I want to."

"All I'm saying is, don't knock it," said Marco.

The next day at work, Oliver dropped off a copy of Rafe's latest Cane Toad video to Barbara Beaver's secretary. He journeyed back to his desk and called Rafe.

"Rafe, this is Oliver from Decamate. I saw your documentary."

"How'd you find it?" said Rafe, quickly standing up and walking out of an old outback bar.

"Come on, mutant toads?"

"Mate, I'm not making this up. They're real, very real. Very frightening. I'm on to something huge here!"

"Please tell me you're making it up," said Oliver.

"Come on, matey. This is real. I stake my name on it."

"Look. The only thing I want to know right now is: Where's the rest of it? I paid you a lot of money and all you gave me was ten minutes of video. You ripped me off!"

"That was just a teaser, there is plenty more video to come. Look, I'm using your funds to upgrade my equipment before I go out and catch me some mutant toads! We're going to go out, my cameraman and me, shortly, and get a live specimen. We'll blow this thing wide open! Now, we're going to need some more funds to do this right. We'll need to buy surveillance cameras and the like."

"Hold the phone! I'm not paying you another dime."

"Look," said Rafe. "This could be the find of the century. Don't you want to be part of it? Ask your company, I know they must have deep pockets."

"We are not paying you any more money. But, I do want to look at all the video you get on this project, and I mean everything."

"Sure."

"For free!" demanded Oliver.

"Come on."

"For free!"

"I'll see what I can do, but believe me, once I find one of these things and once the media gets hold of this, you won't need a copy of the video. It's going to be spread across the globe like wild fire."

"I'll believe that when I see it, but at least send me every bit of research video you shoot, you owe me," said Oliver, as his boss Peter arrived at his desk.

"I'll see what I can do," said Rafe.

"You owe me! Goodbye!" said Oliver. As he hung up the phone, he turned to Peter and said, "What's up?"

"I want to see you in my office, now," said Peter.

Oliver got up and followed Peter down a long corridor to his office. Peter sat down behind his big, paper-laden desk. Oliver hovered over Peter's desk anticipating an argument.

"Oliver, why was I not informed of this new toad video?"

"I just got it!"

"Oliver, as your boss, I need to know what you're working on at all times."

"I've been sending you a weekly progress report."

"Do you have a copy of the latest version of that report?" asked Peter.

"I emailed it to you Friday! Is the 'Print' button broken on your computer?"

"Oliver, why must you always be so difficult?"

"I am not being difficult! Just open the email I sent to you," said Oliver. Peter rolled his eyes and retreated to his computer. He took a few minutes to search for the document. "Oliver, just give me a verbal progress report," he said, frustrated.

Trying to hold back his anger, Oliver said, "I received two videos so far both concerning Cane Toads in Australia from a documentary guy in Australia. I just got off the phone with him, and he's going out to do some more research on what he describes as a 'mutant' Cane Toad disturbance or something like that. He said he'd try to send me the footage once he shoots it."

"Now, that wasn't so difficult was it? By the way, Barbara wants us to refer to this mutant thing as a 'variant'."

"So is it true? Are there mutant toads or variants of mutant toads ravaging Australia?"

"I don't know, but I need two things from you. First, I need a copy of both of those videos. Secondly, you are now to find a local documentary crew to go to Australia and try to film this mutant; I mean this new variant of the toad." Oliver's eyes lit up. "And, you are to report to Barbara Beaver directly on this. She wants to see you this afternoon."

"Is it true? Are there mutant toads roaming free in Australia? And if so, why haven't we heard anything about them?"

"I don't know," said Peter. "All I know is that you are supposed to report directly to Barbara on this. Is that clear?"

"As clear as mud."

"Oliver, don't be difficult."

"Peter," he said, staring down at his boss. "This whole thing sounds way too far-fetched and way too out of the scope of my job description!"

"Oliver, you are to do what your bosses say, do a good job, cash your paycheck and do whatever it is in your free time that you want to do. However, while at work, try, and I mean this seriously, try to get along and not give people this negative Oliver attitude all the time."

"I'm not negative. I would simply like a little respect once in a while. I get paid to do my job and not to do everybody else's job, which I inevitably have to do every five seconds."

"Oliver, every job takes on new challenges now and again. We are an evolving organization and jobs in this company are organic. They sometimes change. You should be excited. This is an opportunity to show people what you can do."

"No, it's an opportunity for you to make me do more work. My desk is piled high with projects that I haven't even had time to get to!"

"I know, I'm in the same boat. Look at my desk. But Barbara specifically requested that you work on this."

"Will there be a raise involved?"

"I don't know. I tell you what, if you do an outstanding job, I will discuss it with Barb and see what she says. How does that sound?"

"It sounds good, if she says yes."

"Okay, in the meantime, I think you should prepare a project update for your meeting with Barb."

"All right, is that it?"

"Yes, thank you for your time Oliver," Peter said, clenching his teeth.

"You're welcome," Oliver said, as he spun around and marched out of Peter's office like a dutiful soldier.

Later that day in Decamate's boardroom, Brudstein and Hu appeared on the video conferencing screen looking tired and disheveled. Lionsgate stared at the two researchers in disbelief as his executive team sat quietly around the boardroom.

"The reason we called this impromptu meeting today is to have a quick update on your progress," said Lionsgate, trying to be patient.

"Yes, we were not fully prepared to discuss the project as we just found out about this meeting an hour ago," said Hu.

"We realize that. Just give us what you have to date," said Lionsgate.

"I'd like to add that it's quite early in the morning here," complained Brudstein.

"I don't care what goddamn time it is," howled Lionsgate. "Now give us an update!"

"Yes, of course," said Hu. "Our team here in Australia is still conducting research and developing new prototypes. A full battery of tests is to be conducted soon on our latest subject, GoMo BoMo version twenty-two, I believe, and then we will be able to update you further."

"We will issue a full report the minute we obtain the data," said Brudstein.

"Have you heard anything about a breach of security," asked

Barbara.

"Security breach? No ma'am. Nothing at all," said Hu, looking quizzically at Brudstein.

"Neither have I. What kind of security breach?" asked Brudstein.

"We have received information that a mutant version of the Cane Toad is running amok in Australia. One that sounds curiously like an earlier version of one of those Gumbos that you showed us during a previous meeting," said Lionsgate, breathing heavily.

"I, I haven't heard a thing about this," said Hu.

"Me neither," said Brudstein.

"You two wouldn't know your own names if you didn't wear an I.D. badge," barked Lionsgate. "I want you to head a thorough investigation. Comb the area outside of the lab for any sign of these mutants out in the wild. I want every inch of soil checked!"

"Yes sir," said Hu.

"Perhaps it's all a hoax, but if it isn't, believe me, some heads are going to roll!" yelled Lionsgate. "In the meantime, I want additional security added to our research site in Australia. Nothing, and I mean nothing, gets in or out of that lab without a certified company ID! Do you hear me?"

"Yes, sir, we'll get right on that!" said Hu.

Later that afternoon, Oliver sat in the waiting room outside of Barbara Beaver's office strategizing about how he could talk Barbara into letting him go to Australia.

"Barbara's ready for you now," said Barbara's secretary.

Oliver nervously entered a large executive office on the top floor of Decamate's corporate HQ overlooking downtown Sacramento. He saw Barbara in a different light after she was on his couch the previous evening arm-and-arm with Marco.

"Oliver," she said with a nice smile, as she looked up from her computer. "Thanks for showing up, have a seat, I'll be right with you."

Oliver sat down on one of her plush leather seats and eyeballed her desk while she typed away on the computer. He looked around the large room wondering to himself whether she and Marco had had sex in her office before.

Her desk was neat and orderly. On one of her walls was a sign that read: We all gotta duck, when the shit hits the fan.

"That ought to be Decamate's company motto," Oliver thought to himself. "All I do, day in and day out, is try to avoid one shit storm after another."

"Yes, Oliver," Barbara said moving her chair from her computer to face him, "I'm ready for you now. Sorry for the delay, I just had to put a few finishing touches on an email. So, how's work going?"

"Okay, I guess," said Oliver cautiously. "I'm so busy I barely have time to think."

"Sounds familiar."

Oliver was going to complain about the special projects that kept coming across his desk, the ones he didn't think he should be doing. But he decided to keep his mouth shut and see what this meeting was all about first.

"Peter said you do good work," said Barbara.

"Thank you," he said, not really sure how to respond.

"Well, the reason I called you into my office today was because of that video you showed me last night."

"I figured as much. Do you think it's real?"

"I really don't know," said Barbara. "I'm sure you are aware that we are currently conducting research in Australia and using Cane Toads to test a new skin cream."

"Yes, Peter told me about it and that's why I was in contact with the researcher who made that video," said Oliver.

"Peter updated me on your little video project this morning. Although it's highly unlikely that the variants mentioned on the video are real and if they are real, had anything to do with our testing. Perhaps our competitors are on to us and are trying to sabotage our project. Whatever the result, we can't afford to take any chances. Any bad publicity at this early stage in product development could destroy our plans to introduce our new product. Thus, I would like you to find an independent camera crew to go to Australia and try to verify the information that was revealed on the video."

"You mean like a biological research crew?"

"Oh no, nothing that elaborate. We believe this video is a hoax, but just in case, we don't need a crew connected to the scientific community or media to potentially damage our reputation or potentially produce the video in some negative way. We just need a normal camera crew from some other industry, perhaps a crew that films sporting events or documents concerts or the like. The main point is we'd like to have a crew that will find just the facts, give us the video and not make any waves. That way we can evaluate the footage and then be prepared for the aftermath, if any."

Oliver pondered this briefly and then said, "So, you'd like to see if it's true and if so, cover it up before anyone gets wind of it?"

"Oliver, we're getting ahead of ourselves. Nobody's covering anything up. We simply want to verify the truth of the video from Mr. McCory, and if it is true, then we'll try to determine the cause of it. Chances are we aren't involved in any way. I think you're smart enough to realize that if a new variant of the Cane Toad is inhabiting Australia then people are going to point their fingers at us because we are currently testing Cane Toads in Australia. In that case, we have to be prepared. Better safe than sorry. Once that video goes out, the press will have a field day, and we will more than likely be accused of causing the problem, even if we aren't. Are you with me?"

Oliver looked off into space wondering when he was going to get off his ass and find another job. He wanted to ask her for a raise, but instead said, "Yes, I follow, but I need more details. Like when do you need the video by? What's the budget?"

"Of course we need this done ASAP. And the budget is wide open. Your first step is to interview some camera crews, tell them what we want, get a proposal, narrow down the list and submit your top three choices to me. Is that do-able?"

"Yes, but I'll have to drop everything else I'm doing."

"I would expect nothing less," said Barbara with a smile. "I need you to report directly to me on this project. No one else is to know that you are working on it, not even your roommate. Okay?"

"Okay," said Oliver sheepishly.

"I hate to put you under a deadline, but I think you can sense the urgency of the situation. I need you to narrow down your top three choices within the next few days, and I hope to have someone in Australia as early as next week."

"Next week!" Oliver said surprised. His initial instinct was to complain, but then he thought that maybe he could finagle a trip to see Zabra. "That's fast. Well, I can fly to Australia tomorrow and start looking for a crew," he said with fingers crossed.

Barbara let out a big laugh and then said, "Well, I appreciate the enthusiasm, but at this juncture, we should stick to finding a U.S. crew and send them over.

"Would you need me to accompany the crew to Australia?"

Barbara laughed again. "No, Oliver, I do not see any reason to send you. However, if you do a good job, I don't see any reason why we couldn't suggest that you visit our Australian branch in the near future."

"Really," Oliver said smiling from ear to ear.

"Why not?"

"Okay. All right, I'll get right on this and try my best to get you a list of potential candidates within the next few days."

"Thank you, Oliver. I can't tell you how much I appreciate this!"

Oliver walked out of her office and down to the elevators with a new bounce in his step. "I might be going to Australia," he said to himself, as he entered a waiting elevator.

Brudstein and Hu waited impatiently for their team of researchers to assemble in the main research room at Decamate's remote Australian research lab. All six scientists eventually filed in.

"Thanks for showing up on such short notice," said Brudstein.

"Look, we know it's early, but we've recently been in contact with HQ," said Hu. "They have come across a vague report of mutant Cane Toads wandering around Australia. However unlikely it is that one of our test subjects has escaped, we have decided to implement tighter security measures, just in case. And HQ has asked that we go out in the surrounding area to look and see if we can find any test subjects in the wild. If GoMo BoMo is out there, it will more than likely only come out at night. So we will go out every night in teams and cover a fifty-mile radius around the lab."

Brudstein put up a detailed map of the area with a red circle marking a fifty-mile radius.

"Wallace," said Hu, "you and Mitesh will have first watch. I want you to cover a ten square mile area here," he said, marking an area on the map.

"What happens if we find something?" asked Mitesh.

"Hopefully, it won't come to that," said Hu. "But if it does, I want you to report back to the lab immediately, and we will devise a plan. Under no circumstances are you to arouse suspicion with the locals. And do NOT, discuss this matter with anyone outside of this room. I'm sure you can all understand how delicate this situation is."

Didier LaFoie, video director and owner of *Out of Mind Video Productions*, walked into his small, downtown San Francisco studio where his cameraman, Fred Mandrake, sat behind his desk cleaning a camera lens while soundman, Patrick Rudis, quietly strummed his guitar behind his desk.

"Okay guys, great news," said Didier. "Are you ready for this?"

"Ready," said Fred, as Patrick made a drum roll on his guitar.

"I just got back from Sac and got us a smokin' deal."

"All right!" said Fred.

"Sweet baby Jesus," said Patrick, as he stood up to high five Fred.

"Can you say two months in Australia?" said Didier.

"Yes, we can!" Patrick and Fred said in unison.

"Can you say outback?"

"Yes, we can," they said, as Patrick beat louder on his guitar.

"Can you say toads?" said Didier.

"What!" said Fred, as Patrick stopped his drum roll and screwed up his face.

"You heard me, toads."

"Dude," said Fred, "we're music video makers. And let me emphasize: MUSIC VIDEO. How do toads fit into the BIG picture?"

"We're a starving camera crew looking for work, and I found work documenting some sort of toad in Australia," said Didier. "They want us to film these toads down under and put a piece together. They're offering us big bucks and a free trip to Australia. As I see it, since we don't have any gigs lined up, this could be a two-month adventure in Australia. And it will surely line our pockets nicely. I say we reinvent ourselves as toad documentarians! Are you with me?"

"Big bucks?" asked Patrick.

"Big Bucks!" said Didier.

"Free trip to Australia," asked Fred.

"Oh yeah," said Didier.

"I'm in," said Fred.

"So am I," said Patrick excitedly.

"Awesome," said Didier, pumping his fist in the air.

"Well all right!" said Patrick.

"When can we start?" asked Fred.

"Get your passports and visas ready, we'll need to be going soon, very soon," said Didier. "As early as next week."

"Sweet," said Patrick.

"Wait, if we're all gone, who's going to take care of my dog and my plants?" asked Fred.

"Worry about that later, get your passports and visas sorted out first," said Didier.

The following week, Fred, Patrick and Didier waited in a San Francisco airport bar for their flight to Australia. Didier munched on a sandwich and read the newspaper; Patrick drank a beer and watched TV while Fred researched the Cane Toad on his laptop.

"Dudes," said Fred, "check this shit out. The Australian government brought in Cane Toads into Australia in the 1930s to control some Cane Beetles that were munching up their sugar cane. It turns out the Cane Toad couldn't climb up the sugarcane to reach the Cane Beetles, which were hanging out on top of the sugar cane plants. Thus, the Cane Toads couldn't eat the Cane Beetles. And then, the imported toads bred like crazy and now Australia can't get rid of the toads. Isn't that fucked up?"

"Shit like that happens all the time," said Patrick, sipping his beer.

"Let me get this straight," said Didier, looking up from his paper. "Cane Toads can eat Cane Beetles, but couldn't get to them. Cane Beetles eat sugarcane. So what eats Cane Beetles then?"

"I don't know. All I know is they screwed up. You can't import another creature to handle an insect problem without really knowing if it would work," said Fred. "I mean, you'd think they'd run a few tests or something."

"Their methods were bad, but their hearts were in the right place, bugs were eating their crops, they had to do something," said Patrick. "You'd think that they would have brought in a few beetle chewing birds or something first though."

"Do you know that when the first settlers came to the great plains of America," said Fred, "they plowed up the soil and immediately birds came out of nowhere to feast on the grubs that were unearthed. The farmers freaked out and began shooting up all the birds. Why the hell didn't they just plant trees around their fields and let the birds eat the insects? Why don't farmers do that now? Why do they have to poison us with all the chemicals that they keep pouring on our food? Why not just let the birds eat up the insects?"

"What if the birds eat up all the seed so nothing grows?" asked Didier. "Or they keep everyone awake with all their squawking?"

"Set up a pen and train the birds to stay in the pen when you sow the seeds or harvest," said Fred. "In between, let them eat all the insects. As for the noise, don't live so close to your fields. How easy is that?"

"Or wear ear plugs," said Patrick.

"Exactly, but don't fucking poison us!" said Fred.

"I trust science," said Didier. "I believe we'll come up with a cure for everything. Take nuclear waste, I believe we'll come up with some bug that will eat that shit and boom, no problem."

"Yeah right," said Fred sarcastically. "What if those bugs fart and their gas destroys the ozone layer, or destroys the creatures that feed on them, then what?"

"You only see the dark side of science," said Didier. "I don't believe Mother Nature is that fragile."

"Come on, we can already blow up the planet many times over," said Fred. "Mother Nature isn't the problem, man is. We're actively destroying a planet that took billions of years to create. Now your precious scientists are unleashing Pandora's box onto the unsuspecting planet. Nuclear Energy's a good example. It's still not safe and may never be and that shit takes eons till it's rendered safe. Why not exhaust all other viable, clean possibilities to create energy first; we have the technology, why not make it happen?"

"Here, here," said Patrick

"All I'm saying is we can now create stuff to help us live better," said Didier. "If we create a better, cheaper grapefruit, why not? If we create a drug to kill cancer, why not? If we create a bug to eat nuclear waste, why not?"

"So what if a nuclear reactor blows up Belarus accidentally, can we handle that mistake?" asked Fred. "What if your cancer cure eats the cancer and years later eats the patient's entire brain, can we cure that? What if your grapefruit causes a mad-cow like disease in humans? Can you cure that?"

"Man, Fred, you only see the dark side, does he not?" Didier said, turning to Patrick for support.

"We just don't know what some of these new cures will do," said Fred. "I'm not saying to stop creating cures and stop creating better products, I'm just saying to test the fuck out of them until you're 150% sure that they're safe."

"Yeah, exhaust all possibilities first before you mess with Mother Nature, before you mess with Mom," said Patrick.

"Okay, just don't stop testing because you're afraid some huge disaster's going to happen," said Didier. "Can we agree on that?"

"I'm just saying control it!" said Fred.

"Amen," said Patrick.

"Hey, I think we should head over to our gate, our plane should be boarding soon," said Didier.

Marco took an elevator to the top floor of Decamate's global HQ and walked down a long, brightly lit corridor to Lionsgate's office. The afternoon sun shone through the clear glass windows. He stopped at the desk of Lionsgate's secretary and announced his presence. The secretary called the CEO while Marco flipped through some golfing magazines.

"He's ready to see you now," said the secretary.

Marco straightened up and then entered an elaborately furnished office approximately the size of his apartment. The walls were littered with pictures, honorary degrees and animal trophies. Lionsgate was hunched over a golf club chipping golf balls into a large net at one corner of the office.

Marco cleared his throat as Lionsgate's very next ball ricocheted off the wall and almost hit Marco in the head.

"Keep your head down, sir," Marco joked after effectively dodging the incoming projectile.

"Been playing this game all my life and still can't seem to find the hole," said Lionsgate. "The story of my life." He walked over to Marco and shook his hand. "I hear you're a computer expert."

"I fix my fair share, and if I can't fix them, then I take a blunt object to them."

"Ha, finally someone with some real skills. All right, here's the situation. We've got a lab in Australia, I'm not sure if you're familiar with it. They've got a full series of surveillance cameras monitoring the place twenty-four hours a day. I'd like to have access to those cameras and to all the devices backing up and storing that video."

"That shouldn't be a problem," said Marco.

"Great. Now, I'm not a computer guy, so I need you to put some easy to use software on my desktop, so I can look in on these lab guys anytime I feel like it, morning, noon or night. And I may need to go back in time to see who's been entering the office and exactly when they entered the office."

"No problem."

"I want to check in on these clowns occasionally just to see what they're up to," said Lionsgate. "Don't want them pulling the wool over my eyes."

"I understand. You just want to make sure they're not having a party way out there in Australia and if they are, you'll want to know why the hell you weren't invited."

"Damn straight. By God, you read my mind. How long have you been working here?"

"Two years since February," said Marco.

"Well, we need more people like you. I like your attitude. Oh, I almost forgot to tell you. This is all on the hush-hush. You are not to tell anyone, not even your boss. If word gets out that I'm spying on people, then everybody'll probably be on alert."

"I understand completely. I won't tell anyone, not even my mother," he said with a smile.

"Good," said Lionsgate. "Now I've got a meeting to run to. You have full access to my office, and if you need anything, just ask my secretary."

"Will do, I should have this up and running in no time."

"Fantastic. Make yourself at home. There's soda and refreshments in the fridge," he said, pointing to a large liquor cabinet. Lionsgate handed Marco his chipping wedge, grabbed his briefcase and then left the office.

"Help yourself to refreshments," Marco said, imitating Lionsgate. "Well, thank you, I don't mind if I do." He shuffled over to the refrigerator and pulled out a soda. He took a few gulps, grabbed a bottle of Rum from the liquor cabinet and then poured in a few splashes of Rum into the soda can.

He walked around the spacious office sipping his soda and imagining the office was his. He set up a golf ball and swung with one hand and netted the ball. "I still got it," he said, slashing the air with his chipping wedge. He stepped back ten feet, set up another ball and took another swing. He swung a bit too hard and the ball ricocheted off two walls and into a trophy cabinet making a loud noise. Lionsgate's secretary barged in and gave him a stern glare.

"Ooops," Marco said, red as a lobster, "that one got away from me!"

"Don't you have work to be doing?" she asked.

"Yes, I do. Sorry about that," he said, as the secretary closed the door never breaking eye contact with him.

Oliver sat at his desk talking animatedly to a coworker about being cut off by a taxi while he drove his scooter to work earlier that morning. The phone rang.

"Oliver?"

"Yes."

"This is Didier, just wanted to let you know that we've made it to Australia. We're in Townsville at the moment and will gather information here, rent a vehicle and then drive around the area looking for this mutant toad."

"Great," said Oliver. "How long do you think it will take?"

"A couple months, maximum."

"What! Look, I specifically expressed to you the urgency of this project! I need something as quickly as possible!"

"Sure, sure, but editing, mixing, etc., all take time," said Didier.

"We don't have time! I want you to send something to me the minute you shoot it. Is that clear? Don't worry about mixing, editing, just send me the raw footage!"

"Okay, okay, keep your shirt on. We will send you the raw stuff the second we shoot anything."

"Okay, and I expect you to send me daily updates via email, so I can track your progress," said Oliver.

"Yes, sir."

"All right, sorry for freaking out on you, it's just that we need footage ASAP. I'll be looking for your email tomorrow. Bye," said Oliver. He leaned back in his chair and grabbed his head. "Man, they'd better not fuck this up," he thought to himself.

Oliver exited a light-rail train and walked into a trendy downtown sports bar after work and located Marco, who had a half-full pitcher of beer in front of him.

"Dude, what's up? Why the urgency?" Oliver said, as he eased into his seat.

"Here, drink up, you're way behind," Marco said pushing a beer in front of his friend. "You are not going to believe this! Drink up first. Believe me, you'll need it!"

"Barbara's pregnant?" Oliver said.

"NO! Worse! Much worse!"

"You're pregnant?"

"NO! Dude, shut the fuck up and drink, bitch!"

Oliver quickly downed the first beer. Pouring Oliver another beer, Marco flagged down a waitress wearing a tight referee's shirt and a short-ruffled skirt. When she made eye contact, Marco pointed to his empty pitcher.

"Pretty cute," said Marco, referring to the waitress.

"What's up, talk to me," Oliver said after checking out the waitress.

"Okay," Marco said, taking a deep breath. "Lionsgate called me into his office yesterday."

"Whoa!"

"Yeah, so I walked in, and he wanted me to add some surveillance features to his computer, so he can keep track of a remote research lab in Australia."

"The one testing those toads," asked Oliver.

"Exactly. So I set up his computer and accessed the remote site's video server. I started checking some recorded data just to make sure everything worked because I didn't want to set up the CEO with some bogus software. I'm flipping through the lab's surveillance cameras, and I came across a room full of cages. I zoomed in and you'll never guess what I saw."

"Toads. Cane Toads."

The waitress came over and set their new pitcher on the table. Marco leaned back in his seat and waited for her to leave. He looked her right in the eye and smiled. She smiled back and walked away, her skirt bouncing back and forth as she left. Marco leaned in again and continued. "Bingo!" he whispered. "But not just any Cane Toads. I'm talking about freaky-looking Cane Toads! Toads the size of a Christmas ham, man, with fucked up heads and all kinds of funky mutated looking things growing all over them."

"Holy shit steak! How many toads do you think there were?"

"A ginormity of toads, man. I mean they had tons of massively mutated toads in cages! Tons! Well, maybe not tons, but a lot."

"Oh my God! Do you know what this means? Did you keep any video?" asked Oliver. "Tell me you kept some video!"

"You know it! I spent the entire night purging Lionsgate's data and saving it along with any incriminating evidence that I could find on the Australian surveillance cameras' servers. I saved all the data onto a remote, secure server. I was so tired at work today that I fell asleep at my desk."

"You fucking stallion!"

"So, what are we going to do now?" asked Marco.

"What do you mean, we?"

"What! You saw that video. Those things are lethal! They brought down a fucking crocodile! Our company is directly responsible for unleashing possibly slews of mutated toads onto the unknowing Australian populous!"

"I'm not supposed to tell anyone this, but Barbara called me into her office last week and wanted me to hire a camera crew to go to Australia to investigate the video that we saw. She said it was "highly unlikely that the video was true," but she wanted me to sign up a camera crew anyway to investigate it. And she specifically wanted me to find a group that had no connection to the science community or to the media. She doesn't want this to get out, just in case it's true. I found three guys in San Francisco that said they'd do it for cheap. I already hired them and they're in Australia right this second."

"Fuck," said Marco. "Barbara must know about these mutants. What should we do?"

"Sell our company stock immediately."

"Then what?"

"I don't know! Should we go to the media and blow this thing wide open?" said Oliver.

"We'd be out of a job the second we did that."

"Do you want to continue working for this company?"

"Hell no, but what if it's a mistake, we'll look like laughing stocks," said Marco.

"How about this?" said Oliver. "We wait for the camera crew that I just hired to get some proof. Then we send everything we have to that Rafe guy, the guy who shot that mutant Cane Toad video that I showed you, and have him take it to the press."

"I like it! That way no one will know it was us."

"Exactly, then we wait for the smoke to clear, and once it does, quit this fucked up company as fast as we can," said Oliver. "In the meantime, get as much proof as you can and hide it on that remote server."

"Sounds like a plan," Marco said, clinking Oliver's beer glass with his own.

"Hey, do you have any idea where Decamate's Australian research lab is? I bet the infestation began somewhere near the lab. If we can find out where that lab is and get the camera crew over there, I bet they'll find this mutant."

Marco whipped out his laptop computer from his backpack and began searching the data he stored on the remote site.

After a few beers Marco turned to Oliver and shouted, "Winton, it's near Winton, Australia!" He suddenly turned to the waitress and yelled, "Two shots of tequila!"

That night Oliver and Marco returned to their apartment drunk. Oliver emailed Didier and told him and the camera crew to immediately go to Winton to look for mutant toads. Afterwards, he phoned Rafe.

"Dude, this is Oliver from Decamate, the world's foremost mutant toad company."

"Hi, are you drunk?" asked Rafe, stuffing clothes into a backpack.

"Shitfaced man, hammered, stick a fork in me, I'm fucked up."

"What gives?"

"What gives? What the fuck gives! I'll tell you what gives! You know those fucking toads? Those fucking Cane Toads, those mutant ones?"

"Listen mate, I'm really busy, if you've got something to say, say it!"

"Okay, okay, look, those mutants are real! Fucking real!" said Oliver, as Marco sat on the couch listening excitedly.

"I know, me and me camera man, Nozzy, are getting our gear together, and we're going to head out and track those buggers down."

"Well all right! It's about time. Look, look, is this line bugged?"

"What? No!"

"Okay then, listen, my roommate found some really important information, and we want to give it to you, but you can't tell anyone that we gave it to you, promise? Swear on a stack of bibles?"

"Sure," said Rafe, "I'll do you one better, Mate, I'll swear on a stack of pancakes and then eat 'em."

"Okay, you're officially weird. All right, now listen, Decamate has a lab outside Winton, Australia, and that's where they created those mutant toads. The evil fucks! Go to Winton and you should find them, but be very, very, very careful! Those things will fuck you up. Those toads are mutants!"

"Right, look mate, I'm glad you called, your secret's safe with me. Nozzy and me'll drive out to Winton as soon as we can."

"Yeah, yeah, but listen, don't tell anyone we told you. Okay? We'll send you more info once we find it. We want you to bring down Decamate. Take 'em down. Knock 'em out!"

"Right, I appreciate the help mate, but I got to be going," said Rafe.

"Okay, but remember, not a word about us."

"Not a word."

"Catch those fucking mutants!" Oliver said and hung up. Marco immediately tackled Oliver onto the couch, shook him playfully and asked him what Rafe had said.

"Dude, he's on his way to find those mutant toads," Oliver said to Marco, suddenly jumping on top of him.

"Outstanding, now get the fuck off me and let's play some video games," said Marco, as he pushed Oliver to the ground and staggered over to his wide collection of video games nicely stacked in a display. He reached for a game and fell right into the entire display, instantly knocking it over. "Whoaaaaa," cried Marco.

"Watch that first doozy, it's a step," said Oliver, as he playfully jumped on the couch.

Marco dug through the pile of video games on the ground, selected one and slapped it into the game player.

"Shit," said Oliver. "I forgot to tell Rafe about the U.S. documentary team."

"If you told him he'd probably get pissed at you," said Marco.

"Maybe. It probably doesn't matter either way," Oliver said, as Marco loaded the game.

"Tell him next time," said Marco. He turned from the game player and launched his body at Oliver's and tackled him on the couch. Marco tried to wrestle Oliver to submission while Oliver squirmed to get the upper hand.

"Get off me, you fuck," cried Oliver, as he punched Marco in the gut and shoved him off.

"Okay, just for that, you're going down! Start the game!"

Rafe and Nozzy pulled into Winton, Australia with Black Sabbath's *"War Pigs"* blaring on their jeep's stereo. Nozzy's dog, Meninga—a black Labrador Retriever and Rottweiler mix—wagged its tail in the back seat as the jeep pulled up to a hotel in the center of the small dusty town.

They checked into their hotel room, unpacked and immediately discussed their plan of action. "I say we conduct a little preliminary research tonight," said Rafe as Nozzy set up his computer. "Oliver said the company's lab is somewhere around here. Chances are somebody knows where it is. You can't keep something like that secret for long."

"Why don't we try to film some locals that have maybe seen this mutant toad?" said Nozzy. "Once we film them, we ask them about the research lab, where they sighted the mutants and then try to pinpoint exactly where these toads are."

"Good idea. Once we establish a perimeter, we'll then need to set up some of those solar powered, cellular surveillance cameras you got from your cousin. Are you sure you know how to work those things?"

"No, but it will be fun trying to find out. I should be able to link the feed to this server and then be able to watch all the cameras simultaneously on my computer. The cameras have motion sensors that will start recording the second anything passes by."

"Will they be able to detect mutant toads at night?" asked Rafe.

"I don't know; I hope so. The cameras have night vision. The quality of the feed might be sketchy, but we can zoom in and zoom out remotely."

"Great! Nozzy, we're going to find those bastards, I can feel it, and then we're going to be more famous than you can imagine!"

"I'm not too keen on being famous, you know that. I prefer to stay behind the camera."

"Either in front of the camera or behind it, you're going to be famous. We're a team! And we're going to find these bleeding monsters! Now, let's see if this one-joey town has a watering hole."

"Now you're talking," said Nozzy.

Thirty miles Northeast of Winton, the American documentary crew camped out in the outback as the sun slowly fell below the horizon. Patrick quietly strummed his guitar while Fred and Didier prepared dinner. The sky was painted in translucent shades of pink, yellow and orange.

"Check out that sunset dude!" said Patrick. "It's so peaceful out here."

"No lie, Australian spring is beautiful in the outback," said Fred.

"It would be great if there weren't so many mosquitoes," Didier said, slapping his neck. "It would be almost perfect."

"What would make this evening most perfect is some tasty weed," said Patrick reaching into his pocket. "And guess who scored some in Townsville?"

"Patrick, your resourcefulness never ceases to amaze me," said Didier smiling.

As Patrick prepared the weed, Fred said, "Did you know that 'Waltzing Matilda' was written about something that happened in Winton?"

"No," said Didier. "What happened?"

"Some guy, a jolly swagman called Banjo, died."

"Patrick, can you play it on your guitar?" asked Didier.

Patrick began trying to hum the few bars that he knew. "Hey, what's a billabong," he asked.

"I think it's a bong for a guy named Billy," said Fred inspecting Patrick's bag of weed.

After dinner, they passed around a makeshift pipe made out of a used beer can and took in the outback scenery. A sparse desert stretched for endless miles. An occasional breeze whipped up some dust and then disappeared. Patrick strummed his guitar while Didier looked off into the horizon. Fred opened a file about toads and began to read next to a glowing fire.

"These fucking frogs and toads are totally cool. Have you read this?" said Fred motioning to his computer.

"Nope," said Patrick.

"Did you know that frogs were around before the dinosaurs ruled the world, and survived the asteroid that killed the dinosaurs?" said Fred.

"Obviously," said Didier.

"I'm just saying they're survivors. And check this out; some scientists believe frogs developed croaking to be heard over the loud thunder of the dinosaurs."

"Cool," said Patrick. "Like it was too loud to be heard so one day one crazy frog starts belching? Pretty nutty."

"Exactly! They're some of the most adaptable creatures on the planet? There's even a variety of frog that lives by a waterfall. Instead of croaking, they use sign language to communicate with other frogs."

"Check out this picture," Fred said, showing Patrick a picture of a frog sticking out one of its arms near a thundering waterfall.

"Wow, I wonder what that frog in the picture is trying to say?" asked Patrick, "Hey babe, I've got a six pack. Let's party!"

"And check this out," said Fred, "one species can be frozen rock solid; so solid that you can actually use it to hammer a nail through a wooden board. Then you can thaw the frog out, and it's fine."

"Crazy," said Patrick. "So like, if you're stuck in the wild, and you lose your hammer, you can use the frozen frog to build you a house and then thaw it out and eat it!"

"Some fish are like that," added Didier. "In the winter when rivers freeze, sometimes you can see fish frozen solid inside the ice. When spring comes, they just swim away. Talk about cryogenics!"

"Wicked cool," said Patrick.

"And check this out," said Fred. "Did you know that the Cane Toad's poison is classified as a Class One narcotic like heroin and dope?"

"What the fuck," said Patrick. "So if we catch one, can we smoke it?"

"No, it says if you lick a Cane Toad, you could die, they are *that* potent."

"Death by Cane Toad," said Didier. "Not a very pleasant way to go, I imagine."

"Wait a minute," said Patrick. "If Cane Toads can kill you with their poison, what can this here mutant do?"

"I don't know, but we'd better be very careful, if and when we run into them," said Fred.

"Hey, what's the difference between a frog and a toad," asked Didier trying to change the subject.

"Yeah, I wondered that myself," said Patrick.

"Me too," said Fred. "According to my research, there is no difference other than slight physical characteristics."

"That doesn't make a lot of sense, they look very different to me," said Patrick.

"Well, I think the easiest way to differentiate them is the ugly factor."

"What's that?" said Patrick.

"If it's ugly, it's a toad," said Fred.

"Nice, now that's easy," said Didier.

"Dudes, these things are badass," said Fred. "All of them. They're really amazingly adaptable!"

"If they're so damn adaptable, why are they disappearing?" asked Patrick.

"Don't know. But good old Bufo Marinus is thriving," added Fred.

"Who?" asked Didier.

"The Cane Toad, Bufo Marinus is its Latin Lover name," said Fred.

"I thought they were imported from the Americas?" said Patrick.

"They were," said Fred.

"So why does it have a Latin name?" said Patrick seriously.

"Because all species are given Latin names when they're discovered, dildo," said Fred.

"Right, right, I knew that," said Patrick. "Now what's its name, Bufo? That's a fucked-up name. Let's call it Bob Martin or something more American. Where is Latin anyway, it's not even a country, man! This thing is American and deserves an American name."

"Its formal name is Bufo Marinus," said Fred. "To be polite, you should refer to it by its formal name until you are properly introduced."

"I don't want to be introduced to it," said Patrick, as he took a pamphlet out of his pocket. "Hey, did you know that there's a park near Winton that has the only evidence in the world of dinosaurs stampeding ninety-three million years ago?"

"Yeah, I saw a poster about that in town," said Didier. "Maybe we could make a day of it tomorrow and check it out."

"I'm totally up for that," said Fred. "I wonder what would cause a bunch of Dinosaurs to stampede?"

"It was probably toads," said Patrick. "I bet the Dinosaurs were afraid of them."

"Doubtful," said Didier. "I bet it was an earthquake or that asteroid that wiped them out. Killer asteroid incoming, quick stampede!"

"Ha! Maybe it was a bunch of mutant Bob Martins," joked Patrick.

"Whatever it was, it must have been wicked badass to make dinosaurs stampede," said Didier.

"We'll probably never know," said Patrick.

"Hey, do you know why they call a group of toads 'a knot' and a group of frogs 'an army'," asked Fred.

"I give up," said Didier.

"I don't know, that's why I'm asking," said Fred. "You've got a gaggle of geese. Now that kind of makes sense."

"A swarm of bees," said Patrick. "A crowd of people."

"A murder of crows," said Didier. "A plague of rats."

"Really?" said Fred. "Now that really makes sense. But why 'a knot' of toads?"

"Maybe because when toads are mating, they're all knotted up," said Patrick.

"Hmmm, that kind of makes sense," said Fred. "But why would they come up with 'army' to describe a group of frogs? Strange. What are they militaristic or something? Maybe they attack in groups. Well anyway, I think a group of mutant Bufos has to be more intimidating than a group of frogs, so I say we come up with a new collective term just for these new Bufos."

"So you just want to change the language to suit yourself?" said

Didier.

"Improve it," said Fred.

"How 'bout a snot of toads?" said Patrick, "or a wart of toads?"

Fred chuckled then asked, "What's more powerful than an army?"

"A platoon," said Didier.

"A battalion," said Patrick.

"A platoon of Cane toads," said Fred. "Now that's nice. A battalion of Bufos. That's good too. Which is bigger?"

"Got me," said Didier.

"A battalion of Cane toads," said Fred. "A battalion of Mutant Bufos. I like that."

"How about a Battalion of Bob Martins?" said Patrick.

"Dude man, get over the Bob thing and call him by his rightful name," said Fred.

"If this is a new creature, it doesn't have a rightful name, so I can call it anything I like," said Patrick.

"Whatever," said Fred.

"Hey, what if these mutants are dangerous?" said Patrick.

"According to Oliver, they are," said Didier. "He keeps emailing me, telling us to be careful."

"Then why are we camping outside?" said Patrick.

"We've got a tent and a raging fire going," said Didier. "I seriously doubt that anything will bother us."

"I hope you're right," said Patrick. "But I'd feel more comfortable if I had my shotgun with me."

"Don't start wimping out on me," said Didier. "We've got to go out tonight and try to find these things again. Oliver's going to blow a gasket if we don't send him some mutant toad video soon."

The following day in the heat of the afternoon sun, Nozzy and Rafe drove around the outback near Winton in their jeep. Meninga sat in back with his head over the side of the vehicle, tongue wagging in the wind. They drove northwesterly to a remote area near Dicks Creek and looked for telltale signs that the mutant toads have been in the area. Nozzy netted a few beak-laden tadpoles that were abnormally shaped.

"Rafe, look here, this might be them," said Nozzy, showing Rafe his net.

"Noz, let's put up a few of those night-vision surveillance cameras on the trees around here."

"Right, we've only got two more cameras left," said Nozzy.

"So let's put them up and then head back to Winton and see if we can determine which location is ripe with a mutant toad infestation."

"I wonder where the adult toads are?" said Nozzy.

"They're nocturnal and burrow in the ground during the day. I bet they'll come out around here to feed at night. Don't worry Nozzy, we'll find 'em."

Later that day, Nozzy and Rafe were sitting on the porch of Teresa Stagpoole's ranch on the outskirts of Winton sipping iced tea.

"Okay love," said Rafe to Teresa. "We're going to film you out in front of the house, and I just want you to tell the camera what you just told us. Act natural."

Teresa wiped her weathered brow as her long skirt blew in the breeze. "I'm a bit nervous," she said. "I've never been filmed before."

"It'll be okay, you'll do great," said Nozzy.

They walked out in front of Teresa's house. Rafe and Teresa stood together while Nozzy adjusted the camera on his shoulder and pointed it right at them.

"Okay love, here we go," said Rafe. "I'm here near Winton, Australia with Teresa Stagpoole, who's about to share with us some incredible news. Teresa, tell us now what happened to your sheep dog, Caesar."

"Last week I was about to go to bed, I think it was a Wednesday, or a Thursday," said Teresa skittishly. "I looked around for Caesar and didn't see him, so I whistled for him. He didn't come to me, so I went to bed figuring he was out finding himself a Sheila or something. The next day, one of our ranch hands, Lyle Foxx, pulled up in his truck shouting for me. I ran out to see what all the commotion was. In his truck bed lay what looked like Caesar, 'cept he was mangled, almost unrecognizable. He was chewed up to the bone and dead as a door nail," she said, wiping away a tear.

"Lyle said," she continued, "that he saw a bunch of strange tracks all around Caesar's dead body. He also mentioned that the night before he'd caught sight of a strange animal he ain't never seen before. He reckoned it was the size of a baby roo 'cept it was hairless and had a deformed, ugly face. He thought it got hit by a truck or something."

"What about the sheep, love?" said Rafe.

"Oh yes, a few days later a couple of sheep were found all chewed up to the bone with the same strange tracks all around the carcasses."

"What do you reckon it was that did them in?"

"Don't rightfully know, could be some new sort of critter running crazy out there. Whatever it is, we're not taking any chances. Nobody's going out alone at night any more. The whole town's in an uproar over it."

The following evening, after visiting Winton's famed Lark Quarry, which boasts that is the only place on earth where tourists can see real Dinosaur tracks, the American documentary crew camped out southeast of Winton. There wasn't a cloud in the sky and the stars glittered brightly as a cool breeze sang across the outback.

"Check out those stars," said Patrick. "I never knew there were so many!"

"The lights and clouds in Frisco block most of them from coming through," said Fred. "Out here, nothing's stopping them."

Patrick passed around a makeshift dope pipe he'd carved out of wood and looked off into the darkness.

Fred took a hit from the pipe and then asked, "What do you guys think about this whole mutant toad thing that Oliver's been feeding us?"

"I think we're just wasting our time," said Didier. "It's got to be a hoax. The townspeople are probably just making it up for tourism or something."

"You think?" said Fred.

"Yes," said Didier. "If it's true, how come no one has captured one yet? It's like the Loch Ness Monster: All BS and no proof."

"It could be like a relic from the dinosaur era," said Patrick. "Maybe it survived the mass distinction."

"Extinction," corrected Didier. "The dinosaurs and most everything from that era are gone-gone. Never to return, unless; we genetically manufacture them."

"Or aliens bring them in," said Patrick.

"Nevertheless, it's gotta be a hoax," said Didier.

"We're still evolving, why can't other species evolve?" said Patrick. "Maybe that's what we have here. This toad just evolved to be better than the rest. It just woke up one day and said, 'Dude, let's rock!' Why not?"

"Maybe," said Didier, "but no toad or frog will ever dominate like we have, unless they fucking evolve to use a computer."

"Or a machine gun," said Fred.

"You know, if there is a mutant toad, I don't know what the fuss is all about," said Didier. "New species have been coming and going for ages."

"Yes, but a new species could totally wipe out local frogs and animals," said Fred.

"So what," said Didier. "That's what's been happening for millions of years. Welcome to survival of the fittest. The vast majority of creatures that roamed the earth are now extinct."

"Yeah, but we can save the ones we have now and learn from them," said Fred.

"Sure, but we can learn from new species as well," said Didier. "I just don't see how one new species is going to ruin the local animal population."

"Look around, Australia's living proof," said Fred. "Rabbits, toads and the white man have ruined this place. They have destroyed the local habitat and in a split second irreversibly damaged most of the native animal life. Haven't you learned anything from our research? Each animal's specific genetic code is valuable. You wipe that out and you destroy variety. If we have a world with only twenty mammalian species, one disease could mutate and wipe us all out. Biodiversity is the key to our survival as a species."

"All I'm saying is creatures have been coming and going for millions of years," said Didier.

"Yes, but they're dying off at a faster rate than ever before, and now we can save them from dying off," said Fred.

"Not all of them," said Didier. "And you can't stop the natural process of extinction. It's just natural."

"Yes, but now we can try," said Fred. "We can try to keep what we have and learn from them."

"We can now replicate anything we have in the wild in the lab," said Didier. "Science will save us."

"Ye have too much faith in science," said Fred.

"You gotta believe in something and perhaps science is the only solution to this problem," said Didier, looking at his watch. "Okay boys, it's about that time to start looking again."

"It's like trying to find a needle in a haystack," complained Patrick, as they all got up and grabbed their gear.

Rafe and Nozzy set up their equipment in their Winton hotel room. Nozzy monitored an array of cameras on his laptop computer while Rafe gazed in wonderment at a large fish tank he'd bought in town, stuffed full of a wide variety of fish as well as the potentially mutated tadpoles that they had extracted from the creek.

"These tadpoles are so aggressive!" said Rafe. "They swim together in packs and use their razor-sharp beaks to tear at the skin of the other fish and use their powerful hind legs to bump other fish out of their territory. At an early age, they are highly aggressive, highly territorial. They're eating up all the fish in the tank like savages. They could wipe out entire fish populations with this kind of aggressive, voracious behavior."

"Oi, I think I've got something," said Nozzy, eying his computer screen.

Rafe ran over to the computer and peered over Nozzy's shoulder.

"Naw, it's nothing, just a couple of people walking around," said Nozzy.

Rafe watched two members of the American documentary crew search around with flashlights. "What are they doing?" asked Rafe.

"Oi, that one's got a camera!" Nozzy said, as Fred clearly came into view with a camera on his shoulder.

"Bloody hell, those fucking wankers better not be trying to film what we're filming!" said Rafe.

"What if they are?" said Nozzy. "Or, what if they aren't and they find the mutants before we do?"

"Right, they'll have to come into town at some point for a drink," said Rafe. "We get them drunk and then sabotage their equipment. We can't take any chances."

Lionsgate barged into Decamate's corporate boardroom filled with his executive team for an emergency meeting called by the Australian research team. Hu and Brudstein's images flickered on screen. Lionsgate addressed the two researchers by saying, "This had better be good news."

"Sir, we have a situation," exclaimed Hu. "We've been sending out teams to scour the area looking for the aforementioned escaped toads."

"And," shouted Lionsgate.

"And you're not going to like this," said Brudstein.

"Try me," said Lionsgate, standing up preparing to tear someone a new asshole.

"Apparently some of the test subjects HAVE escaped, have grown, have mated and are starting to wreak havoc," said Hu.

"You fucking idiots!" yelled Lionsgate. "What do you mean havoc?"

"I mean havoc with a capital H," said Hu. "The test subjects that have escaped are extremely dangerous. The escapees are an earlier test subject. A more aggressive variety, with beaks, extremely potent poison, exceptional jumping ability, and are very territorial. And they could possibly lay up to one hundred thousand eggs in a clutch. A group of our researchers patrolled the area and found kangaroo carcasses completely consumed and surrounding the carcasses were unmistakable GoMo BoMo tracks. The researchers actually drove right into a swarm of GoMo BoMos butchering a cow at night. The two researchers killed a few of the toads and have verified that the escapees are GoMo BoMo version thirteen. If you'll recall, that's an extremely aggressive variant weighing up to twenty-five pounds. The two researchers were actually attacked while trying to catch a few specimens and were sprayed with repetitive streams of highly toxic poison and repeatedly bitten all over their entire bodies. They're currently in the hospital recovering."

"Fan-fucking-tastic!" said Lionsgate. "How in God's name did this happen?"

"We have no idea," said Brudstein.

"You incompetent fucks!" screamed Lionsgate. "You've ruined the entire project! What do you have to say for yourselves?"

"Uh, sir, I don't know," said Brudstein, throwing up his hands.

"That's what I thought. You fucking imbeciles!" Lionsgate yelled at the top of his lungs and paced the room. "All right, we have to abort. I want you to destroy all evidence in the lab. And I mean everything! And kill every single escaped toad. Poison the rivers if you have to!"

"What if word gets out about these toads?" said Tourterellie. "It won't take long."

"What's the name of that town near the lab?" asked Lionsgate.

"Winton," said Brudstein.

"How big is it?" asked Lionsgate.

"It's a tiny, one-horse town," said Hu.

"Quarantine it," said Lionsgate. "Jam all communications and don't let anyone in or out until this entire mess is cleaned up."

"Sir, we're not a military outfit, how do you propose we lock down an entire town?" asked Hu.

"I don't care how you do it, but do it!" screamed Lionsgate. "Get everyone you can from our Brisbane office to head up there and lock it down if you have to. Hire the militia. Spare no expense and leave no stone unturned until you destroy every last one of those ridiculous toads!" Lionsgate turned to Tourterellie and fired off, "Alan, I need you to head the clean-up of this project and fly out to Brisbane as soon as you can. Hire a team of mercenaries if you must, but I do not want anyone to find out about this, no one!"

Later that same day in the early evening, Rafe and Nozzy strolled down the main street in Winton and noticed a rented blazer filled with camera equipment parked outside Banjo's Last Stop, a small bar in Winton. They walked in and immediately ordered two beers and scanned the place for likely suspects.

Rafe couldn't help noticing three men sitting at a table drinking beer and loudly talking in an American accent. Rafe walked over to the table while Nozzy perched himself at the bar.

"You blokes Yanks?" asked Rafe.

"Absolutely," said Patrick.

"What're you doin' all the way out here?" asked Rafe congenially.

"Shooting a documentary," said Fred.

"You don't say," said Rafe, pulling up a chair. "I'm kind of a documentary buff myself. What's your topic: Outback, roos, koalas?"

The Americans looked at each other and smiled. "We probably shouldn't be telling you this," said Didier smiling proudly, "but we're documenting a toad."

"The Cane Toad?" asked Rafe.

"Yes," said Didier. "Do you know anything about it?"

"Ha! I've got tons of video myself, I'm a local expert," said Rafe.

"No way!" said Fred.

"Abso-bloody-lutely."

"Well, maybe you can help us," said Didier.

"You wanna see my footage?"

"Maybe later," said Didier. "But we've been hearing strange reports about the Cane Toad up here. We've heard that it's," he said, looking around and then lowering his voice, "mutated."

Rafe signaled to Nozzy who immediately began chugging his beer.

Rafe then turned to the Americans and said very quietly, "Who are you working for?"

"A U.S. company called Decamate, have you heard of them?" asked Patrick.

An older man wearing an old leather hat abruptly barged into the bar hooting and hollering.

"Check out that old-timer," said Fred.

"Shhh, what's he saying?" asked Didier, as they all listened in.

"Calm down ya crazy digger," said the bartender. "What's all the commotion about?"

"There's a band of people in spacesuits on the outskirts of town blocking the road," said the old-timer. "They tell me I can't go home. They say the town's been quarantined!"

"How much have you had to drink, Ral?" said the cocktail waitress.

"Nothing, I'm as dry as the desert! I'm telling you the truth, I was just out there," he yelled.

Rafe looked at Nozzy and then at the Americans. The bar's TV set suddenly turned to static.

Rafe, Nozzy and the Americans frantically ran out of the bar in unison and into their vehicles.

That evening in the outback, the American documentary crew drove their blazer west of Winton along the Diamantina River in search of GoMo BoMo.

"This is too weird," said Didier, trying to get a signal on his cell phone.

"What's with the reception, out here?" said Fred. "I'm getting nothing on my phone."

"If they locked down the town, they probably knocked out communications and that can only mean one thing: we're not getting out of here," said Fred.

"Why did they lock down the town, man?" said Patrick. "Do you think it's because of those toads?"

"Maybe it's some sort of funky virus," said Fred.

"Whatever it is, let's get the fuck out of here," said Patrick.

"Let's not lose our heads," said Didier. "We don't know what it is, but I'm sure we'll find out in due time. Let's look for those toads and try to stay clear of the town. When the coast is clear, and after we have our footage, we bolt out of here."

"Why take chances?" said Patrick.

"We don't know why they're quarantining the town, so let's just act like we don't know," said Didier.

"But we do know that something big is happening," said Patrick.

"Right, and maybe it is all because of those mutant toads," said Didier. "If we are the first to capture them on video, we could make some serious money out of it," he said, as he parked their blazer by the river. "Let's camp out here and see what we can find."

"I'm telling you, something is fucked up," said Patrick.

"Keep your shirt on, we'll be all right," said Didier. "Let's put the campsite together and then go out there and find us some money-making mutant toads!"

They grabbed their gear out of the back of the blazer and began making a campsite near the Diamantina River. Once they finished putting up their tents Patrick said, "I don't think we should start a fire, it could attract unwanted attention."

"Yeah, but it could protect us against any unwanted pests, like the mutants," said Fred.

"No fire, we'll have to chance it," said Didier. "Now let's get out there, time's a-wasting."

They put their gear on and ventured out into the outback in search of GoMo BoMo as the wind began to howl and the dust began to rise.

"I have a good feeling about this river," said Didier, shining his flashlight around the edge of the river. "They probably mated around here, dropped their eggs in the river and then didn't venture very far."

Carrying his camera on his shoulder and filming as he walked, Fred kicked over a rock and shined the camera's light on a small frog that jumped out from underneath. "Here's a small frog," yelled Fred. "Maybe it's a mini mutant."

Looking over and shining his flashlight on the creature Didier said, "No, it looks like a normal frog. We're looking for something much bigger."

"How big," yelled Patrick, walking towards a bush away from the river carrying a big microphone, a flashlight and wearing headphones.

"I don't know," said Didier, "but think big toad."

"Big toad," Patrick repeated. He shined his flashlight underneath a bush and saw a pair of shining eyes. "Hey," whispered Patrick loudly. "Check this out."

"Whaddaya got?" asked Didier, running over.

"Don't know," said Patrick, easing towards the pair of eyes and shining his flashlight. "It's funky looking and bigger than a toad."

"Turn on the camera," demanded Didier.

Fred carefully walked up, aimed the camera light at the bush near Patrick and started filming. A strange creature stood on its back legs and seemed frozen in the light.

"What is it?" said Patrick crouching close to it.

"I don't know," said Didier getting closer.

"Is it Cane-cer?" asked Patrick.

"It doesn't look like a toad, but whatever it is, it's huge!" said Didier.

"Maybe it's a kookaburra," said Patrick.

"Naw, a kookaburra is a bird, I think," said Fred, still filming.

"Maybe it's a wallaby, or a wombat," said Patrick.

"No, it looks kind of, sort of like a big featherless chicken with a super large head," said Didier.

"The biggest toad is the Goliath Toad which is about seven pounds and about twenty-five inches long," said Fred. "It's way bigger than that!"

"Whatever it is, it's a biggin'," said Patrick, still looking at the creature and inching his head closer to it. "Sure is a big, fat fuck."

"Watch your language, we're recording this," said Didier.

"You sure are a big chubby fella, aren't you?" said Patrick inching closer.

"Look, there are more of them," said Fred, pointing the camera around the bush. "The camera light must be attracting them."

Patrick picked up a twig and rubbed the creature's belly. "That's a good boy," he said. "Are you Bobby Martin? Do you know where he is, because we've been searching all over for..."

A long stream of white liquid squirted out of the back of the creature's big head and hit Patrick squarely in the eyes. Patrick quickly stood up and began clenching his eyes in pain.

"Aggggh! I've been maced," yelled Patrick.

Didier and Fred couldn't help but laugh.

"Dude," yelled Fred, "he pissed on you!"

"I think not," said Patrick, "it burns like hell!" Another creature leapt up and latched on to Patrick's nose. "Aggggggghhhhh!!!! Motherfucker," Patrick screamed, as he flailed around psychotically. "GET HIM OFF! GET HIM OFF!"

"Keep filming," demanded Didier, as he hurried over to help Patrick.

Patrick fell to the ground and quickly tried to unwedge the creature from his nose. The creature secreted more and more poison, while more and more of the creatures joined in on the attack.

Quickly reaching Patrick, Didier immediately fell to the ground, grabbed the creature attached to Patrick's nose carefully and tried to shoo away the rapidly advancing horde.

The creatures sprayed Didier repeatedly with poison while they jumped onto his upper body and began taking huge chunks out of his neck and face. "Arrrgh," yelled Didier. "Fred, where are you, I can't see.

THEY'RE ATTACKING ME! DO SOMETHING!!!" Didier ripped one of the creatures off of his neck and a huge stream of blood began gushing out. "FUCK!" Didier screamed in extreme agony.

The toad attached to Patrick's nose jumped to Patrick's right eye and took a big bite. "FUCKING BASTARD," screeched Patrick, as he began to puke. "HELP!!!"

"HOLY SHIT, HOLY SHIT," yelled Fred, as he started jumping up and down with the camera on his shoulder. Fred finally ran over, tossed the camera on the ground and dove down to help his two friends who were wailing in pain and slapping wildly at the creatures attacking them. Fred desperately worked to pull the creatures off his friends as more and more of the mutants came out of the woodwork clucking wildly like a band of crazed chickens. Fred was sprayed repeatedly with poison and temporarily blinded.

Fred managed to drag his two friends close to the river, planning to splash water on the creatures and distract them long enough so he could run and light a fire. As he approached the river, the poison overcame him and he bent over and started vomiting uncontrollably. The creatures quickly swarmed onto Fred's back and worked their way up to his neck where they bit ferociously. He swatted at the creatures blindly as they bit off chunks of his skin.

The mutant toads methodically closed in and savagely consumed the American documentary crew.

Later that evening in Sacramento, Oliver met Marco at a small Thai restaurant for dinner. It was early October and still hot in the daytime, but the evenings were cooling off nicely. They sat in a quiet booth towards the back of the restaurant.

"Dude, check this out," said Marco. "I was like repairing a few surveillance cameras in the system near Lionsgate's office today. Out of the blue, a bunch of execs tore into the main conference room. I was right near one of the doors, so I stuck my ear to the crack."

"And?" said Oliver.

"They were talking about toads running amuck near our lab in Australia. And not just any toads! I swear to God someone called it 'GoMo BoMo'! Then I heard the word 'quarantine' as clear as day. I have total access to Lionsgate's computer; it's nice being an administrator. So I spent the entire afternoon rifling through Lionsgate's emails, and you won't believe it!"

"What?"

"Lionsgate gave the orders to close the Australian lab and destroy all the evidence. And he wants to close down that little town near the lab called Winton as well as poison all contaminated rivers!"

"Dude, it's happening! They're going to try to cover it all up! We have to do something!"

"Like what," asked Marco.

"Stop it!"

"How?"

"Can you say road trip to Australia," said Oliver.

"Now you're talking!"

"Have you sold your company stock?"

"Yes, have you?" said Marco.

"Yes."

"Sweet!" said Marco. "That stock's going to take a serious nosedive once word gets out about these mutants. Lionsgate's emails alone should implicate the company."

"Dude, this is so huge. However, nobody will believe our story, unless we have a real live sample and actual footage of the town being quarantined, but if we go to Australia, they'll know it was us who let the cat out of the bag."

"Can't we just wait for the sample and the footage from Rafe and the American documentary crew?"

"Maybe," said Oliver. "But if we take off, we can help."

"On the other hand, if we stay here when the shit hits the fan, and Decamate finds out what we've been up to, we could be marked men."

"No doubt about that! We gotta make sure they don't find out. However this pans out, I say we go. I feel useless waiting around!"

"In any event, you gotta call that Rafe guy and tell him what's up and call the American documentary crew as well."

"Rafe and the American crew are in Winton," said Oliver.

"I know! If Decamate closed down the town, then they might be shut down as well. People walking around trying to film toads or film anything are going to be the first people targeted!"

"We don't know what Lionsgate is capable of. He could have the whole town silenced, or destroyed as well as any and all evidence destroyed, and we can't let that happen. We must go to Australia to make sure this thing goes public, before everything gets shut down and all evidence vanishes!"

"Hey, what about that Aussie babe you know? Call her up and tell her we're coming into town, and we need her to chauffeur us around. And make sure she brings a hot friend along. But first call Rafe and the American crew."

Oliver walked outside to call Rafe on his cell phone. He waited until a half-full tram whizzed by. He looked up into the evening sky and noticed the lights of an airplane. "That's going to be me baby, very soon," he said to himself giddily.

"Rafe! This is Oliver. Look, my friend just found out that Decamate is going to try to cover everything up. Going to try to poison rivers and close down the town of Winton!"

"Crikey!" said Rafe, shaking his dick after a long satisfying piss on a bush. "We found out about the quarantine last night. We're safe, for the moment. We're far out of town camping in the outback."

"Great," shouted Oliver. "Me and my roommate are flying in to help you out. This thing has got to go public!"

Rafe's phone suddenly went dead. "Bloody wankers," he shouted, "they somehow killed the phone transmissions. Nozzy, we could be in for a long fight."

"Wouldn't prefer it any other way matey," Nozzy said, while petting Meninga and shading his eyes from the bright morning sun.

"Right, let's get mobile!"

That afternoon in the outback, Rafe and Nozzy pulled up to the American documentary crew's campsite. They had trailed the Americans the previous evening and camped out a distance away. Seeing no signs of movement from their campsite, Rafe and Nozzy moved in to investigate.

"Oi, here's their camera," Nozzy said, as Meninga started to bark near the river.

They walked over to Meninga and noticed three entirely consumed carcasses.

"For fuck's sake!" said Rafe, as he looked away in horror.

Nozzy ran to the jeep to get his camera equipment. He returned and started filming.

Rafe tried to collect himself. He gathered his strength, picked up a microphone and motioned for Nozzy to point the camera on him. "We're here in the outback hunting for evidence of mutant Cane Toads and this is what we ran into," said Rafe trying to stop from choking up.

"We met these three Americans a few nights ago and shared a few beers and a few laughs. We noticed their campsite and pulled up to say hi and ran smack dab into this," he said pointing to the carnage. "It looks like we've uncovered the first physical evidence of this mutant varmint attacking and killing humans. These toads have chewed up the Americans right down to the bone. They're vicious! It's not safe, we're not safe! This is chilling, bloody chilling!"

Rafe lost his concentration for a second and then continued, "What makes it difficult to locate these mutants is the fact that they only come out at night. They must burrow deep into the soil, somewhere during the day. They're crafty. I haven't been able to find out where they're holing up. But now we have three very dead people, and still no specimen. But we are close!"

Nozzy slowly zoomed in on the dead bodies and then stopped filming. He shook his head in disbelief and suddenly remembered the American crew's camera. He quickly ran over to it and tried to view their footage, but the camera's battery was dead.

Rafe scanned the area with Meninga and then walked over to Nozzy who had managed to hook up the America crew's video to his own camera's monitor. They viewed the footage in stone cold silence.

Afterwards, Rafe stood up and told Nozzy to film him crouching next to the bodies. Nozzy readied his camera and then gave Rafe a nod. "I've just viewed a horrifying video that these brave Americans took before they were savagely attacked by these malicious mutants. I can now give you a more accurate description of these abominable creatures. They're big, brown and ugly, very ugly. They're about forty centimeters high and stand on their powerful hind legs while their arms hang at their chest like a mini version of Tyrannosaurus Rex. Their hind legs are enormous, capable of jumping a great distance. They seem to have a hard mouth, like it's solid bone or something. And they're much bigger than any toad I've ever seen. They've gotta weigh 10-15 kilos. They have a huge head and their tympanum, or toad ear, seems to be enlarged to quite possibly hear over vast distances. They have two potent sacs of poison behind each eye. They attack in massive groups and have a voracious appetite. First, they spray a long stream of poison right into the eyes of their victims. Once the victim is temporarily blinded and semi-subdued, the group moves in and bites at the eyes and neck. Once the victim is completely overcome by the poison, the mutants maniacally move in and eat every ounce of meat clean down to the bone. We now have video evidence to back this up thanks to these three stone dead

Americans, who gave their lives so that this video can be shared with the rest of us. This is not a hoax. I repeat, this is not a hoax! I'm afraid these mutants are real, very real, and nowhere is safe! This is Rafe McCory in the outback of Winton, Australia; signing off."

Rafe looked at Nozzy and said, "All right mate, that's enough for now. Let's set up camp here and catch us some mutants!"

Oliver's mobile phone rang while he was asleep in bed. "Hello," he said groggily.

"Matey, this is Rafe, listen, I don't have much time."

"Hey," Oliver said. "We got cut off last time. I tried to call you back but couldn't."

"I know. We were being jammed; the whole city lost all communications. We just managed to get out of range. The whole town of Winton is locked up. We were spotted today and chased out of our campsite. Luckily, we got away before they could catch us. We're close to a town called Kynuna at the moment. Listen, do you know anything about an American crew coming out here to film the toads?"

"Yes, Decamate hired a team that's been in Winton for about a week. They were hired to see if your last documentary was true."

"Well, that American crew is now very dead. We just came across their bodies."

"Dead?"

"Yes, dead. They were attacked by the mutant toads."

"Oh, my, GOD!" screamed Oliver, as he sat up in bed. "OH, MY, FUCKING, GOD! ARE YOU KIDDING ME?"

"Absolutely not! Listen, notify the Australian government that these Americans are missing, presumed dead and last seen near Winton. I'm afraid to call it in myself, because I don't want to be tracked down, have to answer questions, risk being thrown in jail, or silenced, and then have someone else be the first to get a live specimen. The entire city of Winton has been quarantined by who knows who, and I definitely don't want the people quarantining Winton to get a hold of me. If you call it in, they can't get to you, and hopefully you'll bring a few media crews out to Winton and they'll see for themselves that the town is under lock and key. No one can get in or out. And maybe, just maybe the media will distract the people quarantining the town long enough for us to blow this whole thing wide open," he said watching the sun slowly descend over the horizon. "Once we obtain a sample of this mutant toad, hopefully tonight, the media will be right here, and we can release it and our video to the world."

"Okay, I'll do it immediately, but I'm coming out there. I want to help."

"No, no, it's too dangerous, and you're already doing enough as it is," he said.

"Oi," yelled Nozzy, "we've got company."

Rafe turned around and noticed a large white truck in the far distance. In the back of the truck was a large spherical telecommunications dish.

"They're on to us," he yelled to Nozzy. "Let's get out of here." Lifting up his mobile phone he said, "Oliver, gotta run, mate," but the line was already dead.

Nozzy, Rafe and Meninga jumped into their jeep and started driving northwest. "The sun's going to set soon," said Rafe. "We should be able to outrun them till then and then circle around back to the dead Americans and camp out until we catch one of those carnivorous mutants."

An hour later the large white truck was completely out of view. "It looks like we lost them," said Nozzy.

"Great, let's circle back," said Rafe

"They might be onto the American's campsite already. S'posin' we go to where we found the tadpoles first, at Dick's Creek, and if we don't find nothing there, we take a chance and head back to the American campsite."

"Now you're thinking, good on ya!"

Very early in the morning in Sacramento, Oliver woke up Marco and told him what Rafe had said. "Dude, we've got to go to Australia ASAP," he said. "Get on the computer and check on flights to Brisbane."

"All right!" said Marco. "We're going to Australia!"

Oliver walked into the living room and called his boss. "Peter, this is Oliver."

"Do you know what time it is?" said Peter.

"It's early, I know, but listen! Remember that camera crew I hired. They're missing and presumed dead."

"What? What happened?" asked Peter half awake.

"Don't know, but we're going to have huge legal problems and insurance issues that have to be resolved. I have to go to Australia immediately to work it all out with the local government. You'll have to work it out here and notify the crew's family."

"Wait, wait. What? You have to resolve these issues?"

"Yes, I will resolve them in Australia, and you need to resolve them here," said Oliver. "I also have to go to Australia because Barbara wants the toad footage done pronto so I'm going to make sure it gets done."

"Wait! What? Who's presumed dead?

"Look, I'll send you a full report later. Tell Barbara that the camera crew that we hired is dead. I repeat, DEAD! Notify their families, I'm going to notify the Australian press."

"Whoa, whoa!" said Peter. "This just isn't making any sense."

"It will soon. Just take care of this, and I'll contact you once I get to Australia."

"Ho, hold on. Let me call Barbara and sort this out. Oliver, we have huge legal teams that can handle this. Do not leave. I repeat, do not leave!"

"Look, times a-wasting. Just do it! I've gotta go now!"

"No, Oliver. Wait!"

"No, just do it! Goodbye," Oliver said, then hung up the phone.

Marco came into the living room and said, "There's a plane leaving at 6:00am. Who were you on the phone with?"

"I called my boss Peter and told him I was leaving for Australia. I told him to notify the families of the documentary crew."

"Oliver! Why the fuck did you do that? He'll call Lionsgate or Barbara, and they'll try to stop us!"

"No they won't!" Oliver said suddenly worried. "Will they? Fuck, what was I thinking? I'm still not fully awake. Okay, focus. We've gotta pack, now! And change our flight to fly out of San Francisco, they won't check for us there."

"Yes, they will. Shit Oliver!" Marco screamed. "Look, let's pack, drive to Reno, take the first flight to L.A. and then fly out of LAX. If we're lucky, they won't expect us to leave from Reno or LAX."

"Sounds good, pack as fast as you can, we don't have much time! And don't forget your passport!"

Fifteen minutes later they jumped into Marco's car and took off for Reno. Along the way, Oliver called Zabra's apartment.

"Zabra?" said Oliver.

"No, this is her roommate, Robyn. Hold on."

Seconds later Zabra said, "Hello."

"Zabra, this is Oliver!"

"Oh, hi!"

"Look, something's come up and I'm going to Australia. We should be in Brisbane sometime tomorrow if we're lucky. I'll email you the exact flight information once I'm certain."

"Hold on, tomorrow as in tomorrow? And who's we?"

"Yes, tomorrow. I'm bringing my roommate, Marco. Listen, remember that Cane Toad video you gave me from that guy Rafe McCory?"

"Kind of."

"Well, it's complicated, but Decamate is directly responsible for creating a mutant version of the Cane Toad, and somehow it got out and is now ravaging a town called Winton."

"Winton?"

"Yes, its West of Townsville. I sent a documentary team out there to film the mutant toads and the documentary crew are all dead. I repeat DEAD! The mutant Cane Toads killed them! Me and Marco are on our way to Australia to gather evidence and then announce everything to the media. I need you to meet us at the airport; we'll explain everything once we get there. I'll send you the flight info once we figure out what flight we'll be on. But whatever you do, don't tell anyone we're coming!"

"Okay, but Oliver, I don't understand," said Zabra.

"Look, I know it's hard to swallow, I'll explain everything in an email, okay? Now, I need you to do one more thing."

"What's that?"

"Contact the local media and tell them what's happening."

"What is happening?"

"Look, I'll explain everything in an email! I've gotta run, see you soon, bye."

"I hope so, see youse soon, bye, have a great flight" Zabra said, and hung up the phone.

Oliver and Marco drove to Reno, purchased a ticket to LA, caught the earliest flight and arrived in LAX. After grabbing their bags, they immediately rushed to the ticket counter wearing baseball caps and sunglasses to disguise themselves in case they were spotted.

"We need two tickets to Brisbane, Australia," said Oliver to the girl behind the desk.

"Today?" asked the reservationist.

"Yes, we need your earliest flight."

"Let's see. The earliest available flight is 11:30pm, that would get you into Australia about 6:30am, it's a long flight."

"11:30pm as in tonight?" asked Oliver.

"Yes, that would be tonight."

Marco pulled Oliver aside and whispered, "Dude, let's not buy the tickets until the plane's ready to go. If they find out we're on the flight, they could try to stop us!"

"Good idea," said Oliver. Turning to the ticket agent, he said, "When is the latest we can purchase the tickets?"

"Two hours before the flight, but you'll need visas if you're U.S. citizens. You do have visas?"

"No," Oliver said. "Where do we get those?"

"You'll have to go to the Australian visa office in LA."

"Where's that?" Oliver said.

The woman jotted down the address, phone number and instructed the pair where to obtain a taxi.

Marco and Oliver stored their luggage and then headed out to get their visas.

They returned to the airport in the late afternoon with shiny new Australian visas in their passports.

At nine o'clock they purchased their tickets to Brisbane.

After checking their bags and clearing security, Marco and Oliver sat down at a bar near the international departure area and anxiously awaited their flight.

A few beers later, Oliver blurted out, "Marco, I just thought of something! What if Decamate tries to stop us from boarding the plane?"

"Don't be paranoid."

"How can I not be? I bet they've been checking every flight out of the country for our names all day. I wouldn't put it past them. We've got to think of something, just in case they do show up."

"Doubtful, highly doubtful, we aren't fugitives or anything." said Marco. "Look, you just told your boss that you're going to Australia. You didn't give him any details to let him think that we know what's going on, did you? I think you're just being paranoid."

"I'm not paranoid, I'm just being cautious! I simply told my boss that the American documentary crewmembers are all presumed dead, and that he should contact their families. I told you this before, didn't I?"

"You probably did, but dude, why did you make that phone call? Now they are going to think that we will let the cat out of the bag."

"I know, but I've got a plan. Let's find two guys on our flight and have them switch seats with us before we board, just in case."

"We're not going to be able to find anyone who'd want to do that."

"Why not? We can offer them a thousand bucks. We'll tell them the whole story."

"A thousand bucks! What are you nuts?"

"Come on, you got it, don't be a tight wad," said Oliver.

"Okay, say we find two numb nuts who want to do this, we give them the money and then what's stopping them from going directly to the police after we pay them? We'll be arrested before we board."

"Arrested? For switching seats? Come on! Look, we just have to find the right two guys."

"Come on Oliver! If two guys came up to you and told you the story, offered you one thousand bucks to change seats, would you accept it?"

"I don't know, maybe, probably."

"It's too risky!" said Marco. "And too expensive!"

"How about five hundred bucks then?" asked Oliver.

"Okay, okay," said Marco finally giving in. "Let's go to the departure gate and see if we can find two likely candidates. I'm not talking about two businessmen; I'm talking about two guys our age who look like they wouldn't have a problem with it. Two backpackers would be ideal."

They eased over to the departure gate and scanned the area. Seeing no likely candidates, they were about to go back to the bar when two longhaired college students arrived, looking like they had been partying all day long. "Marco, do me this one favor, go with me and talk to those guys. If they say, 'yes,' then we do it. If they say 'no,' then I won't bug you again."

Marco looked at the two students and thought about it. Finally, he agreed, just to get Oliver to shut up.

Oliver and Marco approached the two guys and sat down next to them. "Hey, you two going to Brisbane?"

The college students looked at Oliver and Marco suspiciously, especially since they were wearing dark sunglasses indoors at night. "Yeah," said one of them.

"So are we," said Oliver. "We're on a business trip, first time to Australia, what about you?"

"First time for us too," said the other one. "We're students on our way to do an exchange program at James Cook University in Brisbane."

"Cool, cool. Hey, listen, we're in a sort of dilemma and kind of need your help," Oliver said as the two students looked uncomfortably at each other.

"Come on Oliver," said Marco. "They're not going to do it."

"Hold on," he said to Marco and then began describing the situation in grave detail to the two university students.

"Let me get this straight," said one of the students afterwards, "you just want us to sit in your seats for five hundred bucks?"

"Yes, nothing will probably happen. It's just a precautionary measure."

"Sounds like easy money," said one of them.

"I don't know, sounds too good to be true," said the other.

"I'm sorry, what are your names?" asked Oliver.

"I'm Zane," said the taller of the two.

"Hi, I'm Riley," said the other.

"Hi, I'm Oliver and this is Marco."

"Look," said Marco. "I know this must sound very farfetched and to be honest with you, if I were you, I wouldn't do it. However, this is an urgent emergency. A mutant species is about to ravage Australia and in two days the whole world will know about it, if all goes well. If we get caught before we go to Australia, countless people could die and this thing could be covered up completely and no one will know about it until it spreads out of control. Completely out of control!"

"This all sounds way too freaky," said Riley.

"Can you give us a few minutes to talk this over amongst ourselves?" said Zane.

"Sure, take your time," said Oliver.

Oliver and Marco stepped aside and stood together anxiously awaiting a decision.

Zane and Riley chatted for a few minutes amongst themselves and then walked over to Oliver and Marco and said, "We'll do it if you pay us up front."

"Yes," shouted Oliver in glee. "Okay, okay, let's go to the bathroom, and we'll give you the money and switch boarding passes."

One hour later Oliver and Marco were sitting in Zane and Riley's seats on the airplane. The stewardesses began closing overhead compartments preparing the plane for departure.

"Oliver, it looks like we just lost five hundred bucks! You're buying me drinks the entire time we're in Australia!"

"Maybe I am too paranoid, but we had to show our passports to get our tickets. We are in the computer system and someone could have easily found out that we are on this plane! And I don't need to remind you how urgent this mission is. Hello, if we don't get to Australia, all hell could break..."

"Shhh," said Marco elbowing Oliver.

Five security guards abruptly boarded the plane, walked up to Zane and Riley and escorted the two unsuspecting university students off the plane as they protested passionately.

Rafe, Nozzy and Meninga spent the entire night looking for toads around Dick's Creek. They arrived back at camp empty handed just as the sun was rising. Rafe and Nozzy sat down and passed a bottle of *Bundaberg Rum* to each other.

"Bugger! Came up flat again, mate," said Rafe.

"I reckon they bred here and followed the Diamantina into Winton in search of food," said Nozzy.

"Well, that only means one thing. We've got to risk it and hoof on over to the American's camp tonight, under the cover of darkness."

"It's going to be crawling with the enemy."

"Right you are, but if we don't find something soon, they could cover it all up. I need this find; I really do! My credibility and career are in the dumps. I called up a few media contacts that I know and tried to get them to come out here and see for themselves, and you know what they did?"

"Laughed?"

"Worse, they told me to have another drink," Rafe said taking a swig of rum. "There was a time when I stretched the truth to get a story out. But you cry wolf once too often and get branded a bloody sensationalist, for life!"

"You were young, mate. Now we're on to something, you know it, I know it and Meninga knows it. All we need to do is drive into the American's camp tonight, wait patiently and they'll come right to us. By this time next week, we'll have the story of the year and be back in the media's arms again."

Rafe put his arm around Nozzy and started singing, "I've got ya back in my arms again, baby..."

Zane and Riley sat nervously in a holding room. After telling a number of security officers the truth as far as they knew it, they sat alone, waiting for the results of their interrogation.

Moments later, Decamate's Chief Operating Officer Alan Tourterellie and Chief Security Officer Willard Boarsbreath were escorted into the room by two airport security officers. "Who are these two?" Boarsbreath asked while closely examining two employee photos of Oliver and Marcos.

"They were sitting in Mr. Dendracopus's and Mr. Columba's seats. According to them, Mr. Dendracopus and Mr. Columba asked these two to switch seats with them. Not knowing this, our security officers took the wrong two people off the plane."

"Is the plane still here?" asked Tourterellie visibly upset.

"No, sir, it's *en route* to Brisbane. It should arrive in about ten hours from now."

"I want those two arrested once they land," demanded Boarsbreath.

"On what grounds?" asked one of the officers.

"On the grounds of stealing company secrets and trying to take them across borders," urged Boarsbreath.

"Sir, that's an international affair, I'm not authorized to issue that statement. You'll have to talk to international affairs, file a complaint, and then they'll have to notify the Australian authorities."

"Okay, let's get on it," said Tourterellie.

As they began filing out of the room, Zane interjected to the last officer leaving the room, "Sir, sir, what about us?"

"You're free to go," he said and left the room.

"Schwing!" said Zane, raising his hands triumphantly in the air. "Five hundy clean and easy just like I said! You owe me!"

"I think this is going to be the start of an excellent vacation," said Riley. "Might I suggest that we enter the bar and begin drinking heavily?"

"An excellent suggestion," said Zane. "But let's book another flight first."

Meninga startled Rafe and Nozzy awake well past noon as he barked at an animal and ran off in the distance. He quickly returned empty-mouthed and licked Nozzy's face relentlessly until Nozzy and Rafe got out of their sleeping bags.

"We don't have much to eat, whaddaya say if I take the dog with me to rustle up some eats," asked Rafe.

"Sure, I'm going to clean up the equipment and get ready for tonight's search. I have a good feeling about tonight."

At dusk, Rafe, Nozzy and Meninga jumped in the packed jeep and headed to the American Documentary crew's campsite.

Just as darkness fell, Nozzy looked back and noticed three sets of headlights appearing out of nowhere racing right towards them. "We've got more company," yelled Nozzy.

"Right, they want to play," yelled Rafe. "Put in some AC/DC, we need escape music!"

"The wind's kicking up, hopefully it will give us some cover!" said Nozzy, and then put in "Highway to Hell" and cranked up the volume. "If we can outrun them, we'll be safe," yelled Nozzy as the music began to play.

Rafe turned off his headlights and drove his jeep like a bat out of hell in complete darkness.

Thirty minutes later Rafe had successfully eluded the three vehicles hot on their tail. He turned the jeep around and headed towards the American crew's campsite without headlights.

Halfway to the site, Rafe drove over a big log that he didn't notice.

"For fuck's sake," said Rafe. "I think we have a flat tire."

They got out of the jeep and discovered that two of their tires were quickly losing air. Rafe dug his boots into the earth.

"I tossed the spare out to make room for the equipment, mate," said Rafe. "It looks like we're going to have to leave the jeep here and foot it."

"For how long?" asked Nozzy.

"It's thirty or forty miles away. We can't walk directly there; they'll be looking for us soon. I reckon we take an indirect route, walk in the dark and hide out somewhere when the sun comes up. Then take off again as soon as the sun sets. We can follow the river to the Americans' camp, should get there by nine or ten o'clock tomorrow night."

"I'm not too keen on that," said Nozzy. "What about them crazy mutant toads?"

"Mate, the way I see it, we have two choices. We can wait here and let whoever in those jeeps find us and lose the opportunity to report this story. Or we can walk to the Americans' campsite, film the toads, get a live specimen, take the American's blazer and report the story directly to the media that will hopefully be camping out near Winton, if Oliver did his part."

"And possibly get eaten at the campsite or along the way."

"I don't give a toss! If we stay here, we don't have a chance at all. If we get to the Seppos' campsite we have a better chance. What do you say?"

"I guess I'm game, but we've got a lot of equipment to carry. We'll have to pack as light as we can and travel fast."

"Now you're talking," Rafe said.

The two began throwing items as fast as they could into their backpacks and then headed out into the wilderness as the wind roared; Meninga followed closely at their heels.

Rafe, Nozzy and Meninga walked through the outback for hours in the dark. Suddenly, they noticed an ominous helicopter looming in the distance, shining a bright searchlight back and forth. "You'll never catch us ya bastards!!" yelled Rafe, as he shook his clenched fist at the helicopter. Turning his attention to Nozzy, he said "Look, it's about four in the morning, I reckon we head over to that sage brush, set up a camp site under the brush, and wait it out till sunset."

The two commenced to clearing out a small area with their hands, large enough for them to sleep in. Once finished, they crawled into their sleeping bags and camouflaged their campsite as best as they could. Meninga snuggled up next to Nozzy.

Oliver and Marco stood in line at the custom's area of the Brisbane international airport.

"Dude, we are never going to make it through," cried Oliver. "They're going to snag us and send us right back!"

"How? They don't have anything on us!"

"They'll find something and if they don't find something, they'll strip search us, a full cavity search I might add, and then plant something on us or up us."

"You watch too many movies!"

"Trust me, we are not going to make it," Oliver said, becoming more and more agitated.

"Chill out!" whispered Marco. "You're making a scene before we even get through customs. Act normal!"

"I can't," said Oliver. "Look, my hands are shaking, and I'm dripping wet with sweat."

"Okay, let's get out of line, go to the bathroom, clean up and calm down."

"We're almost to the front of the line! Talk about looking suspicious!"

"All right, then just take a deep breath and calm down. If they catch us, they can't hold us, remember that."

"Shit, here I go," Oliver said, as he walked up to the customs window and nervously handed over his passport and customs' forms.

The officer slid Oliver's passport across a computer barcode reader, verified Oliver's forms, stamped Oliver's passport and said, "Welcome to Australia." Oliver walked past the booth, turned to Marco and smiled.

Marco walked to the window and calmly handed over his passport and forms to the officer. He watched carefully as the officer processed his information, stamped his passport and then returned it to him.

"Thank God," Marco said to himself. He walked past the booth and turned down a hallway and immediately noticed that Oliver was surrounded by several security guards. His first instinct was to run; instead, he reluctantly walked over to the group.

"Hello officers, what seems to be the problem?" he said, trying to smile cheerfully.

For the next three hours Oliver and Marco endured a long line of questioning by a wide variety of men and women in uniform. Every single item that they had brought to Australia was thoroughly examined and much to their chagrin, they were given a complete strip search.

Afterwards, Marco and Oliver waited alone in a small plain detaining room. The two friends stared off into space, exhausted from their ordeal. "We're so fucked," said Marco.

The door abruptly opened and four high-end officials walked in.

"We're going to go over everything one more time," said one of the officials.

"Look," cried Oliver. "Enough is enough! We've been over and over the story umpteen times. We've been here for hours and haven't eaten a thing. We're starving, tired and fed up! I demand to see a lawyer. I demand some respect," he said, as Marco elbowed him to settle down.

"We realize that this is a difficult process," said one of the officers, "but we ask that you please bear with us."

Oliver and Marco went over the details as clearly as they could and then found themselves waiting again. Both of them put their heads down on the table and tried to go to sleep, but sleep wouldn't come.

The door opened again and three of the officers walked back in. "As far-fetched as your story sounds, we've decided to let you go," said one of them.

"Hallelujah," cried Oliver.

"We will look into your story, and if it is true, we will be in touch and if it is not true, we will also be in touch," said another officer sternly. "During your travels in Australia, you are to stay in continuous contact with us. We need to know your whereabouts at all times. Any breach in this agreement will cause us to immediately deport you. Is this understood?"

"Yes, but what are we supposed to do, call you every hour on the hour or something like that?" asked Oliver.

"Here's my card," the officer said sliding two cards on the table. "Call me every time you change locations. We want to know where you are residing at all times."

Oliver and Marco both grabbed one of the cards and put it in their wallets.

"Your things are located in the office next door, you are free to go," said the third officer. "We contacted Ms. Zabra Moineau and she said she will be waiting for you at the international point of entry area."

Oliver and Marco walked into the room next door and all of their stuff was splayed out across a large table. "The least they could have done is pack it back up," whined Oliver.

Zabra met Marco and Oliver at the international point of entry. She gave Oliver a long kiss and hugged Marco. "My God, what did they do to you?" she asked.

"Full strip search and prolonged interrogation," exclaimed Marco.

"Oo, well the strip search can be fun, can't it?" she said, trying to cheer the two up.

"Yeah, about as fun as being butt-raped by an inmate!" said Marco.

"I really can't believe they let you go," said Zabra. "If you told them what you told me over the phone, I would have locked you away."

"Actually I'm pretty surprised as well," said Oliver. "It all seems like a dream. I guess we're just lucky."

"Well anyway, welcome to Australia, I'm really so happy to see you!"

"Me too," said Oliver.

"I've never been so happy to see anybody in my life!" said Marco. "Can we eat, I'm starving!"

"Sure, sure, we have a lot to talk about," said Zabra.

"Before I forget, did you get a chance to call the media about the three dead Americans?" asked Oliver.

"Yeah I did," said Zabra. "And, well, they thought I was joking. Seriously, they wouldn't believe a word of it. I told them exactly what you wrote in your email, and they just laughed and hung up. Can you believe it?"

"Figures," said Marco. "The second you need the media, they're too busy covering real news like which famous movie star is under the knife, or under the wagon or under their director."

"Did you show them the video clip of the toads in the cages that I sent?" asked Oliver.

"Yes! I even posted it all online and someone took it down the second I posted it!"

"I can't believe it! Well, I guess we'll just have to show them solid, unflinching evidence," said Oliver. "There's nothing like the real thing, real physical proof to wake them up."

The threesome walked to Zabra's car, Oliver and Marco put their luggage in the trunk. Oliver walked to the front passenger side. He opened the door and noticed the steering wheel was on the passenger side.

"Oops," said Oliver, "I guess we really are in Australia."

"Want to drive?" said Zabra, holding out her keys.

"Oh no, I'll probably kill us all," said Oliver.

While eating at a local restaurant Zabra revealed that half of her Decamate branch office coworkers had gone to Winton. No one would say why they needed to go; they just suddenly left.

"Zabra, we are onto something very, very big," said Oliver. "We need to go to Winton immediately."

"Oh, but I was going to show you around town," said Zabra.

"Sorry, we'll have time to look around once this all gets cleared up," said Oliver. "Look, we need to ask you a huge favor!"

"Sure, what is it?"

"We need you to go with us to Winton," said Oliver.

"I can't! I've got work tomorrow!"

"Zabra, once this gets out, you won't have a job," said Marco.

"We won't have a job," said Oliver.

"Guys, listen, I don't want to get wrapped up in all this."

"You'd rather have your country ravaged by mutant toads and have done nothing to help?" said Marco accusingly.

"It sounds really, really dangerous. I don't have a gun or even know how to use one. What would happen if we got attacked by one of those things?"

"We need you for your brain, not your brawn," said Oliver. "And the second there's any sign of danger, we're out of there! Nobody wants to get hurt. We just want to find out what's going on and alert the international media once we have proof."

They entered Zabra's apartment as her roommate, Robyn Ridgeback, looked up from her textbook and greeted them.

"Marco and Oliver, this is Robyn," said Zabra as Robyn got off the sofa and extended her hand.

"Hi ya," said Robyn.

"Robyn hun, look, something's come up, and I've got to take off with these two to Winton." Turning to Oliver and Marco, "Look, you two explain it to her, I'm going to pack."

Marco turned to Oliver and whispered, "She's hot." Oliver nodded in agreement.

Marco and Oliver explained the gravity of the situation once again. This time Marco was a bit more animated.

After telling the story, Marco turned to Oliver and smiled and then said to Robyn, "I've got an idea! Why don't you go with us?"

"Oh no," said Robyn. "It sounds like fun, saving the world and all, but I've got a report due soon for uni."

"This is an emergency of the utmost importance," said Marco. "You've got to go with us."

"I'm doing nothing of the sort,' exclaimed Robyn.

"We'll pay your way," said Marco.

"Ooh, paying my way to Winton, my dream vacation!" said Robyn sarcastically.

"We really need you to go, to uh, keep Zabra company," said Oliver.

"I think you two guys can keep Zabra very good company."

"You could have a chance to become a national hero," said Marco.

"Not interested."

"And if we're successful, we may cast you in the movie," said Marco.

"Oh, right, let me get my things," she said sarcastically. She looked at the two Americans sternly. "You really want me to just give up everything I'm doing and go on some crazy trip?"

"I'd do it for you," said Marco.

"So would I," added Oliver.

"So would I," yelled Zabra from her room.

"No you wouldn't Zabra," yelled Robyn. "You'd leave me alone in a pub if you had the chance."

"Ha, I would not," Zabra said, as she entered the living room.

"Look Zabra I don't even know these guys. I just can't toss everything I'm doing on a whim. I'm not like you. Plus, I've got a report to do."

"We'll write it for you," said Marco.

Robyn gave Marco another stern look. Marco turned to Oliver and whispered that he should have Zabra try to talk to Robyn privately. Oliver winked in agreement.

Oliver took Zabra into her bedroom to confer with her privately. After a few minutes, Oliver and Marco stepped outside while Zabra crouched down next to Robyn, clutched her hands and began trying her best to get her to go.

Fifteen minutes later Zabra brought the boys back inside.

"Okay, okay, I'll go on one condition," said Robyn. "You two pay for everything, and I mean everything. And I'm only going for three days maximum, and then I'll have to be back. All right?"

Everyone agreed and Robyn walked into her room to pack.

After arriving at the Brisbane airport that same afternoon, they discovered that all flights close to Winton had been canceled. They immediately bought four tickets to Townsville.

Upon arriving in Townsville, they rented a blue four-wheel drive blazer, purchased some supplies and headed to Winton. Zabra drove with Robyn sitting in the front passenger seat while Oliver and Marco slept in back.

In the late afternoon, Zabra woke up the boys and parked the blazer on the side of the road. "We've got about one hundred more kilometers to go till we arrive at Winton, what's the plan?" asked Zabra.

"Plan?" Oliver said groggily.

"Yes! You do have one, don't you?" asked Robyn.

"I don't know, I was hoping we'd come up with one by the time we got there," said Oliver.

"Great!" said Robyn, as she glared at Zabra.

"Right, need a plan. One plan coming up," said Zabra, as she began scratching her head. "Hmmm."

"What is it again we are trying to accomplish other than saving the world?" asked Robyn.

"We'll probably need to talk our way past a roadblock, find Rafe, get his video of the mutant toads, and if he doesn't have it, shoot our own, get a living sample of the mutant, fight our way through another roadblock, and then give everything to the media," said Oliver.

"Shoot our own?" asked Robyn. "Of these man-eating toads? How do you propose we do that?"

"I've got a video camera," said Marco, taking it out of its case and quickly filming Robyn.

"I think I might have something," said Zabra. "If there is a roadblock, we have to hope that the government isn't manning it. If it's people from Decamate, I think I can talk our way through. Then we snoop around and see if anyone knows where Rafe is or where the toads are, and then we go find one or the other or both. Easy peasy."

"Zabra, have you gone troppo?" said Robyn. "I'm not going anywhere near those toads!"

"It'll be okay, Robyn, I'll protect you," said Marco.

"I feel so much better," said Robyn, rolling her eyes.

As evening fell, Rafe and Nozzy packed up and headed towards Winton along the Diamantina River with Meninga following close by. They spotted several jeeps in the distance zigzagging across the outback.

Meninga barked at something in the brush, several birds took flight.

"Meninga, shush!" said Nozzy.

"You might have to tie up his muzzle, mate," said Rafe.

Nozzy bent down, shushed Meninga again and then petted him on the head. "He'll be all right."

Zabra drove the blazer up to a makeshift roadblock five miles outside of Winton. Two people in protective spacesuits stood by the roadblock.

Zabra rolled down her window and said, "How ya going?"

One of the spacesuit-wearing guards peered into the driver seat while the other suspiciously wandered around the blazer.

"This town's been quarantined, missy," said the guard. "You'll have to head back."

"We're here with Decamate and we're here to help," she said, smiling cheerfully.

"Hold on," said the guard. He walked over to a group of large trailers parked near the roadblock.

Five minutes later a diminutive blonde-haired woman wearing

overalls walked over to the blazer.

"Hi Gail," said Zabra. "How ya going?"

"All right, what brings you out to our wonderful wilderness?" Gail said, as she rested her arms on the driver-side window.

"I received an email from Don saying that he needed volunteers to head up to Winton, so I volunteered."

"Who are they," she asked, referring to the others.

"They're from HQ; the CEO sent them out here. And Robyn's a new hire, works part-time down in shipping."

"Hi ya," said Robyn sheepishly.

"Hi," blurted out Oliver, "I work in the marketing department in Sacramento. Lionsgate gave us direct orders to come out here and help clean this mess up."

"Really?" said Gail. "I didn't receive any information about anyone coming from HQ today. I do know that Barbara Beaver and Alan are coming tomorrow."

"Barbara and Alan are on their way?" said Oliver, concerned. "Oh yeah, right, I knew that," he said, trying to sound convincing.

"Lionsgate directly sent us here," added Marco. "He wants a minute-by-minute report of what's happening here."

"Well, we certainly can use all the help we can get," said Gail. "Are you aware of the gravity of the situation?"

"We've all been briefed," said Zabra.

"All right, why don't you park your vehicle over there, and I'll show you around," she said pointing to an area near the trailers.

"Cheers," said Zabra, and then drove away to the designated parking area.

They all walked into a large white trailer and immediately noticed a long table covered with laptop computers, used coffee cups and old dirty dishes.

"This is our surveillance area," said Gail. "We've got remote cameras situated around the perimeter of Winton."

Walking further back in the trailer, Gail pointed out a small kitchen, bathroom and a bedroom with cots tightly placed together.

"That's it," said Gail. "It's pretty small, but it gets the job done. It's not four stars by any stretch of the imagination."

"How many people are helping out?" asked Zabra.

"We've got over a hundred now," said Gail.

"And you're all sleeping in these trailers?" asked Robyn.

"Oh no, thank God! Some people are living in town, some sleeping in their campers and others are sleeping in other trailers positioned around the perimeter."

"How long do you reckon you'll be here?" asked Zabra.

"Wow, I wish I knew. We have to wait till we contain the outbreak."

"Outbreak?" said Oliver.

Gail looked at him strangely and then turned to Zabra, "I thought you said they have been briefed?"

"Yes, we have," said Oliver, "Lionsgate refers to it as..." he said, turning to Marco for help.

"As a debacle," chimed in Marco.

"Yes, yes, a debacle, I couldn't think of the word," said Oliver.

"That's a good word," said Gail. "It definitely is a debacle."

"What happens if the outbreak spreads beyond Winton?" asked Robyn.

"We all hope and pray that it doesn't, but if it does, it could spread exponentially."

"Are we talking about a virus here?" asked Gail.

"I don't really know. Everyone just keeps referring to it as 'an outbreak.' I'm really in the dark."

"Where are all the other people working in this trailer?" asked Marco.

"We had a perimeter breach and have located two unknown vehicles in the area, but haven't found the people driving them yet. So now everyone is out trying to find them."

"They didn't take their computers with them," asked Robyn.

"They have all of that in their vehicles including Global Positioning equipment."

"Do you mind if I have a look at the computers?" asked Marco. Gail looked a bit nervous so he added, "I work for MIS in HQ. Lionsgate wants me to link his computer up to your surveillance cameras, so he can access the scene from anywhere."

"Oh right, right. Sure, have a go," said Gail, to the delight of everyone.

Robyn and Zabra kept Gail busy with chitchat while Oliver looked at maps of the perimeter tacked on the walls of the trailer and Marco hammered away on a computer.

Oliver worked his way closer and closer to a walkie-talkie plugged into a cradle near the kitchen. When Gail wasn't looking, he put the walkie-talkie into his pocket and then walked back to join the group.

Ten minutes later, Marco stood up, stretched and said, "I'm pretty much done, for the moment. I'll probably need to come in tomorrow to run some tests. But I'm beat, I really need to crash."

"They just flew in from the States," added Zabra.

"My dear, you must be terribly jetlagged," said Gail. Oliver nodded and yawned for effect. "Heavens, we really don't have space for you here."

"That's okay," said Zabra. "We've got plenty of room in the blazer."

They walked outside and Gail recommended a restaurant in town for dinner.

"Is it safe to go outside?" asked Robyn.

"I was told to stay inside at all times, and if you do go outside to wear a protective suit like our guards have on. I'd offer you some of ours, but we're all out, so just stay inside and you should be fine."

The group sat at a small restaurant in the heart of Winton whispering to themselves.

A wiry-haired waitress came up to their table. "You part of those scientists?" she said studying the foursome carefully.

"Heavens no," said Zabra. "We're students from Brisbane; we've come up to see what's going on."

"How'd ya get through the roadblocks?" she asked.

"We snuck through," said Marco.

"That's not too bright, now you'll all have to stay. They ain't letting anyone in or out of here, you know. No communication either. No calls coming in or going out. No computers. They jammed everything and once they know you're here, they'll probably throw youse all in jail as they did to a bunch of protestors already."

"They threw protestors in jail?" shrieked Zabra.

"Yes, these people are crazy. Sez we got us a viral outbreak. Virus my ass! We all know better. We heard they manufactured some strange critter that thrives on human flesh. Apparently, it eats anything and everything. We had a mob of kangaroos stampeding the town the other night. Sounded like thunder. Never seen that before. We also had a drunkard in here the other night go off in the wilderness by hisself looking for them mutants and no one's seen hide nor hair of him in days. My advice to youse is to watch yourselves, especially at night, that's when they come out clucking like chickens. You hear that clucking, you better run fast for shelter!"

"Yes ma'am, thank you," said Zabra.

"Have you seen one?" asked Oliver.

"My dog, Ginger, was killed by a horde of them things. I found her lying outside eaten alive. In her mouth was one of them things. It looked like a big lizard and was ugly as the dickens. Its hind legs were as big as a turkey's. I hear it can jump like a roo and stands on its two hind legs like a roo as well."

"Do you still have it," asked Oliver.

"Nope, I turned it over to one of those snoopy scientists, and he took it away for examination."

Marco's stomach was growling uncontrollably. "Sorry, I'm starving, could we get a menu?"

"We don't have no menus," said the waitress. "We've got two items, fish and chips and burgers and chips. How many of you want the fish?" Robyn raised her hand up. "Right, one fish and three burgers," said the waitress. "What'll ya have to drink; we've got beer and coke. How many beers?" Nobody raised their hand up. "Right, four cokes then."

After dinner the foursome sat in their blazer while Marco hacked his way through the jamming device on his computer.

"I'm in," said Marco victoriously. "Now all we can do is sit and wait till I spot something. I have absolutely no idea where Rafe is or where the camera crew is. But hopefully we can track the search crew and figure out where they are."

Oliver pulled out the walkie-talkie and said, "Look what I snagged from the trailer!"

"You cheeky monkey," said Robyn as Marco gave Oliver a slap on the back.

Oliver turned on the walkie-talkie. "Let's just listen in and see what we can find out," he said.

"Jim, any sign of them up there?" came over the walkie-talkie.

"No," said another voice.

"Jerry, any sign?" said the first voice again.

"No," said Jerry.

"I'll sweep north on the Diamantina and you sweep south again," said the first voice.

"Roger that," said Jerry.

"They must think Rafe or the documentary crew is hanging out around the Diamantina River, or else they wouldn't be patrolling that area," said Oliver.

"Maybe they're patrolling for the toads, you ever think of that?" said Robyn.

"That's true," said Oliver. "In any case, we can sneak in, get our video and then sneak out."

"With jeeps patrolling the area, how do you reckon?" asked Robyn.

"We just drive slowly with our lights off," said Oliver. "We've got a walkie-talkie and surveillance of the area, so we know where they are, but they don't know where we are."

"And if we get caught," said Zabra, "we can just tell them that we are helping out."

"With our lights turned off?" asked Robyn.

"We can say we didn't want to attract the toads," said Marco.

"Then they'll know that we know about the toads," said Robyn.

"Everybody in town knows about the toads," yelled Oliver frustratedly. "We need to get that video tonight before Barbara Beaver, my big boss, comes and exposes us. If we can obtain the video tonight, then we can give it to the media and bring the whole shithouse down! Robyn, you just heard that waitress, this is very real!"

"Okay, but I am NOT, getting out of this vehicle for any reason whatsoever," Robyn firmly stated.

Thirty minutes later the blue blazer was inching along near the Diamantina River with its lights off when Robyn declared, "I've got to pee!"

Marco looked at a map of the area that he had downloaded onto his computer. "We're pretty close to the area being searched," said Marco.

Zabra stopped the blazer, pointed and said, "There are some nice bushes over there. I've got some tissue in my bag, here," she said handing the tissue to Robyn.

"Is it safe?" Robyn asked.

Oliver looked outside the window and yelled, "What was that!"

Robyn screamed. "What was what?"

"Just kidding," said Oliver.

"Don't do that! Look, I don't want to go outside," said Robyn sheepishly. "You two men have to go outside first and make sure it's safe before I'll go out."

"Be careful," said Zabra, as Oliver and Marco jumped outside making wild kung-fu gestures. After a minute, they hollered to Robyn that it was safe. She gingerly stepped out of the blazer and found a large bush to crouch under.

The wind blew thick clouds of dust across the dry landscape as a full moon loomed overhead. Oliver wiped his eyes to remove the dust while Marco looked around for one of the missing vehicles.

Out of the blue, Robyn yelled, "I hear clicking! I hear clicking!!!" She quickly pulled up her pants, screamed at the top of her lungs and ran hysterically back to the blazer.

All three of them jumped into the blazer and slammed the doors shut. Robyn was beside herself. "I felt something wet and slimy hit my bum," she said while Zabra tried to calm her down.

"Shhh, I hear something," said Oliver.

Marco whipped out his video camera and started filming.

"I see something," whispered Zabra.

Marco couldn't see anything on his camera. "I need light," he said. Zabra turned on the headlights and immediately screamed. Directly in front of the blazer was a horde of GoMo BoMos. They jumped on top of the hood and began spraying the windshield repeatedly with poison.

"Get in back," yelled Oliver to the girls. "I'm driving! Marco you get in front and film!"

They switched seats and Oliver sped away as the mutant toads sprayed the blazer with white goo and launched their bodies at the windows. Zabra and Robyn screamed uncontrollably in back.

"Look," cried Oliver. "There's another blazer!"

Oliver drove cautiously along the river as the mutants followed closely behind and launched their bodies at the moving vehicle.

He slowly drove around the other blazer and immediately noticed that all four tires were flat. The toads continued to spray and pelt the moving blazer with their bodies. It sounded like a hailstorm inside. Oliver had his windshield wipers on high and was continually using washer fluid to wipe the window clean of dust and the constant barrage of fluid ejected by the mutant toads.

Oliver quickly drove away from the abandoned blazer and then stepped on the gas to go up a hill. When he reached the top of the hill, two people appeared directly in front of him. Oliver turned the steering wheel as quickly as he could to avoid hitting the people and the blazer flipped over, landed upside down and slowly slid down the hill eventually coming to rest near the bottom.

Two men wearing bandanas over their mouths and goggles over their eyes ran over to the blazer screaming and pounding on the driver-side window to let them in. Both men were surrounded by toads.

"Go around to the back," yelled Oliver hanging upside down and struggling to undo his seatbelt. "Is everyone okay?" he said. Robyn and Zabra dangled upside down and held tightly to one another.

"Is everyone okay?" screamed Oliver.

"Yes," muttered Robyn and Zabra.

"Marco?"

"Yeah, I'm fine," Marco grunted. Hanging upside down, he reached for his seatbelt, unbuckled it and crashed to the ceiling of the blazer.

"Get in the front," cried Oliver to Zabra and Robyn. "I'm going to have them open the back hatch, so they can get in."

Oliver climbed in back and yelled to the two men, "Come in through the back window."

The two men managed to open the back latch and jumped in. A wave of mutants entered with them.

"Squash the bastards," yelled one of the men, as they quickly shut the back hatch.

A frenzy of screaming and swatting began. The mutants inside the vehicle sprayed their poison all over the blazer and jumped around frantically.

The blazer rocked back and forth as all six people beat, stomped and jumped around the small-enclosed space in total fear.

A mutant bit Robyn right on the arm. She slammed her arm into the side of the blazer, immediately crushing the creature. Blood splattered on the window and on her face.

"Shit, I just got sprayed," yelled Oliver, temporarily blinded. "I can't see," he said, as he flailed around accidentally hitting Marco in the face.

"Ouch," yelled Marco. "Watch it! Awwww, I just got sprayed in the mouth!"

Minutes later everyone looked cautiously for any sign of a living mutant in the vehicle.

"I think we're good," said Marco.

The two men removed their bandanas and goggles. It was Rafe and Nozzy.

"Rafe," yelled Marco, before projectile vomiting between his legs.

"Right, who are youse?" asked Rafe, wiping off the vomit splatter.

"I'm Marco and this is Oliver, from Decamate," Marco said, wiping his mouth.

"I can't see," cried Oliver. "Give me some water, my eyes are burning!" Rafe squeezed a stream of water into Oliver's eyes from his water bottle.

The mutant toads continued to pound the outside of the blazer.

"Boy are we glad to see you," said Nozzy, clutching his camera.

"This is my cameraman, Nozzy," said Rafe. "Who are the Sheilas?" he said, referring to the ladies.

"I'm Zabra and this is Robyn," she said, holding onto Robyn tightly.

Oliver turned around squeezing his eyes and Robyn screamed.

"There's one on the back of you," yelled Zabra.

"Don't kill it," yelled Rafe.

A mutant clung tightly to the back of Oliver's collar. Marco felt around for his backpack. Upon locating it and emptying its contents, he tossed it to Rafe, who then moved in slowly to Oliver. "Don't move matey," whispered Rafe.

Rafe eased in next to the toad and slowly put the backpack under the toad. He put his do-rag over the toad's poison sacks and gingerly slid a big knife into the mutant's mouth to pry it free of Oliver's collar. The creature eventually let go and Rafe slammed him into the backpack and zipped it closed.

"Gotcha, you bugger," yelled Rafe. "Now," he said, addressing the others, "What brings you to our neck of the woods?"

Marco passed his water bottle to Oliver, who quickly began pouring water over his eyes. "We came to find you and get some proof of these crazy toads," said Marco.

"Good on ya," said Rafe. "How do you like this proof: We've got some fairly decent video footage ourselves, and now we've got a live specimen thanks to you!"

Rafe informed them about his and Nozzy's ordeal. "We finally arrived here on foot only to find that those bastards following us had flattened all the tires to the vehicle over there. You all came just before Nozzy and I were about to be eaten alive."

"I think the bastards got Meninga," said Nozzy quietly to Rafe.

"Who's that?" asked Robyn.

"His dog," said Rafe.

"Oh! I'm sorry," said Zabra consolingly.

"Maybe he ran away, dogs are smart," said Marco reassuringly.

Robyn and Zabra began to scream.

"What's wrong?" yelled Oliver holding his eyes in pain.

"They're breaking the windows," yelled Zabra, as she and Robyn moved away from the side window.

Everybody looked through the poison-coated side windows. "Blimey," yelled Rafe. "What smart fuckers! They're clutching rocks in their hind legs and kicking at the windows. They're using the rocks to crack the windows! Quick, everybody, use your feet to hold the windows in place."

They all spread out and put their feet on a separate windowpane. They braced the windows as best as they could as the mutants pounded the windows relentlessly.

"The windows won't last long. What do we do?" cried Zabra.

"We gotta hope they hold until daybreak," yelled Marco.

"There's no way," yelled Robyn pointing to the driver side window covered in fissures.

"We've got to find a way," said Nozzy. "These things will retreat once the sun comes up."

"That could be seven to eight hours from now," yelled Marco whose back was against Oliver's and his feet against one of the passenger side windows.

"The walkie-talkie," yelled Zabra. "Call for help!!!"

"Where is it?" cried Marco.

Everyone scampered around the blazer looking for the walkie-talkie. The toads began to make larger cracks in the side windows.

"I found it," cried Zabra. She pressed down on the talk button and yelled into the walkie-talkie, "Help, help!!! We're by the Decamate documentary crew's blazer, next to a small river, and we're swarmed by toads. They're breaking into our blazer!!!"

She released the talk button and listened. There was no sound. "It's not working!!!" she cried.

"It's probably out of power," said Marco.

"Figures," said Rafe. "Okay, don't panic. Nozzy and I can go outside. Maybe we can draw the toads away from the blazer, then you all get out and try to tip it back over."

"I am NOT going outside," yelled Robyn.

"I got it," said Nozzy. "Let's draw them to the other blazer, light a big fire and maybe the smoke and heat will scare them off!"

"Great," shouted Rafe. "I've got a lighter somewhere, there it is," he said digging in his pants pocket. "Okay, we're going to have to open the back again."

Robyn screamed in fear. Nozzy and Rafe put on their bandanas and goggles and eased over to the back door.

"Ready," asked Rafe. Nozzy nodded like a man possessed, "Go!"

They opened the back door and quickly jumped outside. Mutants launched themselves into the blazer as Nozzy and Rafe slammed the door shut behind them. The group inside began swatting crazily at anything that moved.

Rafe and Nozzy used their hands and feet to try to clear as many mutants as they could away from the blazer while the creatures incessantly jumped, sprayed and bit at the two men outside.

Nozzy ran off to find some dry brush. Rafe uprooted a small dry bush and lit it, then ran back to the upside-down blazer and used the fiery bush to swat away the mutants.

Nozzy ran to the documentarian's blazer and started to pile scrub brush near it while toads slashed and bit at his clothing and exposed skin. Rafe ran over with his burning bush and tossed it on to the mound of dry brush near the documentarian's blazer. Afterwards, he bolted to find more burnables to stoke the fire as he swatted away the ever-increasing mutants clinging to his clothing by their long claws and weird beaks.

Covered in mutants, Nozzy used his hands to rip the toads off his body as he ran at full speed looking for more dry brush. A strong breeze blew the pile of flaming brush right into the American documentary crew's blazer. Both Nozzy and Rafe came back with a huge load of wood, dropped it on the ever-growing fire, and then quickly ran for more combustibles. The fire appropriately repelled the aggressive toads from its perimeter.

Meanwhile, the windows of the upside-down blazer were giving way as the team inside frantically squashed the mutants that had jumped in.

"One's got me in the neck," yelled Oliver.

"I'm blinded," yelled Marco, as he scampered to find Oliver and help him out.

Marco located the toad on Oliver's neck and pried him off. A gaping hole squirting blood flowed out of Oliver's neck.

Nozzy and Rafe, arms loaded with brush, both ran back to the documentary crew's blazer and noticed it had caught on fire. They struggled to throw the brush off of the blazer and pound out the fire on the vehicle. Without warning, the documentary team's blazer blew up, sending Rafe and Nozzy flying.

"What the hell was that?" yelled Oliver.

"The other blazer just blew up," cried Zabra.

"Are they okay?" yelled Robyn.

"I don't know, I can't see them, my eyes are covered in mutant toad gunk," yelled Zabra.

"There's a huge hole in the back window," screamed Robyn as the mutants jumped into the blazer. "They're coming in!"

Marco and Oliver threw everything they could grab at the back window while kicking and stomping crazily.

The mutants poured in and quickly began attacking the humans inside.

"Motherfuckers," screamed Marco, flailing wildly. Two toads gnawed at his arms. Marco slammed them against the sides of the blazer.

Another toad jumped up and latched onto his chin. He ripped it off and squeezed it to death and then slammed it to the ground.

"One of the side windows is giving in," yelled Robyn.

Oliver cranked his neck sideways trying to stop the blood from flowing while grabbing mutants latched to his body and flinging them against the wall. Marco caught a mutant in midair and immediately crushed it on his knee.

A huge wave of fire swiftly approached the overturned blazer.

Robyn screamed as the window next to her completely shattered. Someone in a dark suit grabbed her and pulled her out of the blazer.

Screaming uncontrollably, she squinted through temporarily blinded eyes. She could barely make out shadowy figures in black.

A group of a thousand Australian paratroopers dressed in riot gear had descended into the area. They used flamethrowers to fight off the mutants.

"Cover your face," one of them said, pulling Oliver from the mutant-infested blazer. Oliver covered his face and the paratrooper doused Oliver with a slimy, cold fluid.

After pulling everyone out of the blazer and flinging them in a pile with Rafe and Nozzy who were unconscious, a group of paratroopers encircled them and began flaming toads as they walked outward in a circular fashion.

An army transport vehicle arrived and rushed the six victims off to a hospital in Winton.

The following morning Oliver awoke in a hospital bed thinking it had all been a dream. He tried to open his eyes and then realized that they were completely covered in bandages, as were his neck and arms. He climbed out of bed, feeling around for the bathroom. A nurse helped him locate it.

After Oliver finished, an army guard quickly escorted him back to his hospital bed.

An hour later, with bandages still covering his eyes, Oliver was escorted to a room to be interrogated by Australian army officials.

He told them everything that he had experienced, over and over again.

"When can we leave?" he finally blurted out.

"Because of the volatile nature of this situation, we are going to have to keep you here until the imminent danger has been resolved," said a male voice.

"How long will that be?" Oliver said trying to direct his voice to the appropriate person.

"At this moment we can't rightly say," said one of the officers.

"Look, I'm an American citizen," cried Oliver. "I came here on my own accord to bring to light this whole mutant Cane Toad debacle. I was interrogated for umpteen hours at the airport, where, I might add, I told high-level officials exactly what was happening! I risked my life and the lives of my friends coming here so the great citizens of Australia could benefit, could learn, and could find out exactly what the fuck was happening here! We were attacked by a swarm of those things and damn near killed! Now I am not going to sit here and let you tell me that after all my hard work and my, my Herculean struggle, that I cannot leave! This is complete and utter BULLSHIT!"

"I realize that you are upset," said one of the officers calmly.

"Really, what was your first clue?" said Oliver, adjusting the bandages covering his eyes and accidentally knocking over a glass of water as he slammed his fist down. A few officers quietly chuckled.

"Oh, so this is funny to you?" screamed Oliver, pounding the desk for effect, and then slightly injuring his hand after he accidentally hit the glass of water again. "Ow!"

Another officer spoke up. "Actually Mr. Dendracopus, it is because you were interrogated at the airport that we found out about this situation. The interrogators at the airport put tracking devices on several of your items. Had you not brought this situation to their attention, you would have all been dead and many more could have lost their lives. So on behalf of everyone here, I'd like to say thank you."

"Oh," said Oliver calmly, "well, you're welcome. I guess. And thank you for rescuing me and saving my friends."

"No worries."

"So does that mean we can all go now?"

"Unfortunately, we are under strict orders to keep you all here until we can contain the situation. We are sorry for your inconvenience and will do everything we can to ensure that all your needs are met."

Oliver ate lunch in silence with Zabra, Robyn and Marco in the hospital cafeteria. The whole group had bandaged eyes as well as various bandages over parts of their bodies. Rafe and Nozzy also heavily bandaged arrived at the table with their lunch trays.

"Hi, hi, how's it going fellow detainees?" said Rafe. "Jeez, youse all look like hell!"

"Hey, I thought you were dead!" joked Marco.

"Ha, no pack of feral frogs are gonna get me, mate. They took one bite out of me and went running the other way."

"We're so glad you made it out alive," said Zabra. "I thought you were goners once I heard that blazer blow up."

"A minor inconvenience," said Rafe. "Only singed me skin a bit and gave me a nagging ringing in me ears."

Rafe leaned in and whispered, "Were you all able to bring anything back, as in a sample of one of them mutant toads?"

"No, they took everything," whispered Marco. "What about the video?"

"No, they took everything from us as well, the bloody wankers," said Rafe.

"This is ridiculous," said Oliver. "They can't keep us here; they can't keep a lid on this forever!"

"Keep it together mate," said Rafe. "I don't give a toss what these scurvy bastards say or do. We'll find a way out of here, and we'll get a piece of one of those bloody jumpers to the media, mark my words."

"At least we're all okay," said Robyn.

"But we could have had the story of the century," said Oliver. "Now no one will ever know."

"They'll find out eventually. No one's going to detain me for long," said Rafe assuredly. "We're going to pop the lid right off this freak show soon. Very soon."

Nozzy walked out the back door of the hospital and squinted in the afternoon sun. Two guards stood on duty. He approached them for a light of his cigarette and then wandered under an awning and quietly enjoyed a smoke. He looked out into the great expanse of desert on the outskirts of Winton. He stood still for a second, eyes fixed on a point out in the distance. He saw something move. "Oi," he cried. "Hey fellas," he said to the guards. "That's me dog!"

He ran out to Meninga who greeted him playfully. The dog had huge clumps of hair torn off of his body, as if he had been through a vicious dogfight. "They didn't get you, buddy, did they?" he said hugging his dog.

Meninga barked and ran off into the desert. Nozzy tried to call him back, but he wouldn't come. Meninga reached a spot in the desert and began jumping and barking. Nozzy ran out to Meninga and noticed a dead mutant toad lying on the ground. "Good boy!" said Nozzy, as he quickly picked up the creature and stuffed it into his shirt.

He walked back past the guards carrying Meninga to cover up the bulge in his shirt.

"Looks like he's been through a struggle," said one of the guards.

"Yeah, I bet he gave them mutants a run for their money," said Nozzy.

"Brilliant," said the other guard, smiling fondly.

That evening, Rafe gave a hospital orderly a clumped-up bed sheet with the dead mutant toad hidden inside. Rafe put a note in the orderly's pocket with a poignant explanation of what was happening as well as instruction on how to access the video that Marco had captured from the Decamate lab.

The orderly gathered the sheet and put it in a large pushcart full of dirty sheets. He stored the cart in a utility closet until his shift was over and then walked out of the hospital with the dead mutant toad hidden in his backpack. Once outside, he jumped onto his motorcycle and took off through the desert.

The following day, the orderly appeared outside of famed documentarian Harold Kinghorn's apartment in Brisbane and handed him a small cooler and a few pieces of paper. Kinghorn opened the cooler and noticed a weird creature inside. The stranger briefed Kinghorn about GoMo BoMo and about the cover up in Winton.

Kinghorn called his long-time friend and colleague Graeme Froggatt. The two retirees worked tirelessly through the day and night to devise a plan after looking over the video that Marco had stored on the remote server. Kinghorn's initial reaction was to go to Sydney, contact the Australian media and hold a national press conference. However, he was afraid the Aussie government would try to stop it. His past experience with the government had not been pleasant. Numerous times during the filming of his documentaries he had been harassed, threatened and even barred in the courts from releasing some of his data.

The two old friends decided to prepare a video based on the data that they had downloaded and then fly to Singapore to announce the news internationally. They hoped that in Singapore, they could get a fair shake from the international press without being barred or subdued by the Aussie government. They did not risk bringing the live specimen for fear of being stopped at the airport.

Several days later, Oliver and Zabra sat on a couch in the hospital lounge watching a movie arm-in-arm. Their eye bandages had been removed, and they felt a lot better physically, but were still not allowed to leave the hospital. None of the detainees were allowed to leave the hospital.

Barbara Beaver and the entire Decamate team were rounded up and admitted to the hospital the previous evening. She sat briefly with Oliver and Zabra in the lounge and tried to make sense of all the madness.

Afterwards, she walked down a long white hallway hoping to find Marco and surprise him. She was a bit miffed that he had not responded to any of her emails or phone calls. She didn't care that he and Oliver had flown to Australia. She was actually proud of them because now the Australian armed forces were helping out with the problem, and with their help, hopefully this whole mess would blow over quickly with minimal damage to Decamate.

She walked into Marco's room and saw two empty beds as well as one bed in the corner with a white curtain completely surrounding it. "He's still in bed," she thought to herself. "It's nearly 2:00pm!"

As she approached the curtained bed, she heard a soft squeaky sound. "He must be sleep talking," she said to herself, as she walked up to the bed. She flung open the curtain, took one look and immediately let out a shrill yell.

Marco was on top of Robyn having sex. His hairy ass was thrusting away when Barbara surprised them. Robyn immediately covered her ample bosom with her arms and let out a shriek.

"Barbara," Marco said, looking up at Barbara while continuing to thrust in and out.

"What's going on?" said Barbara.

"What do you mean, what's going on?" said Marco. "We came here to bring this mutant Cane Toad thing to the attention of the Australian media."

"Excuse me," said Robyn.

"No, not that, this!" said Barbara. "You don't answer any of my calls or my emails and now this!"

"EXCUSE ME," screamed Robyn. "Do you mind?"

Marco turned to Robyn while he continued to slowly thrust in and out rhythmically. "It'll be okay," he said, as he leaned down to kiss her.

"Honey," said Robyn putting her hand over Marco's mouth. "Get her out of here!"

"Just give me a few seconds to explain this to her," said Marco, after he removed her palm from his mouth. Robyn turned her head away from Barbara in disgust.

"This ought to be good," said Barbara.

"Look Barb," said Marco. "All forms of communication have been blocked here. Believe me, I haven't been ignoring you. But I kind of met someone else, someone who I really care about. You're a great person and I still have feelings for you, but Robyn... Oh sorry, Barb, this is Robyn."

Robyn, still looking away, feebly waved at Barbara.

"And," said Barbara, as she crossed her arms waiting impatiently for a viable explanation.

"And, Robyn and I just hit it off," said Marco. "We've got a lot in common, and we've been through a lot together. Believe me; I didn't want to hurt you. I was going to tell you once we were released, but no one knows how long we'll be here."

"So it's over then?" said Barbara.

"Yes, I guess you could say that, but hey, really, I had a great time with you, and I want to remain friends," said Marco, as Robyn let out a groan.

"It's over," said Barbara, throwing up her hands. "Just like that?"

"Come on Barb, don't be angry," said Marco.

"That's it, it's over between you two," said Robyn. "*Finito!* Now get out!"

Barbara shook her head and quickly exited the room, slamming the door as she left. Marco closed the curtains and held Robyn's head and said, "Sorry babe."

"I hate you," said Robyn.

"No you don't," said Marco, trying to kiss her. "Come on now, don't be like that. It's over between me and her, you're my girl now."

"Who was that obnoxious woman?" said Robyn. "She's old enough to be your mother!"

"We were dating before I met you," said Marco.

"Oo," cringed Robyn.

"She's cool, and works for Decamate, but it's over between us now. You're the only one I care about now."

"Really?"

"Really," he said, as he rotated Robyn on top of him.

Kinghorn and Froggatt arrived in Singapore a few days later and held an international press conference. They sent out a detailed press release to the international media as well as uploaded pictures and video onto a website dedicated to the mutant Cane Toad problem in Australia.

One day later, Kinghorn and Froggatt, dressed in suits and bow ties, carrying one very dead GoMo BoMo specimen, arrived in Sydney and held a standing room only press conference amidst a throng of reporters.

"It has happened," Kinghorn said, "that science has failed us to such a degree that our beloved homeland may never be what it once was. A new genetically modified creature has been accidentally released in the wilds of Queensland. This creature, dubbed GoMo BoMo, is not much larger than a turkey, but has a voracious appetite and has, to date, killed three human beings that we know of. I have with me here, a sample of the new species," he said holding up a large plastic bag with the mutant toad inside. "Your government, the Australian government, has recently locked down Winton, Australia; and is trying to clean up the mess while they keep a tight lid on it. The government has cordoned off an area one hundred kilometers in diameter and will not allow anyone in or out. The government is holding captive a small group of people that were directly responsible for bringing this information to my attention and have risked their lives in an attempt to obtain this here sample. The government is hiding GoMo BoMo from the good people of Australia and is not allowing news concerning this incident in or out. I simply ask that you, the local media, bring this out in the open so that the Australian people can now know the dangers that are lurking on our doorsteps."

That night the news hit the Australian airwaves like a bomb blast. Winton and its surrounding area quickly became inundated with local and international media personnel, just what the Aussie government hoped to avoid.

Due to the extreme pressure from the media, the army reluctantly released all the detainees to a shower of media attention. Oliver, Marco, Robyn, Zabra, Nozzy, Rafe and even Meninga were all suddenly famous.

A few months later, a team of international scientists entered the

Australian Prime Minister's office and sat down to debrief him on the recent events involving testing of GoMo BoMo.

"Sir," said the lead scientist, John Wolfe, "preliminary tests are in and they reveal some interesting things about this GoMo BoMo, as the press calls it."

"Well, don't be shy, let's hear it," said the Prime Minister.

"We've pitted GoMo BoMo against a variety of local animals and not one of them has a taste for the new toad. It seems the toad's poison is too much for them to handle. Nothing we've tested can stomach it."

"Nothing?"

"Nothing. And they are ferocious eaters, capable of consuming up to twice their weight in food per day. We've seen it take down roos, cows and horses."

"It's an amphibian, right?" said the Prime Minister. "Why not try attacking it in an earlier stage of development?"

"They can lay up to one-hundred thousand eggs in a clutch each. The eggs are solid-ish surrounded by a hard membrane. If a fish swallows one, they can't digest it, so the egg just comes out the other end, undigested and unharmed. The eggs are very poisonous and can even survive in saltwater. The tadpoles are extremely aggressive and territorial, which gives them much higher survival rates than other amphibians. Their three-stage developmental cycle protects them from most biological attacks. If we develop something that gets most of them in the egg stage, some still make it, develop immunity in the other stages and then pass that down. Making matters even worse, they are nocturnal creatures, so they can hide fairly well in the daytime. They are earthen colored, and disguised well at night. To make matters extremely urgent, we have just been notified of unconfirmed sightings in Brisbane."

"So what do you recommend?" asked the Prime Minister. "I've got a nation of very concerned citizens."

"The solutions we are thinking about are number one: pesticides. We realize that no one wants this, but we may have no other choice. Unfortunately, the only pesticides we've found so far that will work are too toxic for humans and other animals. Second, we can create another species that will prey on GoMo BoMo, but we run the risk of creating an even more powerful species than GoMo BoMo that could cause an even bigger headache. Third, we could try to change their genes and introduce genetically inferior females, but you never know what would happen with the crossbred result. And fourth, we could create a virus that could kill GoMo BoMo, but we run the risk of directly harming other animals including humans."

"If we were to do nothing, what do you think would happen?"

"At their current exponential increase in numbers coupled with their voracious appetite, there may be only humans, birds and GoMo BoMos in Australia in the not too distant future. Which may not be such a bad thing. Once their food supply dies off, GoMo BoMo too will die off. We can protect our native species in zoos and when the time is right, reintroduce them into the wild once GoMo BoMo has run its course. Plus, there's a slight possibility that some creature in the wild may develop a natural defense against GoMo BoMo and then we could use that to determine an adequate course of action."

"These are trying times gentlemen. I'll need to consult my advisors and then devise a plan. But please, in the meantime, throw everything you can at GoMo BoMo!"

Three months later.

Oliver sat on a sofa in his Brisbane apartment watching the news on TV while eating a vegemite sandwich.

"GoMo BoMo hysteria has gripped Australia," said the newscaster. "The Australian government has launched a multi-million-dollar prize for anyone who can come up with a reasonable solution. And the government is encouraging everyone in infected areas to stay in at night."

"In related news," said the newscaster, "The Australian government is vigorously pursuing claims against the U.S. conglomerate Decamate, the company directly responsible for the creation and subsequent accidental release of GoMo BoMo into Australia. Thus far, the case is tied up in the courts. Wharton Lionsgate, CEO of Decamate, adamantly claims no responsibility for the problem plaguing Australia.

"Standing on the footsteps of Australia's main court amidst a horde of angry protestors, Lionsgate's corporate attorney had this to say, 'Decamate will fight these allegations tooth and nail. We are not in any way responsible. And might I add, our research was completely funded by the Australian government. They were totally aware of what we were doing'."

"Decamate stock has lost ninety-five percent of its value in recent trading," said the newsman. "And now, time for sports."

A few minutes later, a public service announcement came on the TV.

"Fellow Aussies and Aussiettes," said Rafe.

"Hey Zabra," yelled Oliver. "Rafe's on TV!"

Zabra ran out of the kitchen to hear what he had to say.

Rafe continued, "The government wanted me to talk to youse about a minor menace plaguing Australia. It's nothing we can't handle, really. It's just a mutant toad. You remember our friend the old Cane Toad? Well, now he's got an even uglier cousin—GoMo BoMo. He doesn't taste too good, and he's got the squirts, meaning he'll squirt ya if ya get too close and it packs a vicious punch let me tell you! Not quite as much as a shot of tequila mind ya, ha, ha. GoMo BoMo can jump like a roo, which makes him great for target practice, and they love to feed on flesh, but who doesn't? The best thing for you to do if you're outside is to carry a certified *GoMo BoMo Brelly* or a *GoMo BoMo Slammer*.

"The Brelly is equipped with a bright beam of light that annoys the poisonous jumpers. It's covered in GoMo BoMo repellant and conveniently has a sharp spear at the top. It can help you defend yourself against a swarm of the buggers like so," he said, as he opened up the umbrella and lunged forward, "and it protects you against the intense sun breaking through the ever-expanding Ozone hole lingering over our fine country. And if an old girlfriend you're trying to avoid walks by, you can cover your face like so. Ha, Ha! Believe me, it works.

"And the *GoMo BoMo Slammer*," he continued, "is essentially a modified tennis racket with a serious electrical charge built right in so you can zap the hell out of the little buggers if they sneak up on ya. And it will help keep your tennis game in top form as well. If a GoMo BoMo servers himself up simply administer a forehand, backhand or overhead smash, like so, voilà," he said, as he eloquently swung his racket towards the camera.

"Now, we've been through some tough times in the past, haven't we? And I'm sure we'll have some tough ones to come. We've learned to live with rabbits, the plethora of dangerous Aussie creatures, Cane Toads and Pommies, which coincidentally are the only things GoMo BoMo doesn't seem to have an appetite for. Ha, just kidding. So it looks like we're stuck with old GoMo BoMo and we're just going to have to learn to live with them just like we learned to live with everything else. Now these guys aren't so bad once you give 'em a chance. So let's forget about the wankers who are responsible for all this and put this whole matter to rest. It's the Aussie way. This is Rafe McCory reminding you: If you venture outside, don't forget your *GoMo BoMo Slammer* or your *GoMo BoMo Brelly*. Fair dinkum!"

Oliver turned to Zabra and said, "It sounds like someone has gotten to old Rafe."

"Yeah! What a cheeky monkey, trying to make a profit out of all of this!" said Zabra.

"I betcha Decamate will probably get away Scott Free without so much as a scratch."

"Not as long as the Aussie government has their way," said Zabra

"The Aussie government, oo, I'm really scared. I'm sure every member of the Australian government has already been paid off by Lionsgate and been made honorary mayors of Sacramento."

"We should send some GoMo BoMo eggs to Lionsgate's home swimming pool and release them, see how he likes it," she said.

"The eggs are probably already on their way to America wedged in the soles of shoes, stuck to clothing, stowed away in cargo ships. It probably won't be long till the entire world is enveloped in GoMo BoMo madness. Then someone will learn how to give it an opposable thumb and rifle lessons, and it will take over."

"Maybe we can make a profit from all this insanity too," said Zabra cheerfully.

"Shit yeah! Like sell T-shirts—already being done. Sell tickets to someone being eaten alive by a bastion of hungry GoMo BoMos—hey, there's a thought."

"I think not little Einstein. Maybe we can make handbags or jeans with their skin or cook them somehow. They are part chicken and everyone always says frogs taste like chicken," she said.

"The handbags will probably rot your skin and GoMo BoMos probably taste like butt."

"Or maybe you can smoke their skin and get high!"

"Smoking it will probably give you ten forms of cancer," he said.

"Hey, maybe its poison kills cancer."

"We'll at least you're optimistic."

"No sense getting all gloomy over it. It could be worse you know."

"Like how, their farts kill as well? Their croaks attract asteroids?"

"No! You're so negative. We're still alive, aren't we? And the GoMo BoMos don't like the cold, do they? Maybe we could go somewhere cold, like Tahoe! What do you think? Come on, why be so gloomy?"

"Why am I so gloomy? Well, let's see. My bosses are all liars, and they fucked up the planet big time. Three people I directly hired are dead because of me. And the entire country of Australia is in a panic over something I was indirectly responsible for. Don't I have a right to be gloomy?"

"Olly, come on, it wasn't your fault. Had you known, you never would have gone through with it. And once you did know, you helped bring it to the attention of the media. You're a hero."

"Some hero! I feel so used, so helpless, so stupid!"

"You have me," she said and walked over to Oliver and rubbed his shoulders.

"That I do," he said, leaning back, looking her in the eyes and gently stroking her arms. "And if it wasn't for you, I probably would have done something really stupid."

"Come on, let's go out for a walk, I bought some GoMo BoMo protective gear, as seen on TV."

"You actually bought that protective shit knowing full well it won't work?"

"The proceeds go to GoMo BoMo research."

"The money will probably all go to buy bigger houses for the people directly responsible for this mess," he said.

"Come on, let's go for a walk, it's a beautiful evening," she said, handing Oliver a *GoMo BoMo Slammer*. "We can go see Marco and Robyn."

"That sounds like a plan," he said, gripping the Slammer. "On the way, I'm going to see if I can whack one of those leaping shitcakes to death."

"No, the newspaper said not to aggravate them, or they'll start to swarm," she said, as they walked outside.

"Come on, just one forehand smash."

"No," Zabra snapped, as she opened up her *GoMo BoMo Brelly*.

"If they attack us, I have to protect you," he said.

"Okay, if you must."

Oliver leaned under her protective umbrella and gave Zabra a long, succulent kiss as they carefully strolled, hand-in-hand, down a large empty street.

The End.

About the Author

Hillel Groovatti is an American writer who has travelled extensively and lived abroad in Europe and Asia for more than twenty years. For more stories and more information, please visit groovatti.com.

- Like Groovatti on Facebook
- Rate this book on GoodReads.com
- Follow Groovatti on Instagram: @Groovatti
- Follow Groovatti on Twitter: @Groovatti

Thank you for reading Totally Losing Face and Other Stories!

TOTALLY LOSING FACE

AND OTHER STORIES

HILLEL GROOVATTI

SELF PUBLISHED

www.groovatti.com

www.ingramcontent.com/pod-product-compliance
Lightning Source LLC
Chambersburg PA
CBHW020443270626
47155CB00022B/1210